NIKKI DUDLEY

Nikki is a poet and novelist who grew up in North London, attended a state school, and completed a BA and MA at University of Roehampton.

She runs an online magazine (streetcake), as well as a writing prize. During the pandemic lockdown, she started MumWrite, a writing programme for mums. Nikki managed to complete her novel, *Volta*, whilst also raising her two young sons and was delighted when the novel won the Virginia Prize for Fiction. She is currently working on a new contemporary thriller, a new poetry collection about dementia and some creative non-fiction.

Previously published work includes: a novel, *Ellipsis,* as well as a poetry chapbook *exits/origins* and a poetry collection *Hope Alt Delete,* with another collection published in 2021.

www.nikkidudleywriter.com

D1355516

First published in the UK in 2021 by Aurora Metro Publications Ltd.

67 Grove Avenue, Twickenham, TW1 4HX

www.aurorametro.com   info@aurorametro.com

Volta copyright © 2021 Nikki Dudley

Cover image: Ronaldo Alves

Cover design: © 2021 Aurora Metro Publications Ltd.

Editor: Cheryl Robson

Aurora Metro Books would like to thank Marina Tuffier, Bella Taylor, Joanna Colton

Printed by Short Run Press, Exeter, UK.

ISBNs:
9781912430550 (print)
9781912430567 (ebook)

VOLTA

BY

NIKKI DUDLEY

AURORA METRO BOOKS

To Joe, Ethan and Caleb
My absolute favourite characters

Volta: 'Italian word for "turn." In a sonnet, the volta is the turn of thought or argument.' (Poetry Foundation)

CHAPTER 1

BRIONY

'Please...' She knew that voice. She heard it over and over in her ears but only realised it was a dream when her eyes flickered open. Like a blind slowly letting in light. She was on the floor, one arm bent at a strange angle as if she had fallen from a great height. It wasn't broken though. It had only gone to sleep.

She rubbed her eyes. She realised her hands were covered in something sticky, but it was hard to see properly. The curtains were closed. The room was lit by one small lamp... she knew where she was. The layout of Ed's flat was almost identical to hers.

The stickiness was red. The stickiness was... *blood.* She tried to wipe it away, but it was flaky and hard against her skin as though she'd been covered in it for a long time. Maybe hours. Her face also felt raw as though she'd been crying for days without a break. She felt dried out on the inside.

She checked herself for injuries but didn't find any. She sighed into the room.

What time is it?

She couldn't see a clock, even though she was sure there used to be one on the side table next to her. It was a small digital clock with angry red numbers.

She got on her knees and crawled towards the other side of the sofa, finding the clock on the floor she picked it up. It was 2:51 pm. She dropped it again.

She concentrated on her arms and hands again. So much blood. It had erupted over her top, down her arms and there were splashes staining her trousers. She touched it. It was dry. She noticed the stain on the floor then. Where she had been lying, blood had soaked into the floorboards. It felt tacky when she pressed her fingers against it.

She used the sofa to haul herself up. Her legs shook but she adjusted after a few seconds.

When had she last eaten?

She couldn't remember. She didn't allow herself to sit on the sofa but forced herself to walk towards the bedroom. The door was partially open.

She hesitated in front of it.

This must be a dream, she thought. More like a nightmare but, regardless, *not real.* She wasn't really covered in blood, she didn't have broken nails, she didn't have a tear in her top. This was all make-believe.

She took a deep breath and pushed the door open. The room was dark. She put her hand on the wall and found the light switch. She pressed it on and that's when she saw it: the bed covered with red, streaks of red up the wall, a leg hanging off the bed. A body.

Call the police. Run away.

The body looked like a mannequin. Blood marked the skin like bright red nail varnish. The uncoated skin still. The eyes were closed, the mouth hanging open slightly. Mid-scream?

Don't look. Don't look. Don't look.

She turned and walked to the front door, leaving it open as she left.

She needed air. She needed Mari. She needed escape.

CHAPTER 2

MARI

Mari was pouring herself a cup of coffee in the break room after a long day of back-to-back sessions when she heard the scream from reception. She left her drink where it was and cautiously approached the secure door that separated the patients from the doctors. She bent down to see through the glass panel and tried to locate the source of the noise.

She could make out a woman standing in front of the receptionist's desk. She was wearing a white top that had an erratic red pattern splashed over it. The splatters continued up the arms. It was only after staring for a few more seconds that Mari realised the red marks on the arms weren't on the material; they were on the woman's pale skin.

The woman turned towards the door, allowing Mari to catch a glimpse of her face. Briony Campbell. Mari gasped and pressed the door release before she could stop herself. She launched herself into the waiting room, causing Briony to turn towards her, with her stained hands outstretched to Mari like a person asking to be pulled out of the sea.

'Doctor Demetriou,' Briony breathed out, as if she'd been holding her breath.

Mari approached carefully, the blood making her wonder if Briony had a weapon on her. She was rehearsing moves in her head from the self-defence course that her brother had sent her on a few years ago. But Briony was her patient. She shouldn't fear her, she just needed to talk to her and find out what had happened. There was no need to start out on the defensive like her brother, Aris.

'Briony, how are you?' Mari forced out, trying not to look at the blood. 'Can I help you? Are you... hurt?'

Briony shook her head and stepped closer. Mari did her best not to shuffle back and glanced at the receptionist, Anna, behind her screen protector. She seemed to be signalling something to Mari with her eyes but Mari didn't have time to comprehend it.

'I need to talk to someone. Didn't know if you'd be here. I didn't know who else to go to.' She held her hands out to Mari, the dried blood smell beginning to reach Mari's nose. She tried not to let her face twitch in response.

'You came to the right place. Why don't we sit down and talk about what happened?' She gestured to a few empty seats in the waiting room. The other two patients had moved away and were now cowering against the back wall, but Briony didn't seem to register they were even there.

'Would you like some water?' Mari sat down, leaving one seat between them.

'Um, okay.' Briony nodded as she examined some blood on her trouser leg.

Mari signalled to the receptionist, who slid the screen across to hear what Mari was asking for. 'A glass of water please, Anna.'

Mari turned to Briony. 'Would you like to tell me what happened?'

Briony exhaled heavily and slouched in her chair. She lifted both her hands up and stared at them as though for the first time. Her eyes widened and her frown deepened as the seconds passed. 'Ed…' Briony whispered, so quietly that Mari almost missed it.

'Your boyfriend, Ed?'

Mari knew about Briony's boyfriend and a lot of Briony's life. Briony had been referred to her for psychotherapy via the GP and had been coming to see her as a client for the last few months. Mari liked the local feel of the surgery, but she also had private patients several days a week who were more her bread and butter.

Briony bit at her cheek and eventually pushed out, 'Yes.'

Mari nodded and waited, suddenly overwhelmed with the stench of blood in her nose.

'I think…' Briony paused, staring at the wall to her left. 'I think I killed him.' She turned her face back slowly as though being controlled by someone else's hand, like a ventriloquist's dummy. Her face was deathly pale and her eyes looked devoid of life.

'Why do you think that?' Mari managed to keep her tone even, as she normally did when patients confided strange things to her. Mari wondered if she had the grounds to contact Aris. Was Briony a danger to herself or others? Was Ed in need of help?

'I don't remember exactly… He's back there, though.' Briony put her head in her hand and started murmuring to herself. It sounded like, *'please, please, please,'* but Mari couldn't be sure.

'Where?'

Briony lifted her head again, focusing her metallic eyes on Mari but it was if she had forgotten she was there. 'The flat.' Briony's eyes bore into her like drills trying to extract something from her. Mari would give it up if she only knew what Briony wanted.

'Can you tell me what happened?'

Mari was distracted by the receptionist furiously motioning to her. 'Sorry, one minute. I'll get your water, okay?' She waited for Briony to nod before going over to the reception desk and collecting the glass. As she picked it up, she saw a note underneath that read: *Called the police and an ambulance. On way.*

Mari's jaw tightened as she tried to stop herself from responding. Anna had taken the decision out of her hands, though she could hardly blame Anna for making that call. There was no doubt something terrible had happened and Briony had been involved. Whether it was self-defence or something else, the sheer amount of blood spoke volumes.

Mari clasped the mug handle and tried to walk calmly back to Briony and hand her the water. She retook her seat and tried to smile but the muscles in her mouth were struggling to work. How would Briony react when the police showed up?

'I came here because you're always such a good listener. Not like… other doctors. You make me feel good,' Briony revealed, staring into her drink.

'I'm glad our sessions are making you feel better.'

'Can I tell you something?' Briony smiled hopefully.

'Of course,' she answered automatically, but her voice was a bit strained.

'I'm not going to hurt you,' Briony said coldly.

Mari nodded slowly, but she remained wary, even though her client had never shown any tendency towards violence before.

'While you tell me this, do you think we should get Ed some help? Should we send someone to the flat?'

Briony shrugged in agreement.

'Okay, let me tell Anna the address, okay?'

Briony told her the details and Anna made a note and said she'd see to it.

'And I think we need to get you seen by a doctor too. Just to check you're definitely not hurt anywhere.'

'I need to tell you about it first,' Briony insisted, leaning forward.

Mari nodded. 'Okay, go ahead. Take your time.'

'I guess I should start with earlier... before it... before we...'

Mari encouraged her to go on, while hoping that it would be Aris arriving from the police station. But they were interrupted by the sound of the siren and the blue flashing light of the ambulance arriving at the surgery.

Briony looked shocked and a little betrayed as they led her to the back of the vehicle and wrapped her in a metallic cape. Mari sagged into a chair, accepting a glass of water from Anna, and waited. She felt drained. After all, it wasn't every day that a patient turned up saying that they'd killed someone.

CHAPTER 3

SJ

My favourite hobby these days seemed to be pretending to quit smoking. In the driveway, I shut myself inside my old BMW and pulled out a cigarette. I struck a match, watching the flame catch the cigarette alight. My eyes followed it every millimetre as it came towards my face. I didn't let it out of my sight until the cigarette was lit and I had shaken it out. Finding an empty and long-since-cold cup of coffee in my cupholder, I deposited the dead match in there. It joined five others. I tried to remember when I'd bought it. Two days ago? Longer? It was a shame being in the car made me want to smoke and also a shame that being in this car was one of the safest places I knew.

I turned on the engine and headed to my afternoon meeting at Thameside Prison. Driving so far on a Monday afternoon wasn't my ideal, especially since my Legal Aid shift had moved to tonight instead of Tuesday this week. Although sometimes clients popped up all over the place. My boss, Rebecca, was close to retirement age so she only did occasional cases, leaving me mostly to my own devices, which was exactly how I liked it.

Thameside Prison was off a dual carriageway and, at first glance, could be mistaken for an out-of-town retail park. It was the security checks that gave it away and, looking past the security guard's hut, there were prison bars on every window.

I was there checking up on a new client who had been accused of robbery with a dangerous weapon. He had a list of convictions as long as his arm and had been recorded on the store video, but he wanted to plead 'Not Guilty'. We'd probably be going to court soon enough with some kind of plea, but it was my job to bring his expectations in line with reality. After I'd explained the options and heard his lame excuses for robbing his local Co-op, it was time to leave. But I was stopped on the way out by the prison officer, Jack.

'Hey, SJ, good call on that young fella Sitko last week.'

I cleared my throat, looking anywhere but at his face. 'Why? Did he go for it?' I mumbled, pretending to be busy reading some papers. In fact, they were all just scribbled doodles from when I had been waiting for a client at some point.

Jack threw a pen in my direction. 'Yeah, used his bed sheets. Not sure how he managed to rip them up… Resourceful buggers when it comes to a way out, aren't they?' He liked a chat, same as most of the prison officers. I suppose sitting on your arse all day made you kind of sociable when the moment arose.

I took my time doing my looping signature, the S and J of equal proportion and my surname Robin much smaller underneath. I'd spent hours practising my signature before qualifying as a lawyer, dreaming of the day when my name would appear on official documents. Pretty sad, really, but everyone has to have a dream.

'Well, anyway, good save,' Jack continued, as if I had responded to his last comment. He was an old-timer, like a lot of the ones they put on the gates.

'Cheers. See ya.'

I walked back towards my car. Sometimes it felt like all my days were like this: prison visits, signing in and out, walking back and forth to my car. It was a strange routine. I went to court sometimes, mostly for my Legal Aid cases. Although most of my private clients made a plea before their case ever got to court. Other than that, I didn't like to show my face in court for extended periods of time. It always felt like the judge believed I was some ex-criminal trying to stick up for one of my own. The scar trailing down the right side of my face didn't help. It wasn't my imagination; I'd been told way back during my training to avoid court if I could by one of the senior partners. Didn't exactly fit in with the clean-cut image of my colleagues.

Inside the car, I threw my briefcase on the passenger seat and thought about my visit the previous week to Marek Sitko. I'd watched him frowning as he'd stared at the page in front of him. Plucking a pen from between his fingers, I'd slid the paper back over and read it aloud to him. He hadn't said a word and had eventually written his name where I pointed, his cheek jerking slightly as if he wanted to cry, but I could see that he was still firmly under someone's control. Probably whoever had got him sent down for murder.

'Do you need anything?' I'd asked him.

When he'd stared at me as if he didn't understand and shaken his head in slow motion, I had seen nothing but black despair in his eyes. Whenever I saw a prisoner now with a certain look in their eyes, I always alerted the warden. I knew only too well what that look meant. Outside the room, I'd immediately asked to speak to the warden.

'Get that kid under suicide watch,' I'd told the warden, who'd barely looked up from eating his sandwich.

'Don't tell me how to do my job,' he'd growled with his mouth full.

'Well, good luck cleaning his blood off the walls.'

Seemed like the warden had weighed up both the cleaning and the paperwork against his pride and luckily found in favour of Marek.

I pulled out a candy cigarette, the type that kids eat, and put it in my mouth. I was trying to limit my cigarette consumption, but giving up smoking was going to lose me my teeth. I pretended to inhale but it felt empty, as empty as my chest.

I'm thinking about her without meaning to.

I spat out the fake cigarette and tried to throw it out the window, but it wasn't open. It bounced back at me and landed on my leg. I shook it off and started the engine instead. I was always pleased when it sprung to life, being as old as it was.

Just drive, SJ. Forget it. Forget her.

The road outside the prison was empty but I could see the cars zooming by on the dual carriageway not far away. People didn't tend to spend much time hanging around outside prisons. Those who got out, ran for their lives, and those who were visiting didn't want to be seen. Me? I just put my foot down and drove, trying to outrun the shadow that loomed behind my every step.

CHAPTER 4

SJ

It was just after 8 pm when I entered Colindale police station. It was an odd-looking building; it had a huge white barrel-like entrance surrounded by brick. Most of the other local police stations had been closed, but this one had survived the cuts and was even due a refurbishment.

When I approached the front desk, one of the regular staff, Petra, put down her Sudoku book and gave me a big smile. She was approaching fifty, always looked incredibly refined regardless of the commotions that came through the door and had a sweet spot for me. I would routinely gift her with a new Sudoku book. I spent a lot of time speaking to the point of contact staff, so being friendly was not only important but useful.

'How are you, Mr Robin?'

'Petra, when will you start calling me SJ?' I started typing my details into the sign-in screen and posed for an unflattering photo for my pass.

'When you get a proper first name. What kind of a name is SJ?' she joked, getting a badge ready for me.

'Did you know studies show that more intelligent people use initials in their names?'

She leaned closer. 'Really?'

I laughed. 'No, my dear Petra, just teasing.'

She sighed and gave me a look as she stuffed the photo ID badge into its holder and threw it across the desk to me.

'I should have known… be careful not to get on my bad side, buddy.'

I slotted my badge through my buttonhole and saw she was already back at her Sudoku book, pretending to have forgotten I was there. 'Thank you, ever patient Petra.'

'Who are you here to see anyway?'

I got my notepad out of the inner pocket of my suit. I read out, 'Briony Campbell.'

She glanced at the whiteboard with the booking in information. 'Holding cell 3. DC Demetriou.'

'Oh, the luck of it,' I pretended to grumble.

'Go do some work, Mr Robin,' she mumbled, half-smiling and pressed the door release.

I knew there were two places I'd find Aris: by the vending machine drinking a Ribena or filling out his paperwork at his desk in his precise hand, waiting eagerly for me to speak to his suspect so he could get on with his job. When I found him in neither place, I went back down to the interview rooms to look for him, scanning the custody notes as I did.

I found him pacing back and forth in front of a door. 'Hey kiddo, you must be on fire today. You've finished your paperwork already?'

Aris stopped and took me in for a moment, as though he didn't recognise me, but finally broke into a tired smile. 'Oh crap, it's *your* shift?'

'No, I just come here for the laughs.' I approached him and held my hand out, which he took and squeezed. I noticed how he wasn't wearing a blazer for once and his shirt was creased. Aris always wore a well-pressed shirt and suit, which clashed horribly with my unkempt attire most of the time. 'You okay, kiddo?'

He took my arm and pulled me away from the door to the other side of the corridor. 'Don't call me that here, Jon. You'll ruin my image,' he joked but glanced around the corridor to see if anyone had heard. It was a bit unfair for me to call him 'kiddo' – he was actually the same age as me, but when we'd first met five years ago and had no idea what we were doing, I'd joked that he was just a kid in comparison to me as he was six months younger. Somehow, the nickname had stuck.

'When Petra told me you did the booking in, I pretended to be disappointed, if it helps.'

He managed a laugh, but his shoulders were tight. 'Yes, well Petra knows we're buddies, so I think you're on a lost one there.'

'Oh no, you mean people have realised we're *not* sworn enemies?' I pretended to gasp. To be fair, it was odd that a detective and a lawyer who were often on opposite sides had managed to forge some kind of friendship.

'I've had comments,' he raised his thick eyebrows. 'But look, I can't say much, as you know, but I presume you're here for Briony Campbell.'

'Yep. She ask for a solicitor?'

He leaned against the wall and crossed his arms. 'She did, but I decided you'd have to do.'

'You know how to make me feel good, kiddo.'

'It's complicated, Jon.' Aris sighed.

'How so?' I leaned against the wall too, trying to ignore the officers and suspects ambling past us towards interviews and holding cells. There was a lot of chinking of handcuffs and the rustling of batons in police belts.

'In many ways… Before you bust my balls or anything; she's been assessed by the custody nurse, and a mental health professional, and deemed fit for interview and detainment. We've been told to handle her carefully but that's it.'

'Thanks for the heads-up.' I was interested to see why she needed to be handled carefully but I'd find out soon enough. Sometimes the custody notes don't tell you the full story. It had been noted that she'd seen a therapist in the past. Even so, there had to be something behind this story of a twenty-seven-year-old woman bludgeoning her accountant boyfriend, but they'd get to the bottom of it.

'The other point of interest is that the crime was divulged to Mari.'

I straightened up at the name. 'As in, *your* sister Mari? How is she involved?'

'Which other Mari do you know?' Aris scoffed, luckily not noticing how uncomfortable I now felt with my body. It suddenly seemed like the floor was made of marshmallow and I might fall over.

'Yeah, of course, sorry.' I made a big point of checking my watch. 'Bit tired today,' I lied.

'Shall I tell that to your client?' Aris pushed himself off the wall. 'Anyway, why are you moaning; you basically don't sleep now anyway. Wasn't that partly why *The Woman* left you?'

I pulled my phone out of my pocket and pretended to check for an incoming message to avoid Aris's probing. 'I'd rather not talk about Claire.' Though part of me was touched he only referred to her as 'The Woman' out of solidarity with me, much like Irene Adler in *Sherlock Holmes*.

'Yeah, well it's been all "no comment" from you since it happened.'

'So, get the hint, kiddo,' I shot back.

'Hey, Aris, you'd better not be leaking all our secrets to that vampire,' a voice interrupted from behind him. His partner, DS Josie Owusu, appeared, giving me her usual disapproving glare. It was safe to say she had never taken to me and I had long-since given up trying to charm her. She was no-nonsense, more like an older sister to Aris because she was ten years his senior. She was brilliant with computers and always followed the money; it was her basic policy for pretty much every case.

'Don't worry, we've even banned using the word "case" in casual conversation. It's a bit limiting but we must uphold your wishes, DS Owusu.' I would never call her 'Josie' to her face, but I normally did in my head.

She rolled her eyes at me and turned to Aris. 'Guv's calling us so let's go update him. You finished the paperwork?'

Aris dropped his head slightly. 'Um, no,' he mumbled. 'I'll get right on it.'

Josie didn't look impressed. 'Well, we'd better shake a leg then.' She marched off and Aris went to follow but I grabbed his arm.

'Are you sure everything is okay?'

'Course, always.' He stepped back. 'Just FYI, we have basically twenty-two hours left on the clock. We want to talk to her right after you before she goes into sleep mode.'

Aris started walking away but stopped outside the door he'd been pacing in front of earlier. He reached over and opened it a fraction, nodding inside. 'Can you just chat with Mari for a minute until I get back, Jon?'

I felt my stomach plummet. 'Oh, I should really, you know,' I checked my watch.

'Please,' he interrupted.

'Of course. Whatever you need.' I stepped towards the door, sucking in my breath.

I nudged the door open and saw a familiar form sitting at a table. When she noticed me there, her mouth fell open, but she quickly clamped it shut when she noticed her brother behind me.

'Get in there then. She doesn't bite,' Aris tried to joke but his voice was flat. Everything he was doing tonight was a show – for me, for Mari, for his partner, Owusu.

'Don't be long,' I warned him as I entered the interview room nervously. But he was gone.

CHAPTER 5

MARI

SJ held his briefcase in front of him as though it would offer some kind of protection. He gave her a brief smile, which oddly, she found she had missed after having avoided him for the last eight months. Actually, she hadn't avoided *him,* he'd avoided *her* at every opportunity.

'Maria? How are you?' he asked with false cheer. 'You look like you need to be in bed.'

She couldn't believe she was sitting in this cold interview room waiting for Aris to say she could go home. What else did he need from her? Or was he just checking she wasn't going to freak out as soon as she was out of his sight?

'You know it's Mari,' she growled. 'And as if you would know anything about my bed,' she spat, half-angry with herself that she still had thoughts about him being in it.

He looked down at his feet and mumbled but loud enough for her to hear, 'I should be so lucky.' Then he cleared his throat and stepped towards the chair on the other side of the table.

'Don't sit there. This isn't an interview.' She pushed out the chair next to her and patted it.

He froze and looked over at the empty chair as though it were a volcano oozing lava and he wondered if he could outrun it. He slid his briefcase onto the table and forced his legs to move towards her and sat down.

As he looked around at anything but her, Mari took the time to take him in again. He was wearing his suit messily as usual (tie loose, his jacket unbuttoned, his shirt slightly crumpled), his hair was longer than she remembered, but he didn't have any facial hair, which made his scar even more prominent. He didn't normally like to draw attention to it. And his eyes... They were the strangest blue. She'd spent a lot of time thinking about their colour and settled on aqua metallic blue, which was actually a type of car paint. It had irritated her for ages after last New Year's.

He unexpectedly met her eyes, and she didn't break contact.

'What are you doing here?' She blinked a few times, waking herself up.

He laughed. 'I think I'm the one who should be asking you that. You're kind of on my territory, Mari.' He dropped his smile then and leaned a little closer. 'Seriously, are you okay? I mean, after what happened today...' He put his hand on the table, edging it closer to hers until his fingers were resting on top of hers. She instinctively turned her hand over.

She realised that he didn't smell of cigarettes for once. He smelt of washing powder and coffee, which was an odd mix, but strangely familiar. 'Aris says I can't talk to you about what happened, but it was pretty... unsettling.'

He nodded gently. 'I get it.' He paused, his eyes moving over her face and down her body, assessing for damage. She felt herself blushing as thoughts of them together last New Year's Eve resurfaced. 'But are you hurt?' he asked quietly.

'Only by men who stick their tongue down my throat and don't call me.'

He lurched back, taking his hand with him. 'Guess I deserved that.' He took a deep breath, and Mari thought he might actually apologise but instead, he whispered, 'Aris doesn't bloody know, does he?'

'I'm sure what you *meant* to say was "sorry."' She grabbed him by his tie and pulled him closer, making him cast a panicked glance behind them to see if the door was still closed. 'And if Aris knew, you'd be toast, SJ.' She managed to keep her tone cool, despite lingering dangerously close to SJ's face.

He grabbed her by both arms and held her still. He seemed to be breathing her in, although simultaneously holding her in place so neither of them could slip any closer. Was it just her imagination? 'I'm sorry, all right?' he breathed, swallowing hard.

'What did you say?' Mari cocked her ear closer.

SJ screwed up his face and sighed. 'You heard me. I was a mess at New Year's.'

'Yes, you were pretty off your face,' Mari agreed. She remembered taking him outside for some air and forcing him to drink water. When he'd arrived at the party, it was clear he had quite a few drinks in his system already. Then he'd proceeded to drink straight whisky for an hour non-stop. How they had ended up locking lips outside, Mari wasn't sure, but despite her anger, Mari had never quite forgotten how hard her heart had thudded in her chest and how her body had responded to his kiss. She'd had a mini-crush on SJ for a while before that night anyway. At thirty-three, she really should know better.

'Look, I think it's time we tried to be… okay… with one another again. What do you think?' He released her arms and sat back, pressing himself against the back of the chair as if to restrain himself from coming closer again. 'Can we do that?' He presented one side of his face to her, making his scar disappear for a moment.

'We can,' Mari shrugged. Maybe SJ was here to represent Briony? 'But sometime you'd better explain why you were such an arse.'

His mouth twitched. 'Maybe it's just my human nature.'

Mari raised her eyebrows and pulled him closer by his messy collar so she could whisper in his ear. 'Sorry to tell you, but I know you're full of shit.'

SJ straightened up and widened his eyes at her, a smile bubbling up on his lips. 'I knew there was a reason I kissed you.'

'Sort your tie out. You look like a fourteen-year-old.' She rolled her eyes.

He frowned and half-heartedly attempted to fix his tie, with an amused grin on his face.

'One day I'm going to ask you to marry me, Mari.' SJ had a serious expression.

'Oh, I've never heard that one before – Mari, mar-ry. But anyway, please do, so I can tell you where to shove your proposal.'

'You know, I'm not sure I remember quite how we ended up kissing.' He stared her down.

'I remember. You said, "Who'd want to kiss a carved-up piece of shit like me?" and I said, "Me, SJ. I think you have a great arse."'

'That rings a bell, especially the part about my arse.' He glanced at his watch pointedly.

Mari snorted. 'It's etched into your heart, I can tell.'

He turned back and smiled but she only saw sadness behind it. What was SJ hiding and why wouldn't he just let the mask slip? 'Really, Mari, I'm pleased you're okay.' He had his hand on his knee, palm upwards, and his fingers were twitching as though wanting to bridge the gap between them again.

They both stared at his hand without moving but the air felt heavy with the gap of eight months.

When the door opened, SJ jumped up and put his hand on his briefcase as though he'd been planning on leaving. Aris stepped in.

'Sis, you wanna go home now? I think we have what we need for now.'

Mari pushed herself up and nodded, glancing at SJ, who had plastered a grin on his face and was trying not to look at her.

'I hope he wasn't trying to have his way with you,' Aris joked.

SJ frowned but covered it with a choked laugh.

'What are you talking about?' Mari stammered.

'You know, trying to get information out of you.' He shot SJ a warning look.

SJ pretended to look offended. 'I won't have you slandering me this way.' He focused on Mari again and winked. 'Good to see you, Mari. Next time, maybe I'll choose the place, huh?'

Despite the disturbing and exhausting day she'd had, she couldn't help but laugh.

Aris nodded towards the door and said, 'Come on, Jon. I can brief you with the essentials on the way.'

CHAPTER 6

BRIONY

She was dreaming about Ed when something woke her. She groaned against the coldness of the 'bed' she was lying on. It felt more like a slab of cold concrete but, in reality, it was one of those thin mats with an equally shoddy pillow to match. It reminded her of the floor she'd woken up on in Ed's flat...

She squinted at the man near the door, who didn't bother stepping closer. 'Got visitors,' he mumbled. He looked like he could do with some more sleep and resented her for being asleep when he'd opened door. He sniffed as if he needed a tissue and stared at her.

'Who is it?'

'Lawyer.'

'What time is it?'

'Coming up to 8:45 pm.'

She stood up, causing him to fall back on his heels. He seemed to finger the baton in his belt, causing her to freeze.

'Can you take me to them please?' she asked, smiling gently. She tried to reposition her mouth, so she didn't look demonic but wasn't sure how she appeared. They'd taken her clothes away for forensics and given her a grey tracksuit to wear.

The officer's face softened a little, as though her manners detracted from her crime. He stepped out of the doorway to allow her to pass. Moving in pigeon steps, she watched the baton in his belt as they walked. Even though they'd let her wash her hands, traces of blood were still visible under her fingernails.

'Second right,' he mumbled from behind her.

When she entered the interview room, she noticed a man sitting just inside. He was wearing a grey suit but the top button of his shirt was undone and his jacket was hanging off him as if he had been roughed up by some bullies on his way in. He was reading something and didn't bother to look up, even when she turned her attention to him.

The officer was trying to close the door and practically shoved her inside.

'Who are you?' she asked the man, trying not to stare at the large scar on his cheek, which extended from his right eye all the way down to his chin.

'SJ Robin, lawyer.' He stood up and held out his hand.

He gestured towards a chair on the other side of the table. 'Can I call you Briony or would you prefer Miss Campbell?'

'Briony's fine.' She paused, sitting down. 'But why are you here? Are you with the police?'

SJ tapped his fingers on the table as if he was in a jazz café relaxing, rather than sitting in a cold police station. 'You have a right to a lawyer. I'm sure they told you that?'

'I can't afford a lawyer,' she blurted.

'Don't worry, it's called Legal Aid.'

'You're working for free?'

'Do I look like I work for free?' He gestured to his appearance with a knowing grin. 'Anyway, this type of case interests me.'

'And what kind of case is that?'

He poured her some water and pushed it across the table. She downed the water in one, suddenly parched.

'A mystery,' he whispered in a secretive tone.

'Is this a game to you? Because it's *not* a game to me.'

'Calm down, Miss Campbell,' he commanded, raising his voice just enough to make her stop short and shrink down in her chair.

'I'm sorry,' she mumbled.

'I'm here to help you, Briony. Can you tell me what happened?'

'Can you tell my mum I'm okay? Tell her she needs to take her medicine.'

'Medicine?' he asked, raising his eyebrows.

'She's got type-1 diabetes. If she gets stressed out, she forgets to take it.'

'Ah.' He nodded to himself. 'I'll get a message to her. What's her name?'

'Jessica Campbell. And thank you, sir.'

'It's SJ,' he corrected her.

'What does SJ stand for?'

'It's just SJ,' he mumbled. 'So, Briony, tell me...' He opened up his folder and slid a fresh piece of paper out, took a silver pen from his inside pocket and wrote the date on the paper in precise curvy handwriting. He looked back up at her. 'They say you don't remember what happened. Can you tell me anything that you *do* remember?'

'You think I'm a liar?'

He moved the pen between his fingers like a magician as he stared her down for a few moments. 'Briony, we need to help you remember so we can get this all sorted. They told me you'd been psychologically assessed.'

She nodded.

'Okay, we need to decide what to tell the police, which may not be much right now, with your memory, and then you'll probably be here overnight.'

She frowned.

'I know, I'm sorry but they get twenty-four hours to detain you and you're entitled to some rest. They'll probably interview you again tomorrow and decide if they have enough to charge you or not.' He paused. 'You're clean right? No prior offences?'

'Nothing.'

'Are you happy with the way you've been treated?' he checked, squinting at her, his blue eyes steely.

'Yes.'

'Good. Look, you'll have to be interviewed. Then hopefully we'll be out of here soon enough. In the interview, I want you to use "no comment" as much as you like, okay? And check with me before you say anything other than the cold facts, like your name or address, or what we've previously agreed.'

'But I already told Doctor Demetriou what happened.'

He nodded. 'Yes… but she's not a witness. She didn't break confidentiality as someone else called it in, so nothing she says can be used as evidence against you, at this point,' he explained and suddenly it felt so serious: *witness, confidentiality, evidence.* And what did he mean by '*at this point*'?

When she didn't speak for a long moment, he asked, 'Briony, do you understand that they might charge you with attempted murder?'

'*Attempted murder?*' she repeated hoarsely.

'I asked if you understood. Can you tell me if you do?'

31

'I heard what you said but *"attempted"*. Why "attempted"?'

He was now holding his pen like a cigarette in his right hand. 'Ed isn't dead, Briony.'

'What?' She sat forward.

'Ed. He's *not* dead, not yet anyway,' he repeated, checking his watch. 'They have about one hour and a half max. until they should probably let you rest for the night, so I think we need to get started.'

'Wait… Ed's alive?' She shook her head in disbelief.

'That's good news. You should be happy,' he informed her gently, meeting her eyes.

'Can I see him?' she asked, before she remembered what a stupid question that was.

'Sorry, no.' He tapped his notepad. 'Right, just take your time Briony. Give me what you know so I can see what we're dealing with.'

'He wasn't breathing when I left. I thought—'

'Yes, but Ed's injuries… Can you tell me what happened?' he asked softly.

'There was so much blood… I… I… can't…' Briony let out a strangled sob.

SJ sighed and waited for Briony to calm down again.

'You can do this,' he assured her, but she saw him glance at his watch again.

CHAPTER 7

SJ

An hour or so later, in another bare interview room, I sat with my notepad open and my pen poised. It seemed fitting that every time I had to write about violent crimes, I used the pen that my father had given me. It was a delicate fountain pen with a robin clip, after our surname – he'd loved birdwatching. I should've got rid of the pen years ago but somehow it had followed me, and I diligently refilled it.

I'd been in this interview room more times than I cared to remember. The walls were white but marked with kick marks from frustrated clients waiting to be interviewed or left alone for a moment to contemplate their crimes. The chairs were plastic and uncomfortable, but my body seemed to have adapted to their unforgiving hardness. Now, I barely noticed. Briony, however, was squirming in the chair next to me while the interviewing officers sat opposite us.

The video recorder had been fiddled around with a few minutes and was now rolling. Briony had given it a distasteful glance but decided not to protest.

'This interview is being recorded at Colindale Police Station in London. It is Monday, 17th August 2020. The time is 9:45 pm. I'm Detective Sergeant 625, Josie Owusu. Also present is…'

'Detective Constable 813, Aris Demetriou.' Aris met my eyes with a subdued smile.

'Can you tell us your name for the recorder please?' Josie directed at Briony.

'Briony Grace Campbell.'

'And your age and date of birth please?'

'29th July 1993. I'm twenty-seven'

'Thank you. Also present is…' Josie turned to me, wearing her standard blank face in my presence. It was either that or her pissed-off face.

'SJ Robin, Stafford's solicitors.'

'Is it okay for us to call you Briony?' Josie asked. It seemed as though she was taking the lead and Aris was playing the silent partner. Perhaps it was because of the link to Mari?

'Okay.' Briony stared down at her hands. She'd been doing it a lot since I'd met her.

'We're going to be talking about the injuries sustained by Edward William Porter in his flat today, the 17th of August. We will ask you questions and whether you choose to answer is up to you. Do you understand?'

Briony flashed me a look before saying, 'Yes.'

'First of all, Briony, can you explain the nature of your relationship with Mr Porter?'

'We're… a couple.' Everything Briony said seemed to open up a maze of possibilities because she didn't sound certain about anything.

Josie tried to stop her eyebrows from raising and focused on her writing for a moment. After pretending to scratch out a few words, she asked, 'How long have you been a couple?'

'Around six months.'

'And how long have you been neighbours with Mr Porter?'

'Around a year.' Briony started pressing her hands into balls over and over. I saw Aris's eyes latch onto it, storing it away for later.

Josie sat forward, 'Can you tell us what happened earlier today, in your own words?'

Briony raised her head, squinting as though she couldn't see properly. 'Starting when?'

'Whenever you feel is relevant.'

'Okay… I stayed at his flat last night and this morning, he went for a run. He was working from home today. When he came back, we had a sandwich and a fruit salad I'd made. Over lunch, we chatted about his run and our plans for the day. We were thinking about going to the cinema maybe. Sometimes we got a drink after in a nearby bar. Then Ed…' Briony stopped short, turning to me again.

'You can answer whatever you like, Briony. You can also choose to say "no comment" if you want to,' I reminded her. I'd told her to tell them what she remembered and if she felt uncomfortable or unsure, she should remain silent. She appeared to be struggling with the concept already.

'He suddenly said, "Beautiful, did I tell you how much I love you?" and I asked him what was wrong, and he hesitated and said, "I just love you. Is that a bad thing?"' Briony covered her face with her hands and let out a squeaking sound. I exchanged a look with Aris who was trying not to look up from his pad, but couldn't help raising his head at the sound.

'What happened after that, Briony?' Josie persisted.

Briony uncovered her face and, surprisingly, it was bone dry. I thought she might have erupted under her hands but, if anything, she looked calmer than ever. 'I don't remember.'

'You don't remember anything at all?' Aris piped in, sounding more incredulous than he probably should.

I raised an unimpressed eyebrow and he looked down again. 'My client has already told you she is suffering from memory loss,' I emphasised.

'Has this happened to you before, Briony?' Josie asked gently.

Briony examined her hands for a moment, moving her fingers back and forth as though moving them through water. 'No.'

The abruptness of her answer said more than she thought it did. She'd told me exactly the same thing back in our brief beforehand and I'd been unconvinced then. I saw Josie's pen jolt on the paper involuntarily, but she straightened it out quickly.

'No blackouts? No history of memory loss? Whether it be after drinking or drugs, or something spontaneous?'

Briony shook her head and then murmured, 'No,' for the sake of the video recording.

'I don't think my client's past activities in relation to drink and drugs are pertinent here, especially when there's no suggestion of her being under the influence of either on this occasion.'

Josie didn't scowl at me, but I heard the pressure of the pen on the paper growing harder as she wrote down a few words. 'Briony, can you tell us what you next remember?'

'I woke up on Ed's living room floor. There was... blood. It was 2:51 pm.'

'That's incredibly precise,' Aris noted.

'I found a clock on the floor. I wanted to know what time it was.'

'Do you know how much time had passed since you had lunch with Mr Porter?' Josie took over again.

'I think he got back from his run around 11:30 am.'

'And when you woke up on the living room floor, can you tell me what happened?'

Briony checked with me but I nodded gently. 'I went to find Ed. The flat isn't that big, so I figured he must be in the bedroom...'

'Do you have a memory of being in the bedroom with Mr Porter after you finished lunch?' Aris contributed, taking a pause from his notes. He didn't look in my direction; he rarely did, unless he was forced to, when we were on opposing sides.

'No.' Briony was staring past his head as if she'd seen a friend across a busy street. 'I just remember... waking up.' She sounded surprised by her own words. I could almost see the CPS green-lighting the prosecution just from hearing Briony's interview.

Josie shifted in her chair. 'Can you tell me what you found in the bedroom?'

Briony sucked in her breath sharply. 'Ed... and blood. A lot of blood.'

'How did you react when you found him?'

Briony started pulsing her fists again. 'I felt numb.'

Damn, numb is not the word to choose...

'Did you think about calling someone?' Josie asked, which was one of the standard questions. A lot rode on the answer to this one too.

I felt myself tense, anticipating Briony's response.

'Who would I call?' Her voice cracked slightly.

'I don't know, Briony. Perhaps the police? A family member?' Josie suggested.

'I was afraid.'

'What were you afraid of?' Her voice was soft, as though they were friends sharing.

'That he was dead, I guess.' Briony grasped the side of the table with her hands now. It looked like she was about to go over the edge on a rollercoaster.

'Were you worried what people would think about you hurting Mr Porter?'

'I think that's a leading question,' I interrupted before Briony could answer.

Josie pursed her lips without looking up. 'Okay, I'll rephrase… Can you tell me how you felt about reporting the crime?'

Briony met my eyes questioningly, and I gave her a nod.

'I wanted to find someone who wouldn't judge me, so I went to my therapist.' Briony zoned in on Aris at this point, obviously having made the family connection. Aris kept his eyes down, but I could see the muscles in his neck were taut.

'This was Doctor Mari Demetriou at the local surgery, correct?'

'Yes, she's my therapist.'

'Okay, and why did you think she would be the best person to speak to?'

Briony smiled for one of the first times in the interview room and clasped her hands together in front of herself on the table. 'She's just always been so… approachable. She's listened to everything; about my life and how my family were… Well, she's never seemed to be thinking horrible things, you know?'

Josie put her pen down. 'Is there something you'd like to tell us?'

'I think I need a moment with my client before she answers that question.'

Josie internally growled; I almost heard it, but on the outside, she returned my smile. 'Briony, is that okay with you?'

'Yes, fine.'

'Interview terminated at 10:07 pm on August 17th 2020.'

Aris stood up abruptly and left the room.

'Let us know when you're ready to continue.' She stood up and followed Aris out.

CHAPTER 8

BRIONY

As soon as they were alone in a different room, SJ gestured to a chair. This room was smaller and painted a cream colour.

SJ had ordered them hot chocolates and they were waiting on the table.

'Proper mugs, wow,' he noted, flicking his fingernails against one as if to check they were real. 'I bet Petra was on drink duty – she loves me,' he joked.

He added, 'I thought it best to avoid caffeine. I know how precious custody sleep can be.'

She shrugged and sat down. 'Thanks,' she managed.

'How are you finding this process, Briony? I know it doesn't always feel like it, but your wellbeing is important.' He took a sip of hot chocolate, pulled a face but immediately took another sip.

She wrapped her hands around the mug, enjoying its warmth at the very least. 'Terrible. Is that normal?'

'Not many people describe it in positive terms. But if there's anything you take issue with or are finding too overwhelming, now's your chance.'

'No.'

'Is it okay if we talk then? I'm interested to continue with what came up at the end of the interview. You mentioned your family and therapy. Is there something there I need to know about?' He put his expensive pen down and gave her his undivided attention.

She sighed. 'I didn't mean to mention it. I don't really want to talk about it.'

He put his hands together on the table in front of him and forced a smile. 'Briony, I appreciate you may not *want* to talk about whatever this is, but anything that may be important to this investigation needs to be discussed.' He gestured to the door. 'Would you rather they dig it up and ask you in the next interview?'

She rubbed her hand slowly down the side of her face, and he could see how tired she was.

'Okay... I lost my brother when I was seven. He was only four.' She came out with it like a recipe she'd reused a thousand times. She'd probably had to tell numerous doctors and professionals about it since that day. It sounded like it had become a cold fact and the emotion had slithered away from it at some point.

'I'm so sorry,' SJ said quietly. His voice was muted and slow, like someone who had felt death standing close to them. 'Could you tell me more about that?'

'Agh,' she groaned. They would never leave her alone. She had to explain it all again. Maybe she would never escape, like a cockroach constantly stuck on its back, unable to crawl away and unable to die.

'We were on holiday. Me and my brother, Jason went for a walk. He drowned in the lake.'

SJ listened and nodded as he considered her words. 'How did it happen?' he asked so directly, she jerked her head up to meet his eyes. 'I'm sorry. I just need the facts,' he quickly added.

'I don't remember what happened. Only waking up beside the lake and trying to find him. He was... floating. I tried to shake him.'

'Okay.' SJ paused. 'What did you do after that?'

'I ran.'

'To your parents?'

'No, I hid in the woods for a while.' It had been cold in the woods, dark, scary.

SJ stared at the wall beside her for a long moment, opened his mouth a few times but didn't speak. Instead, he picked up his pen and made a few notes. He seemed to deliberately write incoherently so she had no chance of reading it.

'I presume you've received help for this issue? From Doctor Demetriou?'

'And others, but she's been... the best.' Thinking of Mari made her feel lighter.

SJ nodded again. 'I have to ask you if I can discuss this with Doctor Demetriou. You need to give me permission to break the therapist-patient confidentiality. We'll have to get it written down and signed too.'

'Okay,' she agreed, staring at the tabletop. She took a minute to meet his eyes again; they were bright and full. 'This won't look good for me, will it?'

SJ glanced down at his notepad as if it held a secret and then looked back at her face, then down to his notepad again. 'I don't know, to be honest. But it's good to be prepared. If we go in blind, there's no point in us doing this.'

42

'Do you think Ed will die?' she asked, clenching her hands into balls again. She'd been taught to do this by one of the numerous doctors she'd had throughout her life.

'I'm sorry but I don't know. What I *do* know is that he's having emergency surgery. We should know more by morning.'

'Oh.'

'Briony, look, what do you want to tell them here?'

'I don't remember,' she repeated. It felt like she could say it forever and no one would hear.

'There's nothing at all? Not an image, anything?' he persisted, leaning in.

She shook her head. 'I don't remember what happened to Ed. Or Jason. Everything is blank.'

He sat back and stared at the ceiling for a long moment. She could see his lips moving but he was silent. Suddenly, he stood up and pushed his chair in. 'There are definitely no other surprises for me, right?' he appealed across table.

'None.'

'We'll work this out,' he informed her but unlike his previous assurances, this one sounded empty.

CHAPTER 9

MARI

As Mari entered the surgery on Tuesday morning, she couldn't stop thinking about the events of the previous day. She hadn't seen pictures of the crime scene; she had no right to, but it didn't stop her imagining the scene and how Briony had got covered in so much blood.

Stop it, Mari.

Aside from Briony and checking her diary for appointments starting later, it was the usual morning madness of trying to keep up with her numerous relatives who had set up about twenty different text groups for the most random reasons. It was as though they came alive at 8 am every morning after someone had thrown them some food.

She had managed to overfill her coffee mug and now there was coffee running down the cupboard door and pooling on the floor. She was trying to mop it up with a tea towel when her supervisor, Ollie, popped his head in.

'Wrecking the joint?' he joked as he knelt down beside her without a second thought and took the tea towel out of her hands. He grabbed another one from the worktop and used that to soak some up as well. He didn't even like coffee so this was a real sign of friendship.

'Sorry. I was miles away.'

He gave her a gentle smile. It was one of the first things she'd noticed about him and, evidently, what his patients noticed about him too. They seemed to soften under that smile. 'Can't blame you after yesterday's shenanigans. Are you sure you're okay?'

She leaned against the worktop, nodding for a long moment but realising she was actually just nodding without meaning. 'I'm… okay,' she finally said quietly.

He raised his eyebrows at her. Ollie could always spot one of her lies.

'That lawyer is outside.'

'SJ?' She straightened up.

'You sure you're ready to talk to him? I can throw him out?' Ollie winked but she wasn't sure he'd ever thrown anyone out in his life.

'No, that's okay. I can handle Mr Robin,' she assured him but inside felt herself melting like she'd been left out in the sun for too long.

'You know him then?'

'You could say that.'

'I'm next door if you need me, Mari. Don't let him step out of line,' he warned.

Little does he know. 'Can you bring him to my office, please?'

Ollie went to retrieve SJ as she made her way to her office. She was rearranging the motivation quotes on her pinboard when she heard a knock at the door. She shouted, 'Come in,' and took her seat.

Before she could catch her breath, in walked SJ, dressed much more casually than normal in a polo shirt and jeans. He even had some sunglasses hanging from his shirt as if he was on his way to the beach.

'Your boyfriend doesn't seem to like me much,' he said as he threw himself into the seat opposite and placed his briefcase on the desk.

'He's my supervisor, actually,' she corrected him with narrowed eyes.

He nodded at her mug. 'Still one sugar, or are you sweet enough?'

'Why would you remember something as random as that? Anyway, you're the one who doesn't take sugar,' she blurted out and instantly regretted it when she saw the smug smile on SJ's face.

'I *knew* you remembered something about me.'

'More's the pity.' She clasped her hands together on the desk and tried to reset. 'So, what is it you want to discuss?'

'Shouldn't your supervisor be in here?' SJ busied himself with pulling out a notepad and pen from his briefcase.

'He knows the situation and I told him I can handle you.' She stared him down.

'Is that so,' he laughed. It wasn't a question. 'Wow, you're really mad at me, huh? It's not like we slept together.' When she remained silent, he sat forward and added in a whisper, 'Did we?'

'Yes, I decided not to keep the baby,' she answered flatly.

'Probably for the best, honey.'

'Don't call me that,' she snapped.

He held his hands up in a sign of peace. 'Okay, look you know I'm here to talk about Briony Campbell. Can I ask you a few things?'

'If you have all the paperwork signed. No funny business.'

He passed across a signed affidavit from Briony confirming he was allowed to discuss her therapeutic history with Mari. She spent a long time examining the signature.

When she looked up, he was grinning. 'Satisfied?'

'Okay,' she said.

'Look, you're not a witness because of your pre-existing relationship to Briony and you didn't call it in so you're not in hot water there. Briony will also be independently assessed by another doctor in time.' SJ paused and looked her in the face. 'This is just a chat.'

'As if I could trust you.' She crossed her arms and sat back in her chair.

He swallowed hard and she wasn't sure if it was because of last New Year's Eve or because of something to do with the case. 'So, Briony's still in custody for now but the clock is running down, which is why I had to make a hasty morning call like this. I'm sorry.'

'All it takes is an attempted murder case and you're all kinds of available, I see.' She watched him fidget with his sunglasses as he digested her words.

He cleared his throat. 'I'm sorry, okay? I was an arsehole to you. I should've called you, at the very least.'

Mari took a sip of her coffee to distract herself from staring at SJ for too long.

'I *did* think about it by the way.'

'Think about *what?*'

'Calling you.' He swallowed heavily.

'Maybe you should have.'

'Is it too late? You're probably taken, aren't you? I mean, come on, look at you. It's like "order-a-Greek-goddess-dot-com".' He chuckled nervously.

'We should probably remain professional until whatever this is gets resolved…' She pulled her eyes away from his searching gaze and lowered them to the paper on the desk.

'Well, look at that. I put myself out there and you give me the brush off.' He stood up as if thinking of leaving but remembering he had things he needed to discuss, slid awkwardly back into the chair.

'Right, *concentrate*… So, as you know, Briony told me about her brother's death and said I could discuss it with you.'

'I still can't believe she told you.'

SJ half-shrugged. 'I think she thought it would come out anyway, especially when they started asking her about the memory loss.'

'That's what she's saying – that it's memory loss?' Mari latched on.

SJ gave her a twisted smile. 'Yes, sorry. We can talk about bare bones, especially as you know her history, but not the meat of the investigation.'

'I understand. But what do you want from me? She didn't say much when she came into the surgery.'

'I appreciate that. I just had a few questions.' He opened his notepad and held his pen over the page, ready to transcribe. If only she knew what to tell him.

'First question is: did you notice any injuries to Briony?'

Mari thought for a moment. 'I think there were bruises. Around her neck.'

'If I told you the victim had similar bruising, would you have any comments on that?' He didn't look up, but she knew he was paying close attention by the way he was so still.

'I don't really think that's my place to comment. Maybe you should speak to Aris about that?' she suggested.

SJ met her eyes. 'I would never put you at risk, Mari. I'm trying to find ways to help her.'

'Are you sure about that?' She stared him down and it felt like she was asking about more than just this situation. It felt intimate in some way.

'On my life.' He paused. 'Second question: would you say it's possible someone's past trauma might influence their current behaviours?'

'Come on, SJ...' she cautioned.

'To rephrase, could a repressed memory re-emerge and cause violent behaviour if there was a particular trigger?'

Mari crossed her arms again. 'I'm not comfortable with where this is going.'

SJ nodded as if he'd expected her to say that. 'Right, some details we can focus on... When Briony came to the surgery, what were her exact words?'

'She said, "I think I killed him."'

'So, she didn't say she had *definitely* killed him?'

'No.'

'How many sessions have you had with Briony?'

'I checked the records, and it was ten over the course of five months. We tried to meet every other week.'

'She told me she was referred to you for anxiety. Is that correct?'

'Yes.'

'That's it.' He closed his notepad. 'Well, more or less... Briony asked if you would continue to be her therapist.'

Mari thought about Briony's flat expression and the blood and didn't know what to say. Of course she wanted to help Briony, maybe to finally unwind the trauma rooted in Briony's brain, but she felt out of her depth with this. 'Could I let you know?'

'Absolutely,' he agreed brightly. 'And there was one final question.'

'Seriously?' she exclaimed.

'Um, yeah…' he stammered to a stop and took a deep breath. 'Are you then?'

'Am I what?'

'Taken? In a relationship? Seeing someone?' he clarified, dodging her eyes.

She tried not to laugh. 'Actually, no. Is that pertinent to the case?'

SJ's face transformed into a grin. 'Oh yes, it's of huge interest to the case.'

'I fail to see how. Can you clarify exactly?' she teased.

SJ looked up at the ceiling. 'Absolutely no comment.'

CHAPTER 10

BRIONY

The night passed slowly. She had almost jumped at the door when the custody officer had come in at 8 am to check if she wanted breakfast. *Crunchy Nut* seemed like an odd thing to eat when you were being detained at a police station, but the options were limited.

When SJ finally turned up at around 10 am, she was moved to an interview room, where he greeted her with a bright good morning, despite having huge bags under his eyes that could compete with hers.

'How did you sleep?' he asked, as he played with his pen between his fingers.

'I think you can imagine,' she answered flatly.

He nodded and gestured to cup beside her hand. 'Tea if you want it. Two sugars.'

'Thanks,' she mumbled but left the cup where it was. She needed to pee, out of nerves maybe.

The door opened and detectives Owusu and Demetriou entered. Briony had spent the night thinking about his connection to Doctor Demetriou. They must be siblings because of their age and physical resemblance. No one had clarified the connection though. She could ask SJ perhaps.

'Morning,' they greeted her.

Then it was questions upon questions about all things they'd already discussed. It was thirty minutes later when they finally moved onto new ground. DC Demetriou had been largely silent until he finally met her eyes.

'Briony, you mentioned something last time about your therapy. Would you be willing to discuss this with us?'

Briony nodded and then remembered she had to speak. 'Okay.'

'I assume you've spoken with your lawyer about this?' he asked, glancing at SJ.

'We've produced a written statement of what Briony wants to say, if I can read it?' SJ sat forward with paper in his hands.

'Please go ahead.'

SJ started reading.

'I, Briony Campbell, would like to share the following information. I have been seeking therapy over the course of my life in relation to the death of my brother, who died at age four. I was seven when he drowned on a family holiday. I have no memory of the drowning. No doctors have been able to help me recall what happened that day. I have most recently been seeing Doctor Mari Demetriou for anxiety, which is linked to my past trauma. I am telling you this because I want to share that I have suffered from memory loss in the past, which is relevant to what happened with Mr Porter.'

SJ put the paper down, signalling he was finished.

'Thank you for sharing that with us,' DC Demetriou commented, but Briony saw him thinking hard. His eyes seemed to be moving in various directions as if he couldn't latch on to a single thought. He blinked for a long moment and then asked, 'Have you ever been given a medical explanation for your memory loss as a child?'

'No.'

'Okay. Is it all right if we move back to the present day?'

She sighed. 'I really don't know what else you want me to tell you.'

DC Demetriou nodded. 'I appreciate this is difficult and we've been asking you a lot of questions. We really only have a few more to ask.'

Briony noticed SJ shifting in his chair slightly.

'Go on,' she conceded.

'Okay, so you said that when you went into the bedroom after you woke up on the living room floor, that you saw Mr Porter and lots of blood. Did you see anything that could be used as a weapon near him?'

'I'm not sure my client would know what kind of weapon you were referring to.' SJ jumped in.

DC Demetriou stared SJ down for long moment and nodded. 'Yes, you're right, Mr Robin.' He paused and turned back to her. 'We were thinking of something blunt – maybe not an obvious weapon. Did you see anything like that?'

Briony looked over at SJ, who was already checking her reaction. She appealed to him with her eyes for help, but he didn't interrupt. 'I'm not sure what you mean,' she eventually said.

'We currently have a forensic team at Mr Porter's flat. They'll be checking every corner, every surface, every inch. Is there anything you'd like to tell us? Anything you think they may find?'

She squeezed her fists together under the table, trying to stop blood rushing so fast to her brain. It felt overloaded. 'I don't know what they might find.'

DC Demetriou cleared his throat. 'Okay, Briony. Though when you went to see Doctor Demetriou, you were covered in blood. Do you know whose blood that was?'

'Probably Ed's.' She shivered.

'Do you know if the blood on you definitely belonged to Mr Porter?'

'She's said multiple times that she has no memory of how she got blood on herself,' SJ reminded them, sounding almost bored.

'Yes, thank you, Mr Robin,' DC Demetriou said. His voice sounded tight, like there was history between them.

'Briony,' DS Owusu finally spoke. 'Could there be an innocent explanation for the blood on you when you were arrested?'

She hesitated for a long moment. 'Not sure.'

'Witnesses at the surgery reported you said, "I think I killed him." Were you talking about Mr Porter?'

'Yes. He looked dead.' The tears began building. 'I thought he was gone,' she whispered.

DS Owusu gave her sympathetic smile. 'We understand this is difficult.' She faced SJ, 'Mr Robin, is there anything else you'd like to share on behalf of your client?'

He shook his head. His eyes were moving between the two detectives as though watching a tennis match. He clasped his hands together in front of himself, trying to appear relaxed.

The two detectives seemed to be communicating silently and after few moments of gestures and nods, DC Demetriou focused on her again. 'Briony, we have decided to release you on bail pending further investigation at this point.'

'What does that mean?' she croaked.

'It means that we are still building a case, but we are allowing you to leave the station until we have further evidence or information that we need you to answer to. Do you understand?'

'I think so.'

'It means you can leave, Briony, with some conditions,' SJ clarified.

'Exactly,' DC Demetriou agreed. 'In this case, we'd like you to find alternative accommodation as we have secured a search warrant for your flat and, unfortunately, you won't be allowed into your apartment building while the investigation is ongoing.' He paused, as though checking a list. 'Do you have someone you can stay with?'

'My… mum?'

'That's fine. And obviously, no leaving the country or contacting Mr Porter. Mr Robin can fill you in on the rest.'

'Is he awake?' she asked quietly.

DC Demetriou examined her face. 'He's in a stable condition but still in ICU. I can't tell you anything else, I'm afraid.'

'Thank you for telling me that much.' She dropped her head to her lap as a few tears started to fall.

'Interview terminated at 10:42 am,' DS Owusu said.

As they both pushed their chairs back and stood, SJ got up and spoke with them quietly in the corner.

'Briony,' SJ said a few minutes later.

She looked up through her tears to see SJ's scarred face. 'Why are they letting me go?' She stood up, wobbled and then used the table to hold herself up.

'They'll only charge you if they think they can get a conviction.'

'Oh… okay,' she breathed out, sagging back down into the chair.

CHAPTER 11

SJ

I met Aris in *The Three Horseshoes* pub in Whetstone on Wednesday evening, the day after Briony had been released. He was undoubtedly playing the new detective app he'd just discovered on his phone (such a cliché but he couldn't seem to help himself), while sipping at a pint, which he'd probably been nursing for at least half an hour. I plonked into a seat opposite, making Aris spill some of his pint in his lap. He scowled at me, but it didn't last long.

'Not seen enough of me lately?'

'Wasn't this meeting your idea?' he grumbled. 'And you owe me a drink.'

'I owe you *a sip* of a drink.'

'Good correction, counsel,' Aris shot back.

I laughed and got up to order two beers. When I slid one across to Aris, he beamed like I'd just given him a bag of cash. I noticed he'd polished off his last one while I was away.

'I concede, sir.'

Aris turned his phone off and slipped it into his pocket.

'What level are you up to?'

Aris grinned. 'Eighteen. Only twelve to go.'

'Amateur,' I pretended to scoff.

He shook his head at me. 'You seen the local paper?' He gestured to a folded paper on the table. 'Page five.'

I opened it and zoned in on the headline: *Attempted Murder in East Barnet.*

The short report was pretty standard: 'Police called to a disturbance. Twenty-seven-year-old woman arrested. Victim in hospital. Stable but in intensive care. Suspect released on bail pending further investigation. Neighbours reported the suspect and victim were romantically involved.'

'Nothing ground-breaking there,' I commented, folding the paper and tossing it back on the table.

'Yeah, no scandals have come out yet.' Aris frowned. A scandalous detail always made his job easier. He sat forward. 'So, what's the gossip, Jon?' He loved to call me Jon as if it were a secret that only he knew. I didn't know what I wanted anyone to call me most of the time, different names pulled at different buried threads in my brain. Jon was probably one of the safer options.

'You don't deal in gossip, dear friend. I can't discuss it with you anyway, can I?' I drank to divert him. 'Now tell me, is he awake?'

'No, still out. Induced coma. Probably just a matter of time though.'

'Don't forget your human suit, kiddo,' I reminded him. Sometimes Aris got so caught up in the detail, the suspects, the evidence, that he forgot there were real people involved.

The pub was full of old men nursing a beer and a few young men, who were pretending to search for jobs, but were really waiting on their bets to come in. It was the perfect place for a police officer and a defence lawyer to hide a friendship. 'She needs help. I'm recommending she see a doctor.'

Aris raised his bushy eyebrows at me. They were like two hairy caterpillars who'd eaten more than their share. 'She's pleading diminished responsibility?'

'We need to stop talking about it.' I tucked a cigarette behind my ear.

'I guess so.' Aris pointed at my ear. 'You light that in here and I'll fine you.'

'Ha ha. Don't pretend you're not a little pussy cat underneath it all...' I tapped my fingers against the glass. I hadn't touched a drop.

'Look, I can only tell you cold hard facts, like Ed's not awake yet. You spoke to Mari?'

I busied myself with moving my chair closer to the table. 'Um, yeah, we talked.' I felt a strange tingle thinking about her more regularly again. I'd deliberately omitted her presence from my mind and vocabulary unless absolutely necessary since New Year's.

'You didn't try to get information out of her, did you?' I was worried he might take me outside to give me a good beating. This was why Mari was a no-go area, but my body didn't seem to be listening to the brain.

Aris rested his elbows on the table. He wasn't wearing a uniform, barely ever did now, but I knew him from back when he did wear one, before he was made detective. He looked better these days, despite having bags under his eyes seventy percent of the time. We were both night owls for different reasons, which was probably one of the reasons we'd connected in the first place. Today, he was wearing a brown suit that complemented his skin and a striking white shirt. Most of my white shirts looked washed out since Claire had left, so I had to keep buying new ones.

'Would I?' I wondered if it was worse that I'd flirted or that I'd asked her some pointed questions that were clearly linked to Briony.

Aris shook his head at me. 'Be careful walking that line, Jon. We might be friends, but I can still report the hell out of you.'

'Don't I know it.'

'Look, she's under her mum's supervision now, right?'

I sat forward. 'Yeah, about that... You must be missing something important not to charge her, huh?'

'Shut up, Jon.'

'Fine, but I already know what it is.' It was the weapon – no fingerprints. It was one of the biggest let-offs, even if the rest of the evidence pointed in one direction.

Aris rolled his shoulders and stretched his neck as though my probing was making him ache. 'So anyway, me and Josie have been thinking, maybe we need to jog her memory?'

'How so?'

'Take her back to the apartment block. We'd have to stay outside the flat, but we could walk around outside, walk down the corridor maybe. It might set something off.' He took a big gulp of his beer, waiting for my reaction.

'I don't think that's the best thing for Briony,' I dismissed.

He sat up in his chair. 'Ask her.'

'What?'

'I said, ask her. Let her decide.' He shrugged. When it came to evidence, he sniffed it out no matter what was in his way. Sometimes he needed someone to taper his hunger.

'She's really fragile, Aris,' I reminded him.

He nodded with flattened lips. 'Surely, the sooner we get the memories out, the sooner she can deal with whatever happened,' he suggested, for his own benefit more than anyone else's.

'Maybe she doesn't remember for a reason,' I forced out, trying not to make this personal but it was. I felt my chest constricting as if someone was tightening a rope around me.

Aris sipped some more of his pint. Thinking time. 'If she doesn't remember, how can you build a defence, Jon?'

I finally picked up my beer and had a long drink. 'I'll think about it. Let you know tomorrow, okay?'

'I've got my superiors breathing down my neck so don't take too long about it,' Aris complained.

'Do you want another beer, kiddo? I promise not to be a wanker for the rest of the night.'

Aris attempted to frown but slowly let a smile stretch over his lips. 'I wouldn't want to make you achieve the impossible there, mate.'

'I'm sorry. Sometimes I'm an arsehole. We've all got ways to get through the day.' I wouldn't say it out loud, but Aris made dark days turn into brighter days, sometimes even emerald green, or ocean blue at the very least. I couldn't help using Mum's scale, even though I knew it was crap. It emphasised why I couldn't go anywhere near his sister.

Definitely. Most probably. Possibly.

'And what are your ways then, Jon?' Aris brought me back to the conversation and downed the rest of his pint, his eyes shining with humour.

'I like pissing people off, of course.'

'I've always wondered… What *did* you do to Owusu before I turned up, Jon?'

'A man has to have his secrets.' I pretended to zip my lips closed and he rolled his eyes.

'Fine… So, you watching the Formula One this weekend?'

'Jesus, Aris, you're lucky I like you because some of your hobbies are boring with a capital B.'

He grunted. 'Oh yeah, and Pilates and football are thrill-seeking activities.'

'Okay, I'll give you the Pilates, but have you tried playing Stoke on a cold Saturday in January? Your fingers could fall off, the likelihood of a dirty tackle is medium to high, you could slip on some black ice on the way home…' I grinned at him until he smiled back.

'Fine, but you're still watching some of the Formula One with me.'

I held my glass up for cheers and he clinked his glass against mine. We both knew he'd probably end up working overtime anyway.

CHAPTER 12

BRIONY

'I'm sorry, Mum,' Briony announced at the dinner table. They had been sitting in silence for about ten minutes, picking at the chicken and leek pie her mum, Jessica, had made.

Jessica lifted her head up and stared into Briony's face like she was a stranger who'd sat down opposite, then, after a few seconds, she forced her mouth into a smile. She dropped her fork onto her plate with a clang. 'Why are you sorry?'

Briony moved her hand over to her mum's, noting how her mum didn't take her eyes off it for a second. Her mum shuffled in her seat as Briony's hand pressed over hers.

'This can't be easy for you.'

Her mum shook her head and delicately slipped her hand out from under Briony's as if she wouldn't notice. She pretended to fix her hair but Briony knew she didn't care much about her hair. Briony's mum wasn't into having a style, not since her dad had died two years before, and she'd cut it shorter. 'Don't be silly. What are you talking about?'

Briony sighed. 'I know you haven't been answering your phone. Who are you avoiding?' Yet Briony already knew the answer; her uncle for one, friends, the women from knitting club who liked to gossip... *Everyone*, in a word.

'I just don't feel like talking…' Her mum picked up the fork again but only held it above the plate as if she had forgotten how to use it.

'SJ called and suggested I go back to the apartment building. See if it brings anything back. What do you think?'

Her mum met her gaze. 'You really don't remember?'

'I don't… think so. My mind is so… blank.'

'Does he know?' Her mum asked and then, as though Briony would have no idea what she was referring to, added, 'About Jason?'

Jason. A name hardly ever mentioned in their house. They thought about him all the time, but the name rarely passed between them. Her dad had been mumbling his name at the hospital, even though he had never fully regained consciousness. Briony supposed when he was dying, her dad's body had finally felt release was possible. He could once again say the name they'd repressed so many years before. The name of the child they had never stopped missing. Briony felt like she been left behind like an inferior model, never quite satisfying them.

'Are you saying you think I did something… to Jason?' Briony asked slowly. She had already had hours and hours of therapy about that day. She told them she remembered walking down to the lake with him, his muddy fingers laced with hers. She remembered the way the lake had looked so peaceful, not a danger at all. The next thing was Jason's body in the water. It hadn't been moving. She had been soaked. There were cuts on her knees, but she had no idea how they'd got to that point. That was the story.

'No,' her mum whispered, pressing the fork into her pastry. It made a slow cracking sound like someone standing on bone and waiting to feel it break.

Briony pushed back in the chair and stood up. 'You always said you believed me.' Her voice came out broken. She downed some water and slammed the glass back on the table. 'You *do* believe me, Mum?' she squeaked.

Briony's mum pushed herself up. She glanced behind Briony as if hoping someone else might appear so she wouldn't have to be alone with her daughter. Then she grabbed her plate and started scraping food into the bin. She'd barely touched it. She took Briony's plate without checking and scraped her food into the bin too.

'You have to eat,' Briony reminded her.

'I might just have something smaller.'

'Mum, you didn't answer me.' She jumped up.

Her mum dropped the plates into the sink with a crash. Briony wondered if any of them had broken. Her mum took a few deep breaths before turning back. When she did, her eyes looked glassy. 'Bri', you know what I think. We've talked about this.' She stepped closer and, for a moment, Briony thought she might be about to give her a hug. But she skirted past Briony without so much as a touch and walked out of the kitchen.

'We never talk about it,' she muttered to the empty kitchen. After a few minutes, she pulled out her mobile phone and called SJ. When he answered, she didn't bother saying hello. 'I think we should go back to the flat.'

'You sure?' he asked shortly. It sounded like she was disturbing him.

'No… Yes. I think so.'

'I'll get it set up. Speak soon.'

He hung up.

She was alone again.

CHAPTER 13

S J

It was a black day, just like every 20th of the month. This was the time when everything stopped – all my clients became shadows in the background. I had passed everything over to Alexis and turned my phone onto silent. At least for a few hours. The 20th was the time my trauma was centre stage. When I couldn't help using Mum's stupid scale of colours to match my mood, like she had daily, because today was a family day in the oddest way possible.

I turned the engine on and sat there for a few minutes, sucking in and out on my cigarette until the car was full of smoke. The car was a BMW 3 series, red, still in pretty good condition. There were a few scrapes here and there I hadn't got round to fixing. What I loved about the car wasn't anything that could be measured though; I loved it because it reminded me of Debbie and of safety most of all. The first time the social worker had driven me to her house, she'd been washing it. She'd thrown me a sponge and said, 'Come on, get stuck in,' like she'd been waiting for me.

I still lived in Debbie's house. She'd left any money she had to fostering charities and transferred the deed for the house to me before she'd died. Not only had she given me a home back when I was a kid, she had given me somewhere to keep living for as long as I wanted to. It helped me take on Legal Aid cases, which also gave me something to do instead of feigning sleep. My boss had told me I could stop doing them if I wanted, or at least cut down, but she didn't realise that I had my own selfish motivations for continuing.

I opened the window and finally put the car into gear. I pulled out of my driveway, still smoking, and drove in the wrong gear for a few blocks. When the engine began to complain, I finally moved up the gears and threw my dead cigarette out the window.

'It's just another day,' I repeated over and over to myself. I must've said it around five hundred times by the time I finally parked. I didn't wait any longer. I staggered out of the car and stared up at Pentonville as though it was the first time I'd seen it. In some ways, it didn't look like a prison due to its proximity to the main road and how its formidable white walls made it appear like a small fortress sitting on a hill somewhere in Europe. Though when you looked closer, there were cracks and huge bubbles in the paintwork from years of neglect. It was unlikely many of the people going in cared what state the walls were in.

Once you were out of the car and walking towards the visitors' entrance, you were met with lots of brown brick and low squat buildings, which didn't appear like a prison at all. They looked like small university buildings where students came to ask about their welfare, not a place that housed category-B prisoners.

I spent so much time in prisons, even *this* prison, yet today I wasn't wearing a suit or carrying one of my folders. My hands were empty.

'Business or pleasure?' Cam, the old prison officer asked without looking up from his book. He asked the same question every 20th of the month as though my answer might change, as he sat at his usual desk at reception, looking even greyer haired than he had just one month before.

'I guess I would have to say… *pleasure.*' I grumbled, sliding my passport onto the desk.

He lifted his eyes up and closed his book. He put it aside and stood up. 'I see.' Then he reached over the desk and brushed my hand slightly. The weird thing was I didn't even move it away. His hands were surprisingly clean looking and if I didn't know better, I'd say Cam had been getting secret manicures.

'All good in there?' I moved my hand back and gripped the side of the booth.

'You mean, good behaviour and stuff?'

I put another cigarette behind my ear and cleared my throat. 'I don't think that's ever been a problem, has it?' I started emptying my pockets of the few personal items I had.

Cam gestured to the cigarette. 'You can't smoke that in there.'

'I've been here often enough to know that.' I checked the clock behind him. Its face was almost as weathered as Cam's, it said 11:13 am. I signed my name on the sheet and wrote the time next to it. Only three other people had signed in today. 'Plus, you remind me every time,' I added.

'When you going to start listening then, son?' He chuckled deeply and waved me through the scanner. He had always called me 'son'. I didn't know if he called everyone that or if he had kids of his own. All we had was this conversation once a month, for ten years of the thirteen I'd been subjecting myself to this torture.

He handed me my possessions and I was escorted by another prison officer to the visitors' hall. All of the officers knew me by name and my face wasn't one you could forget too easily. After going inside, we were buzzed in and out of about ten gates. Eventually, I was standing outside the visiting hall with my fingers on the door handle. It always felt so cold.

Inside, there were a few occupied tables, but my eyes immediately locked in on a man who was sitting upright in one of the chairs at the back. He always chose that table. I tried so often to call him 'Dad', but the word retreated back inside quicker than I could think it. When he saw me enter the room, his mouth stretched into a smile, but it died down halfway when he saw I didn't return it. He should have been used to it by now, but he seemed to live in perpetual hope. I slipped into the seat opposite and placed my hands on the table, using it as a scaffolding to stop me sinking into the floor or maybe into the past.

His hair was thinning but had retained its brown colour. He was losing his sight now, so he was sporting unfashionable prison-issued glasses. His skin was pale because he barely ever saw the outside; they had assigned him to laundry services to keep him away from some of the other prisoners. He was fifty-eight after all and not up for a fight.

'Stanley,' he croaked. He had taken up smoking a few years after he came here, and his voice hadn't reacted well. He sounded like a creaky step that I wanted to forget but kept stepping on in the middle of the night when I was half-asleep.

'I prefer Jon,' I reminded him.

He bowed his head and nodded, dropping his eyes to the table. He then recomposed himself and met my eyes again. 'Sorry, you know what my mind's like.' Yet I knew it wasn't his mind at all. He was hoping that one day I would let him call me that again.

'Cigarette?' I asked.

He gave a wonky smile and accepted the fake cigarette I passed across. They were made of sugared candy. I wasn't sure when the habit had begun but we'd done it for years. The prison officer didn't even move from his desk, although he was new. Someone must've told him about us. I took one out of the packet for myself and we both pretended to inhale. The real cigarette behind my ear was calling out for me but I was determined to quit. However, the 20th of the month was no time to stop smoking.

'How are you?' He pretended to flick ash on the floor.

'Same old, same old.'

'Why do you come to visit just to tell me that?' he complained, but quietly as though he didn't actually want me to hear. He always looked at me like I was a firework he'd just lit in his hand.

'Would you prefer me *not* to visit?'

He squinted at me behind his glasses. His eyes looked bulbous and bloodshot. 'Jon... I *live* for your visits.' He hesitated on my name, but I wouldn't let him call me the name he wanted. It made me think of her, the way her intonation always rose at the end. Despite her nastiness, I'd never heard anyone say my name, like she had, when she loved me; not since my face got carved up. Well, maybe only my foster mum, Debbie, but I'd soon told her to call me Jon.

'Everything okay here?' I turned to look at the wall. I couldn't keep looking at him leaning closer as though he might reach out for me. The table was a barrier, not a bridge. I pressed my hand into the wood to remind me of how much of an obstacle it was.

'You don't need to check up on me. I'm not one of your clients.'

I turned back to see him chewing on his cheek. Sometimes he looked just like he had when he was younger. I saw flashes of him, and every flash left me straining to see properly again. The tears kept building but I kept blinking them away. 'I know that, William.'

'You don't need to call me that.'

'I'd prefer to—'

'Is it so hard for you to just say it?' he mumbled, putting his head in his hands.

'Actually, yes.' I sighed and pulled the cigarette out of my mouth. It was sticky, wet, and didn't seem much fun anymore. I tossed it on the table.

'When will you stop being angry with me?' he whispered. He lifted his head up and stared at me. To him, I was the only person left in his world.

'When you can tell me why you did it?' I suggested, pushing away from the table.

I often pictured the headlines about it. They were imprinted on my brain.

Family man slaughters wife in front of young child.

Father executes innocent wife, leaves child scarred.

Man who stabbed wife multiple times sentenced to life.

All of them factual but never getting past the superficial details and digging out the why.

'Stanley, I can't—' he started, trying to follow me but stopping when the prison officer sitting nearby jumped to his feet. He lowered himself into his chair again and could only watch me stand up. He closed his mouth, not knowing what else he could say. He'd been trying to find the right phrase for twenty-two years already.

'I'm glad you seem okay. I'll see you next month.' I turned my back on him but stopped a few steps away, waiting.

'I love you, Jon.'

As I did every month, I tried to get myself to say it back, but her face always appeared in front of my eyes and I clamped my mouth closed. 'Bye.'

Then I was walking down the corridor and out of the prison, waving to Cam and unlocking my car. Only once I was inside did I rest my head on the steering wheel and allow a few tears out.

CHAPTER 14

BRIONY

SJ looked tired when he picked her up. He didn't say much as they drove towards the place where she'd last seen Ed, where her life had started to finally unravel.

She was shaking when they pulled up outside. It felt hot and uncomfortable as he turned the engine off. Briony could see DC Demetriou and his partner standing beside a car near the entrance. They looked over when they heard SJ's car approach and shared a few words.

'Do you think I'm evil, SJ?' She was squeezing her fists again but couldn't stop.

'I don't think you're evil,' he tried to reassure her. His voice was flat though. 'Even if you did something to Ed, it doesn't mean you're evil, okay?' He craned his head to look in her eyes, but she continued to stare out of the windscreen.

The officers approached, waiting for her to open the car door. She didn't move, so in the end, SJ leaned across and opened it for her. She flashed him a dirty look but swung herself out of the car and stood up, still shaking.

'Miss Campbell,' DS Owusu greeted her.

'Briony is fine,' she told them again.

'We can't go inside because it's still an active crime scene, but we thought it might be useful to be outside, and think about what happened that day,' DC Demetriou suggested, cocking his head at her, assessing her already.

They all walked closer to the front door of the apartment block. She remembered thousands of times she'd walked up the path. She'd been living a semblance of a normal life at some of those points. She'd actually loved someone like she hadn't before.

Inside, her home was lying empty. As empty as her heart inside her chest was these days. She peered up at the glass windows and thought about her neighbours. What did they think about her? They had to be talking about it. She couldn't see her flat because it faced the courtyard at the back. It was right next to Ed's, where his blood had stained the walls. Blood always looked so odd when it'd dried and aged, like paint, suddenly unreal.

When she thought of blood, she sagged onto a wall beside the entrance. The detectives stayed back, watching her. SJ hung closer but even he was removed, constantly stifling a yawn. She wanted to tell him to leave but she needed him.

'I know this is hard for you,' DC Demetriou said in a quiet voice, crouching down in front of her. Briony saw a silver tooth in his mouth glint at her. 'We're not doing this to punish you. We just want to find out what happened.'

'I told you I don't remember,' she repeated, but her voice sounded hollow.

He nodded gently. 'I know. This might help though.' He gestured towards the building.

She closed her eyes then and thought about that day. Which parts should she tell them, which parts should she keep for herself? Maybe nothing was hers anymore.

'He told me he loved me,' she whispered, barely audible. 'He seemed upset… strange,' she added, fiddling with the hem of her jumper.

'You told us that at the station. Do you remember what happened after that?' DC Demetriou asked.

'He kissed me,' she said abruptly, as if the memory had just popped into her brain.

'Okay…' the detective urged.

'I think we went into the bedroom… Had sex,' she revealed, staring at her feet.

'And?' DS Owusu asked.

Briony looked up at SJ then. His lips were tight. What would he tell her to say? There was no indication in his face.

'I don't think I want to do this anymore,' she blurted and stood up. She spun away from the detectives but SJ caught her arm and pulled her back.

'Briony, you asked for this. Are you sure you want to stop now?' he whispered, appealing to her with his eyes.

She covered her face with her hands. The pleading was getting louder. 'Please… please… please…' she mumbled over and over.

A hand on her arm made her uncover her face. SJ was still there, frowning.

'Briony, what is it?'

She whimpered but the tears stayed inside. 'SJ, there's this voice in my head. I don't know if it's Ed or someone else… What's wrong with me?' She threw herself into him before he could move away. He didn't comfort her, but he didn't push her back either.

'What does the voice say?'

Briony moaned and moved back. '*Please*... it just says please again and again.'

'Is it a man's or a woman's voice?' he asked.

'I can't tell. It just sounds like *me*.' She paused, glancing at the detectives again. 'Everything's so mixed up in my head.' She sighed.

He said something under his breath and turned back to the detectives. 'I think that's enough. She's not ready for this. Sorry.'

The detectives regarded her for a long moment, slowly nodding in tandem. They must spend far too much time together. 'Your call, Briony,' DS Owusu said.

She nodded in agreement. Too many memories were battering against the sanity barrier in her brain. 'I thought I could, but it's too much.'

'Let's go back to your mum's,' SJ suggested and guided her back to the car.

As she settled into the seat, she noticed that SJ lingered by the door, staring towards the detectives. She watched as DC Demetriou lifted his hand and waved, smiling in SJ's direction. For the second time, she felt like she was stepping into a maze they all knew the solution to and could only think about what that meant for her. Was anyone really trying to help her?

CHAPTER 15

SJ

When I sat down opposite Mary Walsh, my body felt heavy. It had been a bastard of a day with my dad and then Briony. In between that, I'd dealt with some outstanding cases too. There were a few court dates coming up. I'd passed on some case notes to my trainee, Alexis, and had a quick catch up with Rebecca via phone. Then, in the evening, a new case that demanded my attention. I wouldn't sleep anyway, so I may as well be working.

The woman in front of me wouldn't meet my eyes, just kept massaging a bracelet she was holding in her palm. I wanted to ask what it meant to her, but I knew she wouldn't say. Her hair was pulled back in a messy ponytail and her custody clothes were hanging off her, as though they'd given her two sizes bigger than they should have.

'Mrs Walsh, my name is SJ Robin. I'm a lawyer who's been asked to come in and represent you during questioning. Would you like to tell me what happened to bring you here today?'

She raised her head and regarded me absently. 'Why do I need a lawyer?' Her voice was muted, and I struggled to catch her words.

'Whenever someone is arrested, they have a right to representation. Someone must have asked you when you were being booked in?'

She nodded slowly. 'Oh yes, that young lad with the glasses. I suppose I thought it would be best. For my children.'

'You have kids? How many?'

Her mouth transformed into an easy smile. 'Two. They're actually adults now. Twenty-six and twenty-four.'

'You don't look old enough to have kids that age,' I teased.

She laughed quietly. 'Don't let my husband hear you say that.'

I raised my eyebrows at her. She had been arrested for attempted murder. The victim: *Connor Walsh. Her husband.*

'He gets jealous,' she explained, shrinking into herself. I had an urge to reach over and hug her. She was visibly trembling, but I knew the lines and I wasn't about to get personal with a client.

'We have a confession from you, Mary. Is it okay if I call you Mary?'

'Do what you like.' She said it in such a way that it felt like a phrase she'd used many times. I wondered in what context but tried to shake it away.

'When you were arrested you told the officers you'd tried to kill him. That you'd finally had enough. Is that correct?' I looked up from my notes to find her staring at me with watery eyes. She had deep creases across her forehead.

'Yes.'

'And by "him", can you tell me who you were referring to?'

She sighed. 'My husband, Connor.'

I nodded gently, feeling like moving too much might harm her. She was so sunken that it felt like the air might push her over. 'You realise with a confession, you'll most likely be charged with attempted murder?'

She nodded, her face finally crumpling. She buried her face in her hands and let the tears come out. I watched the clock, shuffling in my chair, until she finally raised her head again two minutes later. I handed her a tissue.

'Can you tell me why you attacked your husband, Mary?'

She shook her head and mumbled something.

'I'm sorry. Could you repeat that?'

She wrung the tissue between her hands, and I heard the sound of it tearing. 'So many years, pushed me so hard,' she said, louder.

I sat forward, placing my elbows on the table. 'Can you tell me what you mean by that, Mary? Do you mean physically or in some other way?'

She turned to the wall.

'Your children are waiting outside, Mary. They'd like to know what happened.'

She moved her head back rapidly, her features dropping. 'I can't see them. I can't tell them what happened.'

I licked my lips, wishing I'd brought some water in. 'You deserve a chance to share your side of the story.'

She scratched at her greasy hair that looked like it hadn't been washed for a few weeks, let alone since she'd been detained. I would recommend they let her have a shower if she wasn't released soon.

'They have no idea what he's like,' she finally whispered, as if her children could hear through the walls. She leaned in. 'He's… a horrible man. A monster.'

'What has he done to you, Mary?' I asked, trying not to let my tone change but it was hard to hold the anger inside.

I pushed my feet down and focused on pressing the feelings into the hard floor.

'I try to make him happy, all the time. I've tried all my life but he just... punishes me. Says nasty things, gets physical... I guess I just lost it.'

I tried to make him happy. I blinked for a long time and tried not to think about my mum, but I did anyway. As a kid, that phrase was basically my mantra. *I tried to make her happy, Dad, but she smashed up the house. I tried but she called me names. I tried but she cut up my clothes with scissors.*

I cleared my throat and shook myself out. 'So, you were standing in the kitchen when this happened? Did you think about picking the scissors up?'

She pressed her fingers into the tabletop and tried to stop herself from erupting into more tears. 'I just grabbed them, and he had his back to me... and–' she broke off with a sharp intake of breath.

'You stabbed him?' I supplied.

She stared without blinking and nodded. She lowered her head to her chest and was silent.

'Just once?' I checked, even though I'd been told by the officers.

'Yes. Just once. When I realised what'd I'd done, I backed away and knocked everything over... I broke the vase Ryan bought me.' She bit her lip, as though the vase was more important than the knife in her husband's back.

'When you stabbed him, how were you feeling?'

Don't think about knives, SJ. Don't think about the one that sliced your face open.

'Frightened. I thought he might hit me... again.' She wrapped her arms around herself like a child hiding in a corner.

'Mary, were you defending yourself?' I asked, trying not to put words in her mouth but not able to hold them back any longer.

She raised her head and examined me for a long moment. Then she nodded.

'Okay, we can build a defence for you, Mary. Let's talk some more and see where we get to. How about a hot drink?'

After she agreed, I brought us both tea and we spent the next forty-five minutes talking about her long history of sustained abuse from her partner. I tried not to think about it too deeply but every now and again, a case got me right in the spine and it flooded into my body like an epidural that slowly took over all my senses.

Though I never wanted to acknowledge it, part of me wondered if my mum's behaviour had triggered the violence that followed. The depression, the alcohol, the pills, the nasty verbal attacks, sometimes even physical attacks.

I left Mary in the interview room, but her story followed me out. Then as I exited the police station, my phone started ringing.

I pressed accept, pleased to have my thoughts broken, and was greeted by a strange voice.

'Can I speak to SJ Robin, please?'

'Oh… speaking.' I slid into the driving seat of my car and slammed the door, throwing my briefcase onto the passenger seat.

'This is Yvonne Kalinca from the prison service.'

'Is he dead?' I blurted out.

'William? No, he is asking to see you.'

I breathed out, not realising I'd been holding it in. 'What? I mean *why*?'

'He will not tell me. He asked me just to call.'

'Can't you tell me whatever it is on the phone?' I jammed the car key into the ignition.

'He wants to see you. Will you come? Whenever is good for you.'

'Fine, Saturday.' Two days' time. I started the engine.

'That is very soon. Are you sure?'

'What did I say? Saturday, 1 pm.'

'Thank you, Mr Robin. I will make the appointment. I am sure he will–'

I cut her off and threw my phone onto the seat next to me. Great, an extra visit to my dad, especially after the interview I'd just had. *Lucky me*. Although he *was* alive and no matter how much I tried to deny it, for reasons I couldn't identify after over twenty years, I still wanted that to be the case.

CHAPTER 16

BRIONY

Another day, another doctor. She counted how many of them she'd seen over the years – she thought the number was around twelve. Some of them just briefly, others for months and years at a time. Her favourite had been Doctor Ahmed, who let her call her Regina. She had had a gentle voice, almost like a lullaby that made Briony feel clean again. Yet she'd moved away and Briony had been left with Doctor Howard, who smelt of rice cakes. He had just about been happy being called Doctor Howard, let alone allowing his first name to be used.

Today's doctor was at least a little different. They were also at Mari's private office, not at the surgery. Mari still had a pinboard of quotes behind her though, which felt familiar.

'Remember to call me Mari,' she reminded Briony as she shuffled the papers in front of her. Mari said it every session.

'I'll try.'

'Perhaps you could start by sharing how you're feeling today?'

'I don't know where to begin. Everything is so mixed up.' She wanted to crumble already but the session had only just started. Yesterday's visit to the apartment building had nearly been enough and now she was expected to share even more.

'We can go slowly.' Mari's voice was calming though, as it had always been. Briony felt Mari was like the captain of a ship, not wanting to let the crew know they were sinking.

Briony wrung her hands. 'They asked about Jason at the police station.'

'How did you feel about that?' Mari had a pen in her hand. Everyone was always taking notes. Briony wondered what all the notes added up to. Could they understand her if they pooled them together?

'I guess they needed to know because of my memory... but I didn't want to talk about it.'

Mari nodded, her dark brown eyes taking her in. 'Are you taking your medication, Briony?'

Mari had prescribed beta blockers about two months ago. Briony mostly remembered taking them but couldn't think of the last time she had swallowed one. 'Think I forgot. I'll take them when I get home.'

Mari made a note. 'Okay, but promise to try and take them? They have been helping you, haven't they?'

'I think so...' Briony had been on so many pills in her life. Everything was merging.

'How are you feeling about the investigation? And remember I'm asking about *you*, not the investigation.' Mari smiled across the desk at her. Briony had some affection for the slightly old wooden desk. She also enjoyed the way Mari often changed what she had pinned to a board behind her – posters with different messages, like 'Take one step at a time' and 'Acknowledging a need for change is positive' and other silly slogans. Briony was mostly touched that Mari went to the effort of changing them.

'Scared. Anxious. Confused.'

'Those sound like valid feelings. And are you working at the moment?'

She shook her head. 'They said I had to take a "voluntary sabbatical", but I know what that means. They did it to Paula a while ago.'

'Paula didn't come back?' Mari raised her eyebrows.

'No. That place is cut-throat. It's only a bloody graphic design office but the boss treats us all like gladiators fighting to the death or something. No loyalty.'

'And your role is Office Manager, correct? Is it a stressful role?'

'The environment is stressful. Probably not good for me to be there anyway.'

'Does it worry you to not have a job to return to?' Mari asked.

'I guess so. I might have to live with my mum for a while...' Briony crossed her legs, uncrossed them and then pressed them into floor.

'How do you feel about that?'

Briony lifted one side of her mouth up and sighed. 'I've told you about our relationship before. It's not exactly close, or even warm...' She stared at the wall to her left, wondering who was on the other side.

'Perhaps this could be a chance for you to reconnect?' Mari suggested with a bright tone.

'I doubt it,' she mumbled.

'Okay, let's move on. How are the nightmares?'

Briony closed her eyes and felt her lungs screaming for air. She could always see her brother's lifeless body floating in the lake as she tried to swim towards him. The lake had felt like an ocean that went on forever. 'Still there.'

'Is this every night or less?' Mari asked, as she routinely did at their appointments.

'Pretty much every night. Especially the last few days.' Briony turned back to Mari and bathed in her calm expression. She was writing something down and some of her hair had fallen down from behind her ear. Her hair always looked so silky. Briony wanted to touch it but knew she wouldn't be allowed into any more sessions if she did.

'How do you think I can help you, Briony?'

She raised eyes to meet Mari's and forced her mouth into a smile. She thought of Ed in hospital, she thought of sharing more meals with her mum, she thought of Jason running out of breath, and she wanted to cry.

'I want to understand all of this and myself. I don't remember being that... happy.' She kneaded her fists into her thighs and tried to stop the tears, but they started coming anyway.

Mari passed over some tissues. Briony tried to wipe her face. Her skin felt raw from the last few days.

'Were you happy with Ed?'

Briony froze for a long moment but finally answered, 'I think we were. I'm not even sure how any of this happened.' The tears kept coming and she pulled tissue after tissue out of box to dry her face.

'We don't need to talk about that now. Let's focus on what we can do to help you in the short term, okay?' Mari spoke softly, as though not wanting to disturb the room. How was her voice so soft, like a gentle kiss?

'Okay,' Briony mumbled.

'Can you continue writing your mood journal for me? And please, take the medication regularly?'

'I can do that.' She had kept a mood journal for the last few months and sometimes brought it to sessions.

'Writing about your mood will really help us, Briony. We need to see what impacts your responses to things. Be honest with yourself in there.' She looked up at the clock above the door and back to Briony's face. 'Did I ever tell you the best comment I ever heard about therapy?'

'No, what?'

'It's all about wading through shit and coming out clean, just like Tim Robbins in *Shawshank Redemption*.' She grinned, hoping to share a joke. Briony kept her mouth flat. After a moment of silence, Mari mumbled, 'Sorry, bad joke.'

'No, I get it,' Briony said, trying to placate her. 'Is SJ a good lawyer?'

Mari's eyes flickered up from the papers in front of her. 'Why do you ask?'

'Just wondered. I'm meant to trust him with everything, aren't I?'

'Don't underestimate him,' she said, without saying much at all.

When they got outside the room, SJ was standing near the doorway. His hands were shoved casually in his trouser pockets. 'Thanks, beautiful,' he directed at Mari.

She snorted, unimpressed, and slammed the door.

SJ nodded towards the exit. When they were back in his car, he didn't start the engine.

'So?'

Briony frowned at the windscreen. 'You know what she said to me? "Therapy is about wading through shit and coming out clean, just like Tim Robbins in *Shawshank Redemption*."'

SJ leaned in closer. 'What?'

'I think you heard me.'

His mouth slowly transformed into a crooked smile, the scar bending with the contours of his face. 'Absolutely fucking amazing.' He started the engine and let out a bubbling laugh. 'She's one of a kind, that's for damn sure.'

'Do you think she can help me?' Briony dug her fingernails into the car seat.

'Well, she can't do any worse than the docs who've already tried to, right? If there's anything to find, I reckon she's the one…'

For some unknown reason, the words echoed in Briony's mind: *she's the one, she's the one, she's the one.*

CHAPTER 17

MARI

She had swum thirty lengths in the twenty-five-metre pool and still not driven her meeting with Briony from her mind. She'd even had two more appointments after Briony's, but they had passed in a blur. Usually, swimming was a form of release but apparently appointments with people who had no memory of whether they were a killer or not seemed to stick.

Mari wanted to help Briony; she'd been trying to for months. Her colleagues were probably sick of the conversations they'd had about Briony, trying to find ways to access her past trauma and get her to really talk. Though what unnerved Mari these days was how Briony's eyes seemed to sweep over her like some human x-ray machine, settling on different parts of her body, as though she were a fly settling down on discarded food and examining what was on offer. Was it simply her imagination? She often tried to remind herself that she'd known Briony before this tragic incident and memory loss was plausible, but all that stuck in Mari's head was the fact that this was the second time this had happened. Could lightning strike the same person twice like that? It seemed improbable but...

Whenever Mari passed a mirror and caught her reflection, she almost believed Briony was standing right behind her. Had her cool eyes grown colder since the incident with Ed? And Briony's voice sounded like it had been stripped bare, like wood shaved to a point.

'Did you do it?' Mari mumbled to herself as she climbed out of the pool. The lifeguard nodded in her direction. He'd been eyeing her up for weeks, but Mari suspected she was one of many and didn't fancy giving out her phone number here. It was a sanctuary more than anything else, but now, Briony was invading it.

She would do this for Aris. And strangely, for SJ, too. Whatever had gone on and was going on between them, she didn't want to let either of them down. She wrapped a towel around her body and shuffled towards the changing rooms.

As she dried herself and changed back into her work clothes, she wished she'd brought something else to wear. She could only think about sitting across from Briony earlier. In some ways, she wished she wasn't Briony's doctor. She hadn't made much progress with her and since she'd come into the surgery to confess to hurting Ed, things had shifted. Maybe it would've been better if Mari worked at a different surgery or if she had chosen not to work that day. Although part of her itched to know the truth. How did Briony end up with blood on her hands? Was she as innocent as she was making out?

After she left the pool in Finchley, she checked her phone. The pool was in a horrible area, right next to a main road that was polluted and busy, so she reluctantly stopped to read a message from her mother. *Maria, do you have a date for the wedding? Selma's doing the seating plan. xxx*

Great, another reason to lament her single status. Not only did she have the checkout girl at her local supermarket raising her eyebrows at her meals for one and solitary peppers, she now had her mother texting her to make her feel bad. Her mother knew she'd been unceremoniously dumped (via email, no less) two months before. Justin had apparently met someone else (*'I never meant it to happen, gorgeous'*) and that was that. She hadn't loved him; she'd just felt embarrassed. Most of all, he had at least given her some respite from being solo at family events and from thinking about SJ.

She texted back, *When does she need to know?*, and shoved her phone in her pocket.

God, a wedding with her whole family was going to be the usual ferry ride from hell. She said 'ferry' because it would be packed to the rafters and there was no way of jumping off while it was in progress, unless she decided to drown herself to avoid all the questions she hated answering.

'Why didn't you become a surgeon?' 'Why do you still live alone?' 'Why haven't you popped out some children yet?' 'Why couldn't you keep hold of Justin or the one before that – what was his name – Peter?' 'Why don't you come and dance with Niko; he's a good Greek boy and he's single?'

And then repeat the same conversation with every single relative in the room. She loved her cousin but wanted to know why she couldn't just elope to save them all the torture.

Mari turned into a quieter road and stomped towards home. Her hair was still damp so she could feel the cold settling around her shoulders like a layer of cold glue coating her. She wrapped her arms around herself tighter and tried not to think of Briony's searching eyes, or worse, SJ's warm skin. She'd thought a lot about their handholding at the police station.

Her phone buzzed in her pocket, so she pulled it out and read another text from her mother: *Now, Maria. That's why I asked. xxx*

Mari sighed, wishing the ground would open up and do her a favour. It was hard to argue with her mother. For example, despite Mari's protestations, her mother still refused to call her anything other than Maria, telling Mari that she'd chosen that name for a reason. Mari just hated how common her birth name was in so many countries and cultures.

She hesitated before responding to her mother's last message with: *Yes, me plus 1. x*

Before she could take ten more steps, her mother responded with: *Ohhh, gossip. Tell me more. Not Justin, I hope? xxx*

Mari snorted, then looked around but the only person out was a man walking his dog across the street and he had headphones in.

I thought you liked Justin. But no, not him.

Her mother responded with a surprised emoji and the words: *Justin never deserved you, honey. Unfortunately, he will be at the wedding though. He's Alex's best man. xxx*

Mari shook her head at her phone. Did her mother think she had forgotten that she would come face-to-face with Justin at the wedding, probably being tailed by the woman she'd been dumped for? Not bloody likely. She'd actually met Justin via the groom, Alex. She wished she'd never gone out that night now. It would have saved her a few months of her life.

'Oh, piss off,' she hissed to herself. Whether it was Justin, her mother, Briony or SJ she was talking to, Mari couldn't decide. She resumed stomping down the street and exhaled in relief when she spotted her building up ahead. She needed to get home and warm up more than anything else. All of the other ghosts and niggles could wait.

Yet, as she opened her door, her phone started buzzing. She expected to see another text from her mother, but it was SJ. She tried to ignore the way her back seemed to straighten up as though someone had poked her with a hot stick. She poured herself a large glass of apple juice as she read his message.

SJ: *Hey Dufresne, get busy living or get busy dying. It's a simple choice really.*

Mari texted back with: *What the hell does that mean?*

She threw her swimming stuff in the machine and downed the whole glass of apple juice. She always wanted something sweet and refreshing to drink when she got home from swimming. As she turned away from the sink, she saw her phone light up. Trying not to rush towards it, she pretended to wipe the surfaces on the way, teasing herself. When she picked it up, she read another message from SJ.

SJ: *Nothing. I just think you're funny.*

Mari: *Piss off. You're laughing at me,* she texted back before thinking about it.

SJ: *Sorry, couldn't help it. I just wanted to chat to someone.*

Mari: *Someone? Anyone will do?*

SJ: *Okay, specifically YOU. Happy?*

Mari sat down on the sofa and considered how best to reply. In the end, all she managed was: *I suppose.*

SJ: *Have you ever had a client that really got to you?*

Mari: *What, like you?*

SJ: *Ha ha.*

Mari: *Why are you messaging me?*

SJ: *Didn't want to be alone.*

There was a pause and then another message.

SJ: *Is that okay?*

Mari: *There must be a reason you don't want to be alone, Tinkerbell.*

Mari sighed in her quiet flat, realising too late that she'd called him the nickname she'd made for him last year. She'd asked him what happened when he ran out of jokes and he'd answered, 'I die. Just like Tinkerbell.' She could almost believe it.

The only sounds were the fan light and the ticking of the overly noisy clock her mother had given her. She should have thrown it out years ago but somehow the ticking was just a feature now, except when she was pissed-off – then it really embedded in her consciousness and made her want to stamp on it. Getting into SJ's world was slow and spontaneous. She wondered who had managed to break through the barrier before? Even his relationship with Aris was full of banter and deflections.

SJ: *Okay, Dufresne. Have a new client. It brought back memories and my brain won't leave it alone.*

Mari sat down on the edge of the sofa. *Something I can help with?*

SJ: *No one can help me with this but thanks for asking.*

Mari: *Do you want me to come over?*

SJ: *Don't tempt me.*

Mari: *I wasn't joking.*

SJ: *I know, that's what I'm afraid of…*

She saw another message pop up from her mum and groaned. Before she could stop herself, she wrote to SJ: *Want to come to a wedding with me?*

He didn't answer immediately and there was no sign that he was typing. Mari busied herself with changing into her pyjamas and brushing her teeth, pretending she was fully involved with what she was doing.

When she returned to her phone, she finally saw a message. She settled on the sofa and turned the TV on before clicking on the message.

SJ: *You can't propose to me first!*

Mari laughed out loud. *Come on, be my wing man.*

SJ: *Not sure my face will fit.*

Mari: *Shut up.*

SJ: *Oh, now you've convinced me! P.S.: Let me think about it.*

Mari: *Okay – let me know and keep texting me if you feel alone.*

SJ: *Where have you been all my life, Mari Demetriou?*

Mari: *I can be here for you if you let me. It doesn't have to be that hard.*

SJ: *I'm really trying (I promise) but I'm not sure you know what you're signing up for. It's not all jokes and rainbows with me you know.*

Mari smiled at her phone. *I'll take my chances.*

CHAPTER 18

BRIONY

'*If there's anything to find, she's the one…*' SJ's words hadn't left her for a moment since yesterday. And here she was again, sitting outside Mari's office on Saturday morning. Waiting. '*Strike while the iron is hot, jog the memory,*' SJ had said in car. He had dropped her off to go and deal with some clients.

Her feet wouldn't stay still and her eyes kept wandering around the room, searching for something. She only realised what it was when door opened: *escape*.

'Briony,' Mari said. She tried to keep her tone light but it seemed to dip in the middle.

God, Briony even wished she was back at work in the bustling office with her terrible boss but that wasn't about to happen. Life seemed irrevocably changed for her and Ed still hadn't woken up…

'Briony?' Mari repeated.

She raised her head to look at Mari who was already sitting in her chair, craning her neck to watch Briony take a seat also.

'So Briony, did you think about our previous session? Any more thoughts?' Mari was staring down at some paper, or pretending to, but glanced up at her without raising her head.

'What was I supposed to think about?'

'I didn't say you were *supposed* to think, I just asked if you *did* think,' she corrected.

'No, not really.'

'How did you sleep last night?' she persisted.

'Are you asking me if I had nightmares? If so, yes... I dreamt about him.' Briony stared down at hands, just as she did in her dream, seeing them moving slowly through water. Gripping at nothing.

'Him?' Mari sat upright in her chair.

'Jason.'

'Still the same dream every time?'

'More or less. Just *that* day... The water, him under the water...' She opened and closed her fists, trying to tell herself her hands weren't wet. She was in a room, not outside. Her body was warm, not drenched with water. No matter what though, Jason was always lifeless at the bottom of the lake.

'You said you tried to save him?' Mari asked in a measured tone as though asking if Briony had remembered to bring an umbrella, carefully laying each word on top of the other and trying not to break anything.

'What do you think?' she half-sobbed.

Mari nodded, pretending to shuffle some papers while she let Briony take a breath. 'You and your brother, you were close?'

'He was only four, but I loved him so much.' She spoke down into her chest, wanting to curl into herself and block her ears. She didn't want to talk about Jason again. He was more of a second shadow to her dead than he would be if he was still alive.

'We've never really talked about how you felt when he came along. Can you remember?'

'I'm not sure exactly but I'm pretty sure I was happy to have a little brother. We were... close. My parents worshipped him.' Briony crossed her arms and sat back in the chair. 'I'm not sure why we're talking about Jason, though.'

'Everything is connected. I'm just trying to work through all of this again.'

'Hmm.'

'You've never told me where your parents were, the day Jason died.'

Her spine straightened out with a jolt. She coughed without needing to. 'Do we have to do this?'

'Only if you want to tell me.' Mari smiled but faintly. Maybe she'd be calling SJ after this and throwing in the towel. Everyone left in the end, didn't they?

'He wanted to see if there were fish in the lake. I was looking for rocks to throw in. We were standing apart. I didn't see him go in,' she explained in a breathless string of words that she had said about a million times in her life, including to Mari.

'Your parents expected you to look after him when you were only seven?' Mari had never asked that before. Briony's features fell at her words. A searing heat flashed over her and she fanned herself as if it would help. No one had ever focused on what *they* had done wrong, so Briony had felt like she was the wrong one all of her life.

'Apparently,' she squeezed out.

Mari pursed her lips together and nodded. 'Tell me again; when was the moment you realised he was in trouble?'

'I woke up by the lake. I saw something in the water.' Her breaths were coming out faster as an avalanche of memories cascaded down like icy water trickling down a body, inch by inch.

'What did you do?'

'I ran into the water, but he had gone under. I tried to go under… to see him…' Briony closed her eyes and tried to picture Jason's still face. But all she could see was Ed's blood-splattered face instead. She focused on Ed's long black eyelashes, the sticky blood gluing them together. Then they jolted open and she threw herself back in the chair. 'Shit,' she spat and opened her eyes again.

'Did you remember something, Briony?'

She shook her head slowly. Would Ed wake up? Would he just float into unconsciousness and death like Jason had? Briony wondered how she could be here again.

'So, there's no memory at all of what happened before you found him floating in the water?' Mari persisted but in her factual doctor way that made it somehow acceptable.

'No…' Briony paused. 'Do you think you can trust your own mind, Mari?'

Mari did a good impression of keeping her expression neutral yet her eyes flickered over Briony's face like a bloodhound sniffing something out. 'Lots of people have problems trusting themselves,' she answered like a robot delivering an undeniable fact.

There was a long silence. The clock ticked on behind Briony's head and she thought about how time had stopped at the lake that day. She had somehow got freeze-framed beside the water; shivering and caked with mud.

'You shouldn't have been responsible for your brother,' Mari suddenly said.

Briony cocked head and tried to see the world from Mari's perspective. Even from this angle, Mari appeared beautiful. 'They said I should have been watching him.'

Mari pulled her ear briefly, considering her next words. 'A seven-year-old shouldn't have been left to look after a four-year-old,' she reiterated, being general instead of specific.

Briony squeezed hands into fists again and tried to store Mari's words. She knew she would soon lose them though and return to her terrible guilt. Like always.

CHAPTER 19

SJ

'I have cancer,' William announced as soon as I sat down. I wished I hadn't skipped lunch to see him because I immediately felt faint.

I froze, the sounds of the visiting hall immediately disappearing as I scrutinised him across the table. Was this his way of trying to finally make me show some love for him? Cancer or not, he had killed *her* and that was impossible for me to forget.

'I'm not sure what you want me to say.' I wanted it to be yesterday again, when I'd been sending slightly flirty texts to Mari. Instead, I was here, trying to conjure up solid emotions for a man I was supposed to openly love.

William bowed his head, and his body shook gently. When he looked up again, I saw he was crying. He cried often and in almost every one of our visits, but he hadn't cried in court. 'I just thought you should know.' He wiped his tears away with his sleeve. I wanted to feel nothing, but I had to hold my right arm down with my left to stop myself from reaching out to him.

'What type?' I mumbled. I tried to breathe in and out deeply, but it reminded me of her, and my stomach turned. I saw her face as I'd turned my head to look up at her and wished I could wipe my mind blank.

'Lungs.'

'Shit.'

He raised his eyebrows at my word, despite me being far from his little boy. Then he gave me a shadow of a smile. 'They say they can treat it if I want to.' He paused. 'I guess I shouldn't expect you to say all that much. Will you tell your Uncle Dean though? He doesn't answer my letters, but I think he should know.'

I growled into my chest. 'Fine, I'll tell him.' They hadn't spoken since the police had taken him away. My uncle had taken me on and had never wanted to mention my dad's name again. But I couldn't just delete the first nine years of my life. In the end, it turned out he had a harder time dealing with it all than me. He couldn't even stand to look at his own nephew. Of course, my dad knew nothing about all of that.

William put his head in his hands and nodded into them. There would be no candy cigarettes today, I guessed. You couldn't make a joke out of the thing that was probably killing you, right? I felt their weight in my pocket like they were rocks.

'How do you feel?' I asked before I could stop myself.

He raised his head. His face had fallen flat as though the cancer had already taken him and he wasn't here anymore. 'It can't come soon enough. Haven't even considered treatment to be honest.'

'That's it?' I sat forward. 'You get to finally escape what you did?'

He baulked, eyeing the prison officer briefly but then looking straight back at me. 'You think it's as easy as that?'

I ground my teeth in my mouth. 'You didn't cry in court. Why didn't you cry in court?' I ordered myself not to get emotional but my voice broke.

William blinked a few times, not crying any more. He glanced over at the prison officer pointedly then down at his hands. Then he leaned closer and whispered, 'Do you ever dream about her, Stanley?'

I didn't correct him about my name for once. The question was more important than whatever he chose to call me. I twisted my mouth up, ready to swear at him but instead said, 'Maybe. Why? Do *you?*' I hoped he woke up every night dreaming about what he'd done; I hoped he barely slept at all.

'Of course.' He stared at the wall behind me – was he imagining her there? The look in his eyes when he spoke about her grated me because all I saw was pure love. How could he have really loved her when he'd stabbed her ten times? 'I dream about her last words, I dream about her hand on the blade trying to stop it, I dream about her not being dead at all.'

'Stop,' was all I could manage.

He slammed his fist on the table, causing the prison officer to look over but he soon went back to the paper he was reading when I shook my head at him. 'I can't stop. It never ends for me.' He croaked, 'Don't you care if I die?'

I fumbled on words for a moment, wanting to lie. 'Of course, I care,' I admitted. 'But too much has happened for me to just care *for* you, don't you understand?'

He turned to the wall for about thirty seconds. There was a lot of wall staring in our meetings. They were like third parties in our relationship. I sometimes thought I felt more affection for them than him. The wall behind us had a small window, high up, that had a view of the prison gardens. It'd taken me five years to stand on a chair to see that. The wall to our right was a nondescript beige. The only defining features were the numerous scratches and bumps from the altercations that had taken place in this hall. Behind me, about four tables away, was the door out of here.

'If I die, there's something I need to know...' he began, turning back. He put his hands together in front of him on the table.

'You need to know something... from me?'

'Yes. I want you to tell me why.'

'I'm sorry, *what?*'

'You heard me. Tell me why,' he repeated.

I looked around the room for someone to help me with his meaning. None of the other prisoners or visitors seemed to be paying attention. I sat back in my chair.

'Are you kidding me?' I finally mumbled.

He shook his head. 'Why is she dead?'

'I'm sorry, I don't understand you. Isn't that *my* question?' I shifted in my chair. 'You knocked me out, you stabbed her, you gave me this—' I gestured to my face.

'No... I didn't.' He grimaced. His voice was weak, but I caught the words.

I leaned forward and cocked my ear towards him. 'Are you going insane?'

He unclasped his hands and stretched one towards me. I glared down at it and felt my muscles tightening. In my head, I saw myself jumping across the desk and grabbing him by the neck. I could get revenge for what he had done. I could help myself sleep at night. Though there was another part of me that wanted to grab his hand, clasp it like I did as a kid, allow myself to love him again.

'I asked you if you dreamed about her,' he reminded me. The fact that his face hadn't changed was starting to make me squirm. If he were insane, surely he would be inconsistent.

'I don't want to share my dreams with you,' I croaked.

'Does she call out for help? Does she try to crawl away? Does she die straight away, or does she take a long time to die?'

'You're a fucking demon,' I whispered and stood up. I pushed my chair in and started moving away from the table.

'Wash the red away, little SJ,' he called out.

I stopped. I felt myself shiver but I didn't know why. 'What?' I asked hollowly, as I backtracked towards him. All of his features seemed shadowed like someone had drawn him with charcoal and he wasn't actually there in front of me.

'I said, wash the red away, little SJ,' he repeated slowly.

I saw hands in my mind then. Small hands. There was soap all over them. They were *my* hands. I could feel the sensation on my skin. The water in the sink was mixing with red. It was the sink in the kitchen, where I had had to stand on a stool to reach it when I was younger. There was another pair of hands washing up my arms, my face, my neck... *Dad?*

I pulled the chair out, making a loud screech echo through the room. The prison officer looked our way as I placed myself back in the seat carefully and put my feet together, telling myself not to run. I pretended I was sinking into the mud, as though I were still in primary school, playing stuck in the mud.

'What does that mean?' My chest felt empty. I tried to remember her voice telling me to breathe but I was hearing his phrase in my mind on a loop: 'Wash the red away, little SJ.' Why had I needed to do that?

No, don't let him manipulate you. He wants you to fall apart.

'I'm leaving,' I announced, jumping up from the seat again and running towards the door. Another visit, another hasty exit. How many times had I rushed out of this hall, wishing I never had to see his face again? To avoid confronting the past.

I wrenched the door open, hearing him calling my name but I kept walking until I reached a metal gate and couldn't move through it.

'Let me out,' I demanded. A prison officer was watching TV to my right and barely looked up. 'I said, let me out!' I shouted through the bars. The officer jerked his head in my direction with an unimpressed stare, slowly leaning over and pressing a button. The gate buzzed and I slammed it open, not looking back.

The image was an invention or a mixture of old memories. The red didn't have to be blood... It could be paint. It could be another time when I'd hurt myself. Just because there was the red and his voice and his hands in the sink, enveloping my smaller ones that were shaking uncontrollably, it didn't mean I'd done it.

I managed to get outside before I collapsed against a wall. I was trying to regulate my breathing and make sense of the images in my head when I heard a familiar voice say, 'Jon?' I looked up and saw Aris standing there. My hands were empty – no files, no notepad, no anything to help me formulate an excuse. I tried to think of words, any words, but I drew a blank. Eventually, I pushed myself up.

'I'm late for something,' I said, stumbling past Aris.

'Jon, wait,' he shouted after me, but I started running, not caring what he thought of me, only hearing my father's voice saying over and over; 'Wash the red away, little SJ.' It was a prayer, maybe *his* prayer, to try and place the blame on me instead of him.

CHAPTER 20

SJ

I was pouring myself a large glass of red wine when the doorbell rang. I'd phoned the office to say I was signing off for the day. I worked so much, including weekends, that they couldn't complain. I was usually on call for emergency appointments, but I'd told Alexis to delay everything she could, even asking her to book a taxi for Briony to get home after her appointment with Mari.

I looked up at the clock and saw that it was 4:23 pm. I'd only been back from the prison for an hour. Aris obviously hadn't wasted much time in coming over. I took a sip of my wine and waited. Maybe he would just go away… Yet, thirty seconds later, the doorbell rang again and didn't stop. He must've been holding the button.

I stormed over to the door and wrenched it open. Aris was standing there, holding out a bottle of whisky with a huge smile. I could see the fake tooth he had to get after a suspect had belted him. I always joked he got a silver tooth to remind him not to be so mouthy. 'When people don't answer the door, it means they're not home,' I growled.

'But you *are* home.' Aris took a step closer. 'You going to let me in or not?'

I stalked back into the house without closing the door. I didn't normally like having people round. It just led to questions. 'I don't think I have much of a fucking choice, do I?' There was a small part of me that was pleased he had come by though. I was always alone when I left the prison. Although I knew today that Aris wanted more from me than banter or to talk shop. Even Claire hadn't been able to get past the superficial details about my family. She'd believed both of my parents were dead.

'I brought this whisky to sweeten you up, but I see I might be too late,' Aris noted as he entered the kitchen. I pushed the glass of wine aside and got out some tumblers from the cupboard. 'Why drink juice when you can drink the hard stuff?'

'Not too early for a stiff drink, is it?' He glanced at the clock.

'It depends if you're working tonight, kiddo.' I broke the seal on the bottle and poured.

'No, free as a bird. I was planning on sitting at home watching some true crime on *Netflix* but I guess that can wait.' He placed a bag on the worktop and produced a dish. 'Now, I know this is leaving me open to a lot of ribbing, but I have some leftovers from last night...'

'You're kidding me,' I mumbled but craned my neck to see what it was.

'Meatballs, stuffed vine leaves... You like Greek food, right?' He pulled the cling film off and pushed it towards me. I hadn't cooked for weeks. I knew how to, as Debbie had insisted I learn how to take care of myself properly, but it had never really been my speciality. I was kind of jealous looking at the perfectly round meatballs and immaculate vine leaves.

'I'll forego the ribbing if you let me eat that,' I promised. I got two plates out and watched Aris as he dished out some of the food onto plates. Then he pulled out a pot of something.

'Yogurt,' he explained.

After we'd heated up the food and moved into the living room with our glasses of whisky, we started eating at the table. I'd grabbed food with Aris when we were out, but it was rare that we'd sat at one of our houses to eat. It had happened only a few times in our five-year friendship – we were usually too busy talking about a case to sit down like this.

'You really can cook, kiddo.'

He smiled into his food. 'My mum thinks cooking is essential. She basically chained us all in the kitchen when we were kids.'

'Me and my mum never really…' I bit my lip, realising what I'd said. I rarely talked about my mum in front of anyone. Aris dropped his fork and stared at me. I took a gulp of whisky, trying to burn my last comment out of our memories.

'You were saying…' he urged.

I shook my head. 'Nothing.'

'Look, Jon–' he started.

'I know why you're here,' I interrupted him. 'You know why I was at the prison.'

He hesitated but slowly nodded. 'The old officer, Cam – he told me.'

'What exactly did he tell you?' I snapped. I could curse Cam if he wasn't such a nice old guy who helped me get through my stupid visits.

Aris cleared his throat a few times. He picked up his fork again and stabbed a meatball but didn't eat it. 'You looked like you'd seen a ghost. I thought it was weird, so I asked the prison officer. Thought you might be seeing a client, but he said William Robin.'

'So, you know...' I sat back in my chair but kept my hand on the tumbler. 'And you thought you'd bribe me with drink and food like some teenage girls at a sleepover. Thought I'd pour my heart out, kiddo?'

Aris chuckled, not fazed by my obvious aggression. He probably expected people to act this way. After all, he spent most of his days with criminals who hated his face. 'You don't have to pour your heart out, just tell your friend something about yourself. No jokes, no deflection, no shop talk... Just why you were visiting your father in prison.'

'You absolute bastard, you already pulled the file,' I told him knowingly.

He opened his mouth to deny it but stopped as I stared at him. He knew I could see through him. 'Okay, I might have... I can't believe you've never told me this.'

I sighed and looked at the wall beside me for a moment. I thought about the walls at the prison, avoiding my father's eyes as he searched me for something I didn't understand. What did the man who killed my mum want me to give him? And today, he'd tried to manipulate me into thinking I was the killer...

'Aris, I didn't tell you because I didn't want to. You've found out because of pure luck... or bad luck, perhaps.'

'Jon, please,' he said gently.

I turned back to look at him. He didn't have his work face on. His eyes were soft, and his mouth relaxed. He hadn't shaved for once, so his face had a fuzzy edge to it. I reached up and felt my shadow coming on too. Today was definitely a black day, blacker than usual because Aris wanted to open me up and see how damaged I was inside.

'Just leave me alone.'

Aris froze, then slowly reached across for the whisky. He poured himself some more and held it out to me. I pushed my glass across so he could fill it and immediately reclaimed it. 'He was convicted of murder in the first degree,' Aris said, as if I didn't know. 'He confessed. Open and shut really. Is that right, Jon?'

I was tracing my scar with one hand and sipping at my drink with my other hand. I could see the holes in my mum, the blood all over my hands. Had I tried to wake her? Had I tried to plug the holes? Why couldn't I remember? Over twenty years and it was still a blank space in my head like someone had removed a few frames. No matter what he said, I knew I hadn't done it, though. I wasn't going to get convicted by a jury like my clients.

'Did you see him do it?' Aris asked quietly.

'I don't… remember,' I whispered. *Don't cry in front of your friend.* My best friend actually. He'd undersold himself. I wasn't that close to anyone; I didn't allow myself to get that close to anyone, but over the last five years, he'd become more than just an officer who chewed me up for not following protocol or simply for being a lawyer at all.

'You don't remember?' he repeated. I could see his brain going into overdrive. I never thought I'd allow myself to be on the end of his inquisitive mind. I didn't want him to liken me to Briony either, but I knew he was.

'This isn't something for the station, right, kiddo?'

'Just you and me, buddy.' He spread his hands on the table, proving how transparent he was apparently being. 'Jon, your scar…' Aris gestured with his head.

I blew out air. 'Yeah, my scar,' I agreed. 'He did it to me. And this.' I pulled my T-shirt up and showed the scar on my stomach. I remembered the paramedic discovering it and asking me to push something against it. *Liam.* I remembered his name even now. I had wondered if I could bleed to death. I'd been trying to get away from my past ever since that day, but the skin couldn't lie; it fastened back together but the joins remained like a crack in a wall plugged with filler.

'Shit.'

'Yeah. I was nine,' I added, focusing on the details because the emotion was too much to process. I'd seen counsellors but how could I deal with the emotions when I had no idea what had truly happened? 'My mum suffered from depression. Alcohol, overdoses, suicide attempts. She could get pretty nasty.'

'Jesus, Jon. I had no idea,' Aris said delicately, not wanting me to shut down.

'That day was a particularly bad day. She was making stuff up. She thought we hated her. She told me she was going to walk in front of a car, take loads of pills, so I locked all the doors and tried to keep her in the house. Keep her safe. I sent a message to my dad at work and he said he'd be right there...' I was picturing my old house, the one I'd never returned to after that day. I could almost feel the material of the knackered sofa where I would lay watching old detective films and *To Kill a Mockingbird*. I'd been fascinated by the world of law even then.

'I remember her screaming at me. She called me all these names. I tried to ignore her, but she was saying all these horrible things about me and my dad. She started throwing things at me. But then... she went quiet. She refused to say anything else. Became a zombie.'

'Then what happened?' Aris encouraged me.

I downed the rest of the whisky in my glass. 'You read the file, didn't you?'

'Jon.'

'I don't remember. The next thing I knew, I was waking up on the floor of the living room. My side was stinging, I felt hot and sticky, my face was burning. I looked over and saw her on the floor. I thought she might be asleep… at first.' I swallowed hard. The tears were coming. I'd pushed them down too many times in my life and here was someone, a friend, asking me for the truth for the first time in… *God, how long?* Since I'd been at the police station when I was nine? No one else had dared to ask me after that day, not once they'd written it down, nor even the few other times when it was absolutely necessary for me to talk about it.

'Kiddo, I can't…' I began and covered my face with a shaky hand.

I heard the chair across from me scrape across the floor and before I could deflect him, he put his hand on my arm. 'Don't,' I half-sobbed.

He kept his hand there. His hand was colder than I'd expected it to be. 'You need to stop running away from this. Come on, Jon. You have to find the truth.'

'She wasn't asleep,' I mumbled. I was gasping for breath as if I'd been running up a mountain. 'I crawled over to her. There was blood everywhere. I pressed my fingers into the holes… It felt so fucking weird touching her skin, her insides…' I let out a growl and pushed my chair back. I stood up and stepped away from him. 'This is meant to help me, *really?*'

'When did you see him?' Aris persisted, unperturbed by my outburst.

'Wash the blood away, little SJ. Wash the blood…'

My body deflated. There was no anger left in me. 'He was standing in the doorway. He had a knife in his hand. When I saw it, he glanced down at it like he hadn't even known he was holding it… I thought he was going to finish me off too.'

'What *did* he do?'

'He said, "I killed her, Stanley." I just stared at him. His voice sounded robotic. I wanted to say so many things to him but when I looked back at her, I just covered my ears and screamed. I didn't even care if he killed me. I just wanted her to get up again, even though she spent days in bed and I never knew what she'd be like, even though we had to lock away the pills, even though I could never bring anyone round... I loved her.' I slammed my hands against the table, wanting to turn it over but it was too heavy for me to even try.

'And you just... don't remember him doing it?' Aris asked quietly.

I shook my head, giving him a pleading look. 'I don't know how the police got there. I just saw him in the police car. He didn't look at me.'

Aris stared at the floor. When he looked up, his lip was trembling, not with fear but anticipation. He had a question on his lips. I'd seen him pull this face in interviews a thousand times. 'Jon, the prison... Why do you do that to yourself? The officer told me you do it every month.' He turned his nose up as if a nasty smell had floated in.

I bowed my head, replaying my nightmares in my head. I was sure I would find blood on my hands when I opened my eyes in the night but every time, I turned the lamp on, my hands were only white and shaking. The blood felt so real, sticky like drying glue, heavy like her whole life was coating my hands.

'Aris, I need to know.'

'Know what?' Aris leaned closer, searching my face. I knew he always took in my scar, but he did it subtly, not like everyone else who either gawped or looked anywhere but straight at it like it was some kind of infectious tissue that would mark them too.

'Why,' I choked out. 'I need to know why.' Then the tears burst out of me as if a pipe had broken open. I tried to cover my face and dive away from him, but Aris pushed me into him. For a moment, I let him because I'd never let anyone before, not properly. Maybe Debbie... I shoved him away from me as soon as I could and staggered backwards.

'Have you seen someone, Jon... about the memory thing?' he persisted, pulling at a loose thread he couldn't stop noticing.

I examined his mouth, the words he wanted to say causing the muscles to jump involuntarily. 'You don't believe me, Aris?'

He straightened out and held up a hand. 'No, I didn't say anything like that.'

I ran my hand down my scar. 'You think I don't know your tells, Aris?'

He shook his head and tried to deny it. 'No, come on...'

'I think that's enough sharing for today. Would you mind leaving?' I asked roughly, picking up our unfinished meals and taking them over to the counter by the sink.

'Jon, don't be an arsehole.'

'Just... *leave*,' I spat. 'I don't need a friend who doesn't believe me.'

I saw his fists clench by his sides and his jaw go tight. He had a big bloody jaw. 'I know you're in pain, Jon, and I'm sorry if I ask questions that are... uncomfortable. It's a habit.'

'Can you just go?'

'Yeah.' He nodded weakly. I didn't know where this left our friendship. He'd dug in the dirt and come back with my whole sorry and bloody past staining his hands. I doubted we'd be able to wash it away that easily. And now Aris knew, he knew why I had permanent bags under my eyes, why I never talked about my family, why I was quiet every 20th of the month.

'Speak later, Jon,' he said pointedly, meeting my eyes.

I nodded quickly but turned away, waiting for the sound of the door closing. When I finally heard it, I grabbed the bottle from the table and slid down the wall, finally letting the tears really flow. It'd been a long time since I had, and it tore me up as much as that knife had torn her to pieces. I wasn't sure I could plug these holes either.

CHAPTER 21

BRIONY

'Briony, someone called for you. She said she was your landlady and you needed to clear out your flat?' Her mum said quietly as she entered the living room.

Briony looked up from her mood journal, having only written one word: *ALONE.* She'd underlined it twice. 'How did she get this number?' Briony asked, doodling down the page.

'Did you put me as a guarantor?'

Briony nodded. Her mum had done that a year and a half ago when she'd moved out. She had given Briony money for the deposit on the apartment but Briony's salary never seemed to go far. She had never missed a payment before the last two months though, and that bitch of a landlady was going to evict her. Talk about not being at all forgiving. The ironic thing was that she had money now, but it sounded like it was too late; her landlady was intent on throwing her out.

'I meant to tell you – I've been having some trouble with my rent.'

Her mum perched down next to her on the sofa, resting her hands on her knees as if waiting for a church service to begin. 'Why didn't you tell me before?'

Briony wanted to laugh. When had they last had an honest discussion? If she had told her mum about the rent, she would have had to tell her about her job, the antidepressants and the therapy. She pressed the pen harder on the page until it broke through. Then she closed the notebook and tossed it aside.

'I can't help you if you don't talk to me,' her mum added after she was met with silence.

Briony sighed and leaned back on the sofa. 'When have we ever talked?' She scoffed but her chest felt heavy. She'd read about criminals being sentenced in the past to 'pressing to death', which meant they had a huge slab put on top of them until they slowly ran out of air. Sometimes their relatives would climb on top to make the process faster. Who would do that for her?

'We've talked, Bri'. I've been your mum for a while now,' she tried to joke but inhaled sharply when she saw Briony's glare.

Briony's resolve crumbled easily though, like someone had removed a brick and the wall had come tumbling down. 'You abandoned me as soon as he left…' She didn't say 'died' – she knew how the word paralysed her immediately. They didn't say Jason's name out loud much.

'I didn't abandon you,' her mum whispered but she was already scratching at her arms, something she did whenever the subject of Jason came up. He was an allergy she could never abate.

'I've been thinking about it… for a long time,' Briony said, staring at television, which was switched off. She would have welcomed the background noise. 'Where were you?' she half-sobbed, digging her nails into her mum's leg, making her jerk at the sudden touch. Briony hoped it was because it was surprising, not because it was her doing the touching.

'We made a mistake…'

'I asked where you were. You shut down as soon as I saw you again. You were holding Jason so tight. You barely looked at me.' She focused in on the memory. She was holding a man's hand – a local farmer who'd helped with the search. She had wanted to see her mum and dad; she had wanted them to gather her up. Tell her they loved her. Instead, it was like she had floated away in the water, not Jason. She had never found dry land again.

'We were in shock!' Her arms were lined with angry red scratches.

'So was I.'

'We tried to get you help, Briony. We saw so many doctors,' her mum reminded her, as if she wasn't aware.

Briony turned her nose up at her mum, staring at her wet eyes. Was her mum crying for her or for Jason?

'Where were you, Mum?'

Her mum's head fell. She was taking in huge gulps of air. Did she feel as if she was drowning like Briony did regularly? Had she lost part of herself under the water too?

'We were making lunch. We didn't know you'd snuck out… both of you. As soon as we realised, we tried to find you.' Her mum grabbed her hand and tugged, trying to pull Briony into her story. Briony knew it was a story because she remembered getting back to the rental cottage that night. There had been no food on the table. None in the fridge either. They were meant to have gone shopping that afternoon.

'I lost my job,' Briony revealed, extracting her hand. She couldn't touch her then. She couldn't touch her mum's lying skin.

'What? When?'

'A few months ago. My boss fired me for being late and missing a few days,' Briony delivered the truth flatly and felt her chest loosen a bit.

'Surely he needs to give you a warning first. Is that legal? Maybe you could ask Mr Robin?'

Briony laughed softly, trying to imagine SJ's face if she asked him to switch from criminal to employment law. 'That place made its own rules. There'd be no way to prove it.'

Her mum screwed up her mouth for a moment. 'So, you lost your job and now you're going to lose your flat too?'

'Yeah, I know,' Briony agreed, wanting to sink into the sofa cushions and stay there for a while. 'What shall I do?'

Her mum kept scratching her arms until the sound started to get inside Briony's head. She tried squeezing her eyes closed but the sound remained. 'We need to get all this stuff sorted with Ed before we do anything else. Then we'll deal with it, Bri,' her mum assured her, sounding more confident than she had in a long time. Briony smiled when her mum brushed her leg lightly.

'You don't think I'm a screw up?' she asked, meeting her mum's eyes.

'For losing your job and your flat? Don't be silly,' she dismissed, standing up. Every conversation they had seemed to end with her mum standing up, walking away.

Her words were meant to be reassuring but Briony heard the unspoken words: *'You're not a screw up for those reasons. You are a screw up because of Jason.'*

CHAPTER 22

SJ

On my third day of self-imposed hermit-dom, it was Tuesday. I'd taken two personal days, instructing my trainee, Alexis, to handle queries and respond to anything she could. There'd been no movement on Briony's case except for the forensics confirming that it was Ed's blood on her when she'd been arrested. Aris had sent a text to say he had missed me at a Legal Aid shift as they'd been subjected to this young solicitor from another practice who kept interrupting interviews every other sentence. I hadn't responded. Apparently, Mary Walsh had been moved to a women's prison in Ashford. I supposed that would be tomorrow's problem. Despite the severity of the crime, I didn't want Mary languishing in prison. There had also been five missed calls from Aris and two from Briony.

When there was a knock at my door around 6 pm on Tuesday, I ignored it. Then they knocked a second time and I ignored it again. I was hoping they'd get the message but the person started knocking in one continuous stream for two minutes straight. I hauled myself off the sofa and wrenched the door open.

'Is there a reason why you're knocking incessantly on my door?' I growled but seeing Mari on the other side, I forced a smile onto my lips, though it felt like I was being told to do so at gunpoint. 'Wait… don't you play Andy Dufresne in *Shawshank Redemption*?' I glanced down at my shirtless chest and recalled my unshaven and unwashed self.

She narrowed her eyes at me. 'What a comedian. Anyway, you've been to my place. You may as well return the favour, surely?'

I shrugged and opened the door wider. Then walked away from her, grabbing a T-shirt that had been discarded on the bannister leading upstairs. I pulled it over my head as she closed the door.

'Nice place,' she noted, examining the walls as if searching for clues about me.

I was never sure what to say. I was bloody lucky to have a house that was paid for, even luckier that it meant I could worry less about money. Not only did I have Debbie's house, I also had the money from the sale of my parent's house. They'd sold it a few years after my dad went to prison and Debbie had kept the money in a trust for me.

'Come on,' I mumbled, gesturing for her to follow me into the living room. 'Want a drink?'

'I'll have what you've been having.' She gestured to the wine on the coffee table. I'd opened it in the afternoon and had been slowly sipping at it since, trying to avoid downing shots of whisky instead. I got out another wine glass from Debbie's ornate glass cabinet. I went over to the coffee table and poured her a medium-sized glass, hoping she wouldn't stay long enough for anything more.

'I take it Aris is okay? Otherwise you would've got to the point much quicker…' I suggested, picking up my own glass and holding it out for a toast. She clinked glasses and held my gaze while she took a sip. She obviously took toasting seriously.

'Aris is fine. He's actually worried about *you*.' She looked down at the sofa and seeing the pile of clothes and the sheet I'd been sleeping with on there, she perched herself in the single armchair beside the sofa. I made space for myself and sat on the end of the sofa closest to her.

'I still don't get what you're doing here… I only let you in because Aris would skin me alive if I left his sister out in the cold, so to speak.' I tried to remain distant but there was something about Mari that messed with my willpower. I liked to pretend I never thought about kissing her but even in my drunken stupor, I somehow still recalled how soft her lips were. *Shit, am I staring at her?* I dipped my head, my shoulders tightening at the thought of Aris sending her round like some emotional search party.

'I'm here in a professional capacity actually…' She took a big gulp of her wine.

'You usually drink at work?' I joked dryly.

'In a good mood I see.'

I sat forward. 'So, he sent you round to save my traumatised little mind?' *That bastard…* I'd shared with him, against my will, and he had already blabbed it all to Mari. Who else knew about my childhood trauma and my murderer of a father?

'It's more your body I'm interested in… I'm a doctor, remember?' she clarified, giving her creamy laugh. It made my chest feel less tight just hearing it.

'You're a therapist,' I corrected. 'What did Aris tell you anyway?'

'Have you been eating?' she interrupted, suddenly business-like. She had even balanced her drink on the edge of the coffee table.

'Here and there,' I answered vaguely.

'Sleeping?' she persisted, gazing around the room.

'Here and there,' I repeated.

'Aris is worried you're not taking care of yourself. He's worried you might be feeling,' she lowered her tone, not wanting to frighten me off, 'a bit down?'

'A bit down? Is that what he said, huh?' I shook my head with a strangled chuckle.

'He didn't tell me *why*,' she emphasised.

'Good to know.' I downed the rest of my wine and poured some more. I didn't offer to fill hers up.

'Look, if you *are* feeling down, I can refer you to someone.' She gave me a flat smile, obviously feeling more awkward than I'd realised. I suddenly felt sorry for her. Aris had sent her round here, probably against her will, and she was trying her best to help me regardless.

'I'm going to be fine. I'm not your bloody patient, okay? Is it a crime to need some time alone?'

'You're the expert there, SJ.' She picked her wine up and narrowed her eyes.

Great, now I have to deal with the guilt of not calling her again?

'It was nice of you to waste your Tuesday evening coming round here and I'm sorry Aris made you do this.' I paused before adding, 'Maria.'

'Don't start that again.' She glared. 'And actually, I volunteered.' She sat back in the armchair, looking like she was planning on staying all night. I considered if I would like her to stay all night. Strangely, she *did* make me feel relaxed, comfortable in my skin, which was actually pretty miraculous.

'I thought you didn't like me, in a non-work capacity anyway?' I dared to ask. I reached over and picked the bottle up and offered it in her direction.

She grinned and held her glass closer for a refill. 'I'm coming round to you again, I guess. And if you think that, why do you keep texting me?'

'I guess it's nice to text you.' I winced as the words came out.

'I was hoping for a little more than nice...' She raised her eyebrows.

'I might be wrong here, but I don't think it's ethical for you to flirt with–'

'My patients?' she suggested.

'I was going to say your brother's friend.'

'You're too modest. You're his *best* friend. He barely talks to anyone else… Well, anyway, I'm not here in a truly professional capacity and Aris doesn't dictate who I can and can't flirt with.'

'So, you *were* flirting?' I checked, giving her a sideways look.

She stuck her tongue out at me. 'Come on, live a little.'

Ah, that makes sense. It wasn't like she was actually interested in me beyond some drunken kiss. The texts lately had obviously been a harmless flirtation. *Never forget your carved up face. Not for one damn second.*

'Look, I'm not sure your beautiful face is helping my self-esteem right now, but thanks for the thought.'

Mari sat up in the chair and put her hand on the arm of the sofa, dangerously close to my skin. I tried not to move away, pretending I couldn't care less that her agonisingly soft hands were only a whisker away from me. 'You think I have a beautiful face?' she challenged.

'Well, obviously… That slipped out. I mean, look at you,' I mumbled, feeling hot suddenly. Was I actually blushing? *Jesus Chris, what am I – fourteen?* I coughed and made myself look her in the face. The best way to beat her was by confronting her. It might be some fun for her to flirt with her brother's damaged best friend, but it wasn't nice. I wouldn't let her get away with it that easily.

'As lovely as this is, I don't need a doctor of any kind. So, you can report back to Aris and tell him I'll be back on duty tomorrow, okay? Just tell him not to send anyone around to mine again. I'm sure he has enough on his plate anyway.' I stood up and downed the rest of my wine. Then I held out my hand to take her glass and she gave it up without a fight.

She stood up and followed me out to the kitchen, watching me put the glasses in the dishwasher and cleaning up some of the mess I had accumulated over the last three days. I spent a few minutes scraping out congealed food from a takeaway container, hoping she was enjoying the show.

When I turned back, her lips were curled into an amused smile. She had bloody amazing lips, I couldn't lie. Yet she was a meddler. Her heart had probably wept when Aris had told her my dad was a murderer and I'd lost my mum at a young age (because no matter what she said, I couldn't believe he hadn't told her). It must have appealed to her doctor complex.

'You're clearly not in the mood to accept help but when you are, you have my number.'

I snorted, unimpressed. She surprised me then by stepping towards me and touching my arm. The lightness of her fingers made me shiver but I tried not to let it show. I hadn't been near a woman since… well, *her* actually, and the last hug I'd had was from Aris…

'Please, eat and get some sleep. The world misses you,' she joked, applying some gentle pressure on my arm.

I nodded slowly, trying to think of something smart to say and failing for once.

Mari came close to me again, standing on tiptoe to deliver a soft kiss to my cheek. Then she kissed the other cheek. *Ah yes, the Greek custom.* I shouldn't take it personally, of course.

Although as she did it, she lingered a second longer than necessary on both cheeks and pressed her hand into my chest. 'Goodnight, SJ.'

I followed her to the door. She opened it without looking back. Not until she was walking away down the drive did I shout after her, 'That's one of the best nights I've had for a while.'

She stopped, looking back with a little laugh. 'You really need to get out more.' Then, she left and when I closed the door, I wondered why I had sent her away.

I picked up my phone and thought about phoning Aris but in the end, I only opened my messages to Mari and re-read them. I left the phone on the dining table as I went into the bathroom and assessed my face. Tomorrow, I would return to the world. First, I had to tackle the messy stubble that had sprouted on my face.

CHAPTER 23

SJ

The phone woke me up at 7 am. I fumbled around in the dark, mumbling apologies to my girlfriend and then remembered she had left me for pretty much this reason. I cursed the hangover I was nursing.

'Someone had better be dying,' I growled, putting my head back on the pillow.

'Jon, it's me.'

'Who's me?'

'Don't. It's too early for your games,' Aris moaned. He'd never been much of a morning person but that was mainly because he spent his nights mulling cases over in his head.

'To what do I owe this pleasure?' I didn't mention that this was the first time we'd spoken in days. What would be the point?

'Ed woke up. He's asking for Briony.'

'Really? Interesting.'

'I don't even want to dissect the layers in that "interesting", Jon.' He sighed. 'Look, she can come to the hospital and we'll supervise. Will you bring her?'

I got out of bed and grabbed a fresh shirt from the wardrobe. I managed to pull it on without dropping the phone. 'She might not want to…'

'Why? What's she got to hide?' Aris dared me and hung up.

I searched for my suit trousers that I hadn't worn since the day at the prison with my father. I put them on and went to make some coffee downstairs as I dialled Briony's number. She answered on the third ring.

'SJ,' she said, sounding wide awake.

'You're up? Good.'

'What's going on?'

'I need you to come to the hospital with me. Ed has asked to see you.'

There was a long pause. I was about to ask if she was still there when she whispered, 'He's awake?'

'Yep. I'll come by and pick you up.'

'SJ…' she faltered. 'What if he says I did it?'

I stopped mixing the coffee. She insisted she didn't remember and nothing had come out of the sessions yet. If he said she'd done it, everything would shift and I'd be fighting for a way out for her, like I had for countless others over the years. The fight was getting a little tiring though and I didn't know if it was this case, the anniversary of the death of my mum or something else... but it was definitely harder.

'SJ?' she nudged.

'Briony, let's worry about that if it comes to it. See you in about thirty minutes, okay?' I hung up before she could answer.

After the short drive from my house in Woodside Park to Briony's mum's house, I saw her standing outside the front door with a big jumper on. She slid into the car with a grateful smile.

'There's coffee in the flask and an extra cup if you want,' I said.

She hesitated but eventually unscrewed the flask and helped herself to an espresso-like shot of coffee. I had already had a cup with the spare sugar I kept in the glove box. She hadn't even asked for sugar before downing the shot.

'This tastes like crap,' she said gruffly. When I looked over, she was smiling faintly as she stared out the windscreen at the city waking up.

'Make your own fucking coffee next time.'

Briony laughed gently and drank some more coffee, seemingly to apologise for her blatant rudeness. 'You haven't been answering your phone. I kept getting some woman called Alexis,' she mentioned.

I let the silence fill the car for a few minutes, before finally responding, 'I've got a life, you know… But yes, I should've answered the phone.'

'SJ, if I did it… Will you still be my lawyer?'

I glanced over at her. She was drawing on the window like a child, afraid to take the question too seriously or look me in the face. I sighed. 'Briony, that's my job. I always defend the reprobates like you.' She turned to see me flashing her a big smile. At least being back at work meant I had to pretend to be happy and shove thoughts of my father deep down inside, like before, like always.

'I wish I could remember,' she said, her eyes fixed on her lap.

We both stayed silent for the rest of the drive. The silence seemed to deepen even further as we locked up the car and walked towards Barnet hospital. Our laboured breathing and every other sound echoed inside my brain. I could only guess how loud everything sounded in *her* ears. She had no idea that this was the hospital I'd been taken to when I was nine. This was also the hospital where my mum's body had laid in the morgue as I'd tried to comprehend how my father had become a murderer and how I was completely alone in the world.

I was the one to ask for Ed's room at the reception, attempting some semblance of being normal. I didn't recognise the place from all those years ago, which helped settle my churning stomach. When the nurse asked who I was, Josie Owusu appeared.

'Mr Robin,' she greeted me as warmly as ever, which wasn't warm at all.

'DS Owusu, you look nice.'

She glanced down at her trouser suit and raised her eyebrows. 'Okay,' she agreed, unconvinced, and pointed to the lifts. 'This way.'

In the lift, there was a heavy and awkward air, with every breath seemingly bludgeoning all of us into shrinking silence. When the doors finally opened on the tenth floor, I rushed out and took a gulp of air to revive myself. Josie stepped out last and kept glancing at Briony as if she expected her to produce a weapon.

As we approached a door, Josie started talking, 'You haven't been formally charged so you can see Ed if he requests it. However, for the purposes of transparency, I would like to record the conversation. Do you have any problems with that, Miss Campbell?' Josie produced a recorder and held it up to show Briony.

She turned her face to me. 'SJ?'

'Your call, boss.'

'Your advice though?'

I met eyes with Josie, whose jaw was tight. 'I don't think there is any problem with it being recorded, as long as DS Owusu allows you access to the recording and it's destroyed should this matter cease to be a criminal matter.'

'Okay, I don't mind,' Briony readily agreed.

Josie nodded as amicably as she could and knocked on the door, keeping her eyes on Briony. At least, for once, she had stopped staring at me. Someone called out, 'Come in' and Josie swung the door open. She went through first, obviously wanting to see Briony's reaction when she came face-to-face with Ed. I nipped in before her too and spun around as she tiptoed into the room, not taking her eyes from the floor as she approached the bed. When she finally bumped into it, she lifted her head and looked at Ed for the first time since she thought she'd killed him.

She sucked in breath and her whole body visibly sagged. She made a real effort to hold herself up though. She glanced at a woman beside Ed's bed, who must have been his mother, but couldn't manage a smile.

'He's not awake,' Briony noted blankly.

We all turned our attention to the bed and collectively the room seemed to contort in irritation. The woman stood up, holding out her hand to Briony to draw her in for a hug but Briony didn't move. 'He was awake until a few minutes ago. He was asking for you.'

'He *was?*' Briony gasped.

Fucking hell, Briony. Don't do yourself any favours...

'Perhaps he'll wake up again soon,' I suggested.

The woman nodded gently and acknowledged me for the first time. 'Are you with the police like PC Demetriou?' Briony had asked me that question when I'd first met her too. Did I give off a policeman vibe? Aris snorted from a corner, where I hadn't noticed him.

'No ma'am, I'm a lawyer. And for the record, it's *Detective Constable* Demetriou.'

'Oh, really?' the woman asked, barely glancing at Aris. Even though I was still angry with him for the other day, my loyalty somehow took over. 'Why does Briony need a lawyer?' The woman stepped closer to Briony again and put her arm on Briony's. 'This is all ridiculous. Briony and Ed are in love.'

Briony's face paled, mirroring the white paint on the walls. Weren't they supposed to make hospitals slightly cheerier places these days? I edged closer and tried to motion to Briony to move away. She stepped away from the woman's hold. 'It's just to make sure nothing untoward goes in this investigation. Now Ed has woken up, I'm sure things can get sorted out. I'll be surplus to requirement then.' I gave her a confident smile.

'I'm Ruby by the way. Ed's mother.'

'SJ Robin,' I responded with a nod. No handshakes were being doled out around here.

'Why don't you sit down, my love?' Ruby asked Briony.

Briony looked to me but I only nodded. Briony stumbled over to a chair beside Ed's sleeping head and fell into it. She gripped onto the side of the bed and stared into his painfully bruised face. I couldn't tell what she was thinking.

After Josie had set her recorder down, Aris pulled me to the corner of the room.

'This is ridiculous. Why did he ask for her?' I knew he wanted to sound angry, but his voice was more strained than anything else.

'You tell me, detective.'

'We have her at the scene and his blood all over her. We can take her to court,' Aris told me, glancing over my shoulder to check in with his partner no doubt.

'No, you couldn't, otherwise you would have charged her already. You need enough evidence to convince twelve strangers that a loving girlfriend bludgeoned her boyfriend into a coma... Now he's showing signs of recovering though, they could be back together before the end of the week, huh?' I patted him on the arm, and he took in the gesture with a scowl. I hadn't realised how angry I was with him for questioning me about what happened the day my mum died, but here we were.

'This isn't about Briony anymore, is it?' Aris whispered.

'Whatever are you talking about?'

'Jon, come on, don't bring your personal shit to work.'

I snorted. 'Me? Not bring *my* personal shit to work? What about you with your obvious vendetta against my client?'

He squinted at me. 'It's called suspicion.'

'Okay, Aris, whatever you say.' I turned back to the bed, just in time to see Ed's eyes flicker open. He took in Briony and suddenly sprang up, grabbing her by the neck.

'You bitch! You tried to kill me!' he screamed.

I ran towards them, but Josie got there first and pulled Briony out of his grip.

CHAPTER 24

BRIONY

Briony tried to hold the pathetic cardboard cup but her hands were still trembling. Eventually, she lowered it onto the table next to her and gave up. Her skirt was soaked with tea and she felt cold as well as shaken. She had been alone in the room for at least an hour. A few people had come up to the door to look in, seen her sitting in the dark, and wandered away again.

It felt like she was seven again; waiting for people to tell her if she was responsible for Jason's death or not. It seemed the jury was still out on that one.

Then the door opened. She tried not to jump up when SJ entered the room. In fact, she pressed her feet into the floor and told herself to stay put deliberately. He sat down next to her.

'I brought you a drink,' he mumbled.

Briony went to shake her head, glancing at her last attempt at a drink spilt all over table, but it was a flask that SJ held out. She took it from him and smelt whisky. Smiling, she took a huge swig. It was good stuff – strong and warming.

'You are probably the best lawyer in the world.'

'Can I have that in writing?' he joked but without his usual vigour. Looking at him now, his eyes had dark smudges underneath them. His voice seemed strained like he hadn't spoken in days and was finding it all an effort.

'Are you okay, SJ?' she asked, holding the flask in her hands like a wonder drug.

His eyes widened. 'Aren't I meant to be asking *you* that?' He shifted in his chair and made a show of straightening out his tie. 'But since you ask, I'm as good as ever.'

Not really an answer, she noted but didn't comment. He had no obligation to tell her anything. She was *his* client, not the other way around.

'Briony, can you explain what happened in there?' SJ unconsciously scratched at his scar. She was pretty sure he had no idea he was doing it because his hand seemed to move to that side of his face independently from the rest of him.

'No… I don't know why he would… do that.' She squeezed the flask to release some of the adrenaline flowing through her, but it didn't seem to help much.

'It seems odd he asked to see you and then did that as soon as he woke up.' SJ spoke carefully, clearly trying to avoid accusing her of anything but doing so regardless.

'SJ, what is it you want to ask?' Briony stared directly into his face. He blinked rapidly and looked at the wall opposite.

He sighed and turned back. 'Look, the bruises on your neck when you were arrested…'

'Are you asking me if he hurt me? More than once?' She cocked her head at him.

'Well, did he?' he asked. He tried to keep his face impassive but his twitching lip defied him. This was a man who dealt with murderers on a regular basis but hated the thought of a man hitting a woman?

'SJ… I…' Briony tried to form words but they all died on her lips.

'Everything you tell me is in confidence,' he assured her, pressing his fingers against her arm to reinforce his point. He had rarely touched her before.

She nodded and took another swig from the flask. 'That day, he got angry... I don't really remember everything, but I do remember him grabbing me, around the neck.'

SJ's features were contorting and his fingers were now clasped around her arm as though he was one who needed to be pulled from the water. Although when she thought of that, all she could picture was Jason. Floating face down, stiller than anything she had ever seen...

Shut up, memory. Not now.

'Then why did he grab you in there?' SJ was sitting forward now; his body twisted towards her, his forehead as creased as his scarred face. His bright eyes were clouded with... suspicion? Had he spoken to Mari? Briony could tell Mari thought she was a criminal of some sort, whether it be simply stealing Polos or attempted murder.

'Is Ed an honest guy, Briony?'

'What do you mean?' She played innocent, though she scratched at her arm, much like her mum did.

'Was he in any kind of trouble? Had he done anything bad?' SJ probed.

'Not as far as I know. Why?' Her voice had gone hollow, but she tried to disguise it with a cough and repositioning herself in the tattered chair.

'Just wondering if there was a reason why things went wrong between you; a reason why he doesn't want to see you again.' He watched her carefully as he spoke.

She focused on holding her muscles still, but emotion was building up like a dam no longer able to stand the pressure. 'He doesn't?' she asked shakily.

SJ shook his head with flattened lips. 'He says he doesn't want to take this any further.'

'Oh,' she sighed. It took all the strength she had left. Though what had she thought – that he'd wake up and tell her he loved her?

'Briony, you could press charges against Ed. If you wanted to…'

'What, *me* press charges?'

SJ grinned. 'Yeah, *you*, press charges, Briony. He assaulted you.'

'But I… I'm accused of…'

'You're free to go, Briony,' he informed her gently. 'Go home, order a pizza or something.'

'If he wasn't going to press charges, why did he…?'

'Attack you?' SJ clarified.

Briony nodded. She watched his earnest eyes cloud with confusion, flicker to the floor and then back to her face. 'Only *you* know that, Briony.' His words were grave. Perhaps slightly disappointed? *Does he think she lied to him?*

'Look, this is no longer a criminal matter. Go enjoy yourself, maybe move to a new place, huh?' He smiled again, more sincerely.

She felt stunned. *Is it really over?*

'I can't thank you enough,' she mumbled.

SJ shook his head and stood up again. 'I didn't actually do much work, Briony. Not going to court isn't exactly ideal money-wise but you stay out of jail, so swings and roundabouts.' He winked and gave her a mock salute. He went over to the door without looking back.

When she was alone again, she reached up and felt her bruised neck. She wasn't a suspected murderer anymore, but she was still breathing fast as if she were being chased.

She told herself she would feel better again. She repeated it to herself as slowly she got to her feet and thought about going home. *Home?* SJ was right. She needed to move, far away from Ed. Evidently, if she stayed too close to him, he might actually kill her.

CHAPTER 25

SJ

When I got home from the hospital, having no work scheduled in, I collapsed on the sofa and slept for five hours straight. I dreamed of my mum for almost every minute of that time it seemed. I mostly dreamed of being in a white bed, examining my body as the blood just kept pulsing out of my stomach and face. I blamed the trip to Barnet hospital for this new nightmare. As well as that, I had the usual dreams; my bloodied hands, her standing before me covered in blood…

I dreamed of Dad too, which hadn't happened in a while. I dreamed we were in our old garden, searching for insects. It was one of those dreams about something mundane that was tinged with sadness when I woke up. I had blocked him out of my mind for a few days, but my brain was working against me, reminding me how much I had loved him back then.

As I lay in bed reviewing my dreams, I thought about texting Aris but then vetoed the idea. It felt like we needed a break from one another, and things were still weird after his being here the other day. Had he meant to imply that I was lying about my memory loss?

I picked up my phone and considered texting another friend, but the problem was I couldn't think of any. Instead, I hovered over Mari's name for a few minutes, trying to ignore the fact that all of my recent social entanglements involved someone from the Demetriou family. Maybe I would start calling Aris's mum next. Eventually, I wrote a text anyway. Then I turned on the Arsenal match I'd recorded from Monday night and ate a hastily made sandwich as I watched.

It was an hour later when the doorbell rang. I opened the door to find Mari standing there. She was looking at the floor but immediately lifted her head to give me a grin, as naughty as ever. It constantly appeared like someone had told her a dirty joke. I felt a stab in my gut at the thought of some colleague at her practice being that person. Maybe her supervisor, Ollie. He had seemed a bit protective of her.

'I don't remember ordering you.'

She squeezed past me without asking and called back, 'You couldn't afford me, SJ.'

She made my stomach shake with laughter; it was a refreshing change. When I caught up with her, she was searching in the cupboards.

'Anything I can help you with?' I asked, taking a seat on one of the stools by the kitchen counter.

'Glasses?'

'Above the sink. What are we having? Greek white wine?' I leaned over the worktop to catch a glimpse of both the bottle and her figure. A nice smooth red and curvy hips.

'Yeah, right. But I guess you'll have to wait and see.' She winked. I swear she must've had lessons in how to tease. Why had it taken me so damn long to talk to her properly? Maybe my friendship with Aris had been an instant repellent or, more likely, my relationship with Claire. I wondered now, however, how I could have ignored her mischievous lips, always ready to give out or accept a naughty joke, the way her eyes softened and hardened in an instant, the way her whole face changed when she was amused.

God, I'm in trouble now...

'I don't actually remember inviting you round...' I feigned mock consideration by placing a finger on the corner of my mouth.

'It was implied.' She uncorked the bottle of wine and poured us two medium glasses. She was staying a while then...

'The mantra of a certain type of criminal.' I raised my eyebrows at her but accepted the glass she was holding out to me. Despite all of this, I couldn't help wondering still if she really liked me or if I was just some pity case for her.

'Will you defend me if I need you to then?' She clinked glasses with me. 'To broadening your horizons.'

We both took a sip. 'I've tried this wine before.'

She leaned over the worktop, giving me a spectacular view of her cleavage and put her hand over mine. 'Who said I was talking about wine?'

My hold on the wine faltered slightly but I screamed at my hand to lower it carefully. I didn't take my eyes away from her and didn't take my hand away either. 'Spoken to Aris today?'

Mari snatched her hand back and sank onto a stool. 'You know, you two should just get married and be done with it. He phoned me in a huff, mumbling something about you...'

'He did?'

'What have you done now?'

'Case went to the wall, but it was just a natural death, nothing to do with me.' I took a gulp of wine and considered how true this was.

'The case as in *our* case?' She narrowed her eyes at me. There was something delicious about the way she said 'our'. I started imagining shared things with her, starting with *our* bed…

'The case is over. No charges filed.'

'Hmm, interesting…' she trailed off, but I didn't get to ask her what her tone meant before she continued, 'Aris is under a lot of pressure from his boss. He keeps chewing him out because he's young,' Mari explained, tapping her glass with her long fingernails. I imagined them scratching against my skin and shivered.

'He did mention it but only briefly.'

'Well, he was playing it down. He's under the cosh to get prosecutions through. But really, do we have to talk about Aris all night?' She did a theatrical yawn.

'What would you prefer to talk about?' I offered, holding onto the glass with both hands. If I kept them there, I wouldn't be able to touch anything else…

'I searched for you online today,' she revealed, squinting at me.

'Hmm.'

'Want to know what I found out?'

'How much of a stalker you are from one to ten?'

'No… You get a lot of hits, SJ. High-profiles cases.' She moved her hand across and wrapped it around mine. 'Personal stuff,' she added quietly.

I jumped up, knocking the wine over in the process. Both of us watched as the red liquid seeped off the worktop and onto the floorboards. The glass was scattered through the red like diamonds winking in the light. Mari finally stood up and came back with kitchen towel. She started mopping it up and I moved in slow-motion to help her.

'I'm sorry, SJ,' she mumbled. 'This wine cost me fifteen bloody pounds,' she tagged on. When I looked into her face, she was suppressing a smile.

I spluttered with laughter. 'You're almost as funny as me, you know that.' I winked at her. She began trying to pick up some of the glass.

'Don't touch that! I'll do it, come on,' I insisted, pushing her aside gently. I picked up a few big chunks and chucked them in the bin. I collected up some more as she threw the sodden kitchen towel away.

'Oh fuck.'

'What?' She turned back to me.

'I cut myself,' I growled but when I saw the unimpressed look on her face, I couldn't help laughing again.

'Are you joking?' She stepped closer, craning to see.

'No, I'm bleeding out here, doc.' I held up my palm so she could see the blood pulsing out of me. It wasn't a deep cut but seeing blood always made me remember... Ironically, I wouldn't have knocked the glass over in the first place if it hadn't been for the image of my mum's unmoving body on the floor, riddled with holes. I swayed slightly and Mari rushed over to take me by the arms. She lowered me onto a stool.

'First aid kit?' Her voice didn't have an ounce of teasing in it now. It felt like she was in work mode, which I supposed was reassuring.

'Bathroom.'

When she came back, she stood in front of me, practically in my arms, as she cleaned and assessed the cut. It was too big for a plaster, but I still felt ridiculous when she started wrapping it up. At the same time, the tender way she held my hand and carefully moved the bandage over and over made my backbone tingle. *Maybe I should cut myself more often.*

'I used to tell people I got this in a fight,' I told her as she tied up the bandage. She kept hold of my hand though and began stroking it. 'I guess it was a fight… in some respects. That article you probably found… It was some do-gooder at university. They got a sniff of it and decided to write some article all about how miraculous it was that I'd achieved things despite my past.' I paused, swallowing heavily. 'I guess it's not a secret. Not really. I started using SJ again, professionally. Most people knew me as Jon by then, and further back than that, I'd been Stanley.'

'Trying to keep your distance with all these names,' she half-chided me. She raised her head, her thick hair falling around her face like silky ivy. She slowly raised her other hand and pressed her fingers along my scar. Usually, I would dodge away or snap. With Mari, I found myself leaning into her touch as if she could somehow absorb the pain of that day and every day since having to acknowledge it in the mirror.

'You can't fix me,' I added hollowly.

She smiled fuzzily, like someone at the end of a long night of drinking, then leaned in and kissed me. My first instinct was to pull away. Why? Claire maybe, Aris too. My self-confidence regarding women being a site of ruin. But my body dismissed all of my concerns and concentrated on her warm, absorbing lips instead.

'You don't look broken,' she muttered, when she'd pulled back slightly.

'Neither do you.' I raised my eyebrows. 'But I definitely am.'

'My dad died when I was at university. Cancer. Do you know how hard it is to realise you can't save everyone, especially the people you want to save the most?' When she met my eyes again, I nodded gently.

'Yeah, I do... And I'm sorry. About your dad.' I put my unbandaged hand in her hair and massaged the back of her neck with my fingers. Aris had told me his dad passed away quite a few years ago but he'd never gone into huge detail. His eyes watered up whenever he mentioned his dad though. Whereas my dad made me feel predominantly empty because there were almost too many emotions for me to process when it came to him.

'SJ, you can talk to me.'

'Really, doc?' I mocked.

She pursed her lips at me. 'I'm only Mari here, off duty.'

'This isn't just part of the service?' I stood up and planted some soft kisses on her lips.

'You're making me sound like a lady of the night...' She tutted, pushing away from me.

'You're anything but... Look, I'm sorry I was an arse to you when you came round to check on me.'

'Wow, it takes a while to get an apology out of you, doesn't it?'

I cleared my throat. 'I don't have many people in my life. Not many friends, no girlfriend, my ex-girlfriend did the dirty on me and left, I'm basically an orphan so, give me a break, will you?'

She scratched at my chin with one of her nails. 'Don't sob story me. Who are you? Oliver Twist?'

I wanted to be offended but the twinkle in her eye made my anger immediately dissolve. 'You're demeaning my childhood trauma by comparing me to Oliver Twist?' I complained, pressing her into me. 'Anyway, I'm far less angelic.'

'Oh good.' She licked her lips incredibly slowly or perhaps I was watching too closely.

'I don't think I'm supposed to be kissing Aris's sister.'

She sighed and moved one of her hands under my shirt, pressing her nails into my skin. 'Shut up and kiss me again. And if you mention my brother again…'

'You'll get Bill Sikes on me?' I poked my tongue out.

'Shut up, SJ. There are more constructive things you could do with that mouth.'

CHAPTER 26

BRIONY

She walked up and down the street three times just to see what would happen. She saw a familiar form in her peripheral vision on the other side of the street, ducking in and out of darkness. He wasn't exactly a super sleuth but was dressed in black for the occasion. After her third tour of street, she crossed the road abruptly and spun around.

'Is there a reason you're following me?'

DC Demetriou was partially hidden behind a tree, but he edged out from behind it, giving her a delayed smile. 'What are you talking about? I was just walking home.'

'Where do you live?' Briony crossed her arms.

'Just a few blocks from here.' He shoved his hands in the pockets of his jeans and tried to play innocent. He wasn't wearing a suit for once, perhaps he was off duty.

'You seem kind of lost. I walked up and down the street a few times and coincidentally, so did you.' She strolled over to a garden wall and sat down. After a moment of shuffling on his feet, he did the same.

'Okay, look, I was worried about you.'

'Worried about *me?*'

He shrugged. He looked more boyish than she had ever seen him. Maybe it was the loose hoodie he was wearing or the way he kept pushing his tongue against that stupid silver tooth, like he wanted her to look at it. She imagined he usually wore suits not only because it was the norm, but it made him look more mature.

'You suspect me of trying to murder Ed and you're suddenly worried about *me?*' Briony couldn't help but laugh, causing him to scowl.

'The case is closed. Just ask SJ,' he snapped.

'So, this makes even less sense…'

He exhaled heavily and stared at the house opposite as if it were the most interesting thing he'd ever seen. It was a few moments before he finally turned back. 'Why did he attack you like that?' He was pushing his hands far down in his pockets, perhaps to squeeze the frustration out. It didn't seem to be working, judging by the tight jaw.

'Did you ask him?' she mumbled, noncommittally. What would Ed have said?

'He won't talk to me. I don't understand why.'

'Maybe he hates police officers.' She shrugged, earning her another hard glare.

'Look, you've been unhelpful from the get-go, but the case is closed unless he decides to press charges so…'

'And you really think I should confide in you, given that he might change his mind?' She didn't shy away from his gaze.

He flattened his lips together and nodded. 'Fair point. I just can't stop… thinking about it. I just want to know.' He kicked the pavement.

'Don't we all.'

'Can I ask you a question?' he asked.

'If you like.'

'Was Ed straight down the line – at work, I mean?'

Does he know?

If he did, she thought he would sound more self-assured in his questioning. But first SJ and now DC Demetriou?

'How would I know?'

'Okay… We never found Ed's phone. It's kind of weird considering people usually keep them so close.' He paused for effect. 'You didn't see it anywhere, did you?'

She shook her head. 'No idea where it is. Did you try calling it?'

DC Demetriou rubbed a hand over his tired face and nodded grudgingly. He pushed himself up and held out a hand to her. This was first time he had offered to touch her when he didn't have to. He pulled her up but immediately let go.

'You're okay for money and everything, right, Briony?' He shoved his hands in his pockets again, pretending to be half-listening.

'Money isn't a big problem.'

He examined her for a moment. 'Heard you lost your job though. Your flat too?'

'Yeah, well… shit happens.' She tried not to let her facial muscles twitch.

'Are you going to stick around, at your mum's?'

She took a step back. 'It kind of sounds like you're interrogating me.'

'I *am* sorry,' he said softly. 'The case is over,' he added, reminding them both.

'I accept your apology and I'd like it if I didn't catch you lurking in the shadows again.' She held her hand out for him to shake. He regarded it for moment before shaking it, not taking his eyes away.

'There is one thing,' he added, still holding on to her hand. 'There was a transfer from Ed's bank the day he was attacked. Sometime around ten in the morning. Do you know anything about that?'

He clearly expected her to react badly, but she only smiled. 'He owed me some money.'

'Eight thousand pounds?' he asked, narrowing his eyes.

She pulled her hand away. 'That's between me and Ed, isn't it?'

'Of course. It's just it wasn't the only one… There were two other transfers in the week leading up to it. Smaller amounts but still quite a lot of money.'

'What can I tell you; we liked to share.' She stared him in the eyes until he turned away as if she'd singed him with fire. 'Did you ask Ed about it?'

He snapped his head back in her direction. 'Of course we did.'

'So?'

'He didn't want to talk about it,' he admitted, with a reserved sigh.

'That's a shame.'

'Isn't it,' he agreed. Then he took a step back and added, 'We are here to protect you, if anything ever changes.' The words sounded hollow.

'If it turns out you were wrong?' Briony offered.

He chuckled briefly. 'Sure, if it turns out *I* was wrong.' Thick with sarcasm.

'Bye, detective.' She gave him a wave as he stumbled back and spun away. He didn't wave, merely scurried off like the guilty man he was. Briony stayed where she was for a few minutes to check he didn't turn back or veer off course. She saw him disappear around the corner at the end of road and decided to go in the opposite direction. Though she periodically glanced behind her, she couldn't see him anymore. He had either gone home or gotten better at hiding.

In the end, she didn't care. Let the idiot follow her if he wanted. There was no real proof she had done anything wrong. But she had to keep it that way.

CHAPTER 27

S J

I waited outside Colindale police station in the morning sun on Friday, sipping at my strong coffee on a small wall at the back of the building. It was where most of the officers came to smoke. I'd already got a few dirty looks. Most of them knew my face; it wasn't easy to forget after all. Somehow, my face felt different today, as though the softness of Mari's fingers had lessened the scar tissue. It would never completely disappear of course.

'You still here?' Aris asked from behind me. I'd texted him a while ago, but he hadn't responded.

I held out a coffee, though it was probably lukewarm. Milk with one sugar. I waited for him to take it. After a few moments of hesitation, he stepped closer and accepted it. Then he motioned for me to follow him.

After we'd perched ourselves on the bonnet of an empty car, he played with the cover on his coffee for a minute before turning to me. 'I'm sorry for what I said. In your flat I mean,' he eventually managed. 'I shouldn't have treated you that way. You're my friend, not a suspect.'

'Don't, kiddo. Not necessary.'

'Don't be all understanding, Jon. It's not your forte.' Aris narrowed his eyes at me.

I chuckled and thought of Mari. Of course, I couldn't tell him why I was feeling so bright at the moment... Even so, I didn't think he'd done anything critical to our friendship. He'd always been nosey.

'Hey, kiddo, I can't say it was nice to be questioned about... my past. I can't say I wasn't upset that you implied I should remember–'

'Oh God, stop. I apologised, okay?' he half-pleaded.

I nudged him. 'Alright, we'll let bygones be bygones. I'm sure worse things have happened in interview room three.'

He raised his eyebrows in agreement. 'You're telling me.'

Maybe he was thinking about the time a man suspected of GBH had tried to throw a chair at us both. Or the time a woman accused of murder had tried to attack us with anything to hand, including my briefcase and Aris's pen.

'Look, the Campbell case ran out of stream, no one's to blame,' I finally addressed what we were both avoiding.

He sighed, taking a sip of his still steaming coffee. 'I shouldn't have taken my stress out on you.' Aris stared down at the cup in his hands to avoid my eyes. 'It's hard being friends with a goddamn lawyer sometimes, especially when we're on opposing teams and it's one as stubborn as you...' He half-smiled into his lap, then glanced at me sideways to see me grinning.

'Never a truer word was spoken.'

'Seriously, what's happened to you this morning?'

Don't say Mari's name, don't say it...

'Look, what's bothering you so much about this case? Or is it something else?'

Aris chuckled at my tactics but shook his head and eventually answered, 'Got a lot of cases on. A lot of stress from top-down and Josie too. Well, ball-busting, you might call it.'

'Why didn't you say? I could've helped. You know, could've tried to get one of my regulars to commit a crime. Make it a really easy one for you to close.'

'Shut up, you arsehole,' Aris grumbled.

'Well, I could've bought you a pint then.'

'Another one? You *always* seem to owe me a pint, Jon.'

This wasn't true. I often bought him pints, but he liked to pretend he earned loads more than I did, as if it was a badge of honour. I never corrected him because it didn't seem worth it.

Aris ran his hand over his thick black hair. Despite the hair, he and Mari still looked different. His wasn't anywhere near as fluffy and silky for a start. Aris's eyes were a few shades lighter than Mari's, which wasn't saying much because hers were like extremely dark chocolate. Mari's eyes also had the ability to turn hard or soft at the toss of a coin, while Aris's were usually guarded as a default setting. I felt myself being guarded too, about Mari, but I knew he'd find out before long.

'I'm tired, Jon. The cases keep coming in but with Briony, there's something about her I don't trust.' He stared at the back of the building, as though analysing every brick. 'Call it a gut instinct.'

'Ah, the famous cop gut feeling?'

'Shut your mouth,' he muttered but with absolutely no menace.

'Kiddo, I'm sorry but Ed doesn't want to press charges, you obviously don't think you have enough to prosecute and

Briony doesn't want to take anything further either.... Case closed.'

Aris was silent for a moment before finally surprising me with, 'I haven't told you about the laptop, have I?'

I tried not to spring forward but it was painful to hold myself back. 'Ah no. Why?'

'Stop pretending you don't want to wet yourself in anticipation.'

'Yeah, well…'

'There were two interesting finds… First was that he had a hidden folder with some real… um, specialised porn, I guess you would call it.'

I nearly spat out my coffee. 'Okay, wasn't expecting that.'

Aris's cheeks were reddening slightly. It was kind of endearing how he looked at mutilated corpses but still found it embarrassing to openly discuss things like porn.

'I don't think any of us were. And Jon, it was really, um, disturbing.'

'Disturbing, *how*?'

He fiddled with the coffee cup, now empty. 'Okay, well, it was kind of, choking porn.'

'Choking porn?' I repeated slowly.

Aris shifted uncomfortably and glanced around us to see if anyone was near enough to hear. 'Yes,' he leaned closer and whispered, 'Like hands and ties around their necks when they, you know, orgasm or whatever. It was pretty intense.'

'You mean erotic asphyxiation?'

Aris's mouth fell open. 'How do you know the term, Jon?'

'Kiddo, I read stuff. And remember the kind of people I represent.'

'Yeah, I guess, look who I'm asking.' Aris laughed.

'And the second thing?' I reminded him.

He shook his head affectionately, knowing I wouldn't forget. 'Looks like Ed might be facing some charges of his own.' He looked over so he could relish in my confusion.

'For the porn?'

'No, idiot, for the money he's been stealing from his company for the past five years. Seems like he was using his accountancy skills for bad, not good.'

I blew out air and took a few moments to think. We both watched the officers around us getting in and out of their cars. 'Do you think she knew?' I finally asked aloud, even though I was sure I meant to only say it inside my head.

Aris clicked his tongue. 'That's the question, isn't it? Feels a bit crappy though – arresting the guy after he nearly died, but the law's the law. I had to hand over the info.'

'Hmm.' I didn't know what to say to that; it was all Aris could do. Aside from that, all I could think about was Briony. If she knew, it was a motive. Maybe they had fought about it, maybe she had threatened to expose him… Most of all, it explained why Ed wanted it all to go away.

'Since the case is over, I don't think even Josie would begrudge me telling you something else…'

I thought Josie *would* mind, but I exclaimed, 'Something else?'

'There were transfers from his account to hers, the week leading up to it. Josie uncovered it pretty easily. Large amounts. Even one on the morning he was attacked.' He watched me attempt to hide the frown on my face and couldn't help giving me a tight smile. 'It's weird, right?'

I was silent for a minute. 'No comment?' I finally offered, smiling sheepishly.

'We don't know if he knew or not. She could have known his login information.' Aris paused. 'Ed won't talk so we don't know for sure.'

'Sounds a little suspicious,' I was forced to agree.

He smiled, victoriously and then in a rush, asked, 'Did she do it, Jon?'

'You mean did she *tell* me that she did it?' I held my hand out for his cup and pushed myself up, going to toss our cups in the recycling. By the time I returned, he had stood up.

'You can't tell me that, I know...' he half-whined and kicked at some gravel. 'If there'd been fingerprints on the weapon, we would've had her. She was proven to be at the scene, Jon, just *not* on the damn weapon...'

I took him by both shoulders. 'If you don't watch it, I'll send your sister round.'

He went to move back but I pulled him into me instead. Strangely, he let me hug him for a moment before pushing away with a blush. 'Hey... Don't give the other officers something to talk about.' He was only half-joking. He flattened his lips together momentarily and I knew there was something else he wanted to say. 'Jon, I haven't asked you since... But are you okay?'

I smiled easily, more easily than I had for a long time. I knew he was referring to my dad, but after last night with Mari, I felt like it had been firmly pushed to the very back of my mind. I was kidding myself of course, but I enjoyed the pretence, for now. 'I'm good. Thanks for asking though. How about that pint in the next few days?' A sure-fire way to drown any sentimentality.

'Sounds good.' He gestured to my bandaged hand. 'What happened to your hand, Jon? Someone close a door on you again?' His eyes had some of their usual spark, but the bags under his eyes seemed to have grown to epic proportions lately. It was a contest between him and me to see whose looked the worst.

'Something like that,' I dismissed, stepping back. 'Hey, kiddo, I've been meaning to ask, is Mari single, as far as you know?' I tried to sound casual, but my voice came out a little strained. I took out a candy cigarette and put it between my lips.

Aris turned his nose up. 'You look ridiculous *and* don't even think about it.'

My heart thudded harder. 'I was just asking.' I shrugged. 'She kind of invited me to some wedding, that's all...'

Aris baulked. 'Cousin Selma's wedding?'

'Um, yeah, I think so.' I crunched on the candy stick to give my twitching mouth something to do.

'You said no, right? Wait... *how* have you been speaking to her?' He inflated his body as if about to strike me.

'She came round the other day to see how I was. She just mentioned the wedding, that her ex will be there...'

'Jon, are you trying to tell me you're dating my sister?' He was squinting at me as though he didn't recognise me. I thought about two nights ago, kissing Mari on the sofa until my lips felt raw. Did I even recognise myself? How could I make out with my best friend's sister and expect it to be completely fine?

'If you don't want me to go, that's fine. I was just trying to help her out.' I forced out.

Aris chuckled emptily and shook his head. 'Hey, her ex is a real prick. He really humiliated her, you know. I bloody hate men being shits to my sister.' He was nearly baring his teeth at me. 'But if Mari feels like she needs a parachute, I guess you're as good a person as any, huh?' He patted me on the arm, which felt like he was patting a dog for good behaviour, then he walked back to the station without looking back.

God, he's right, isn't he? I was just her parachute to help keep her safe from her stupid ex. Had she even been enjoying our kisses the other night? Surely, someone couldn't be that insincere, could they? We'd sent a few messages since but we'd both been busy with work to chat properly but had it all been fake?

I got my phone out and jabbed out a message, pressing send before I could reconsider. I had work to do and I certainly didn't need any more complications in my life.

CHAPTER 28

BRIONY

Briony had the laptop balancing on her knees when her mum burst into the room. 'What is it?' She shut the lid. She never usually burst into rooms. Her mum was far too polite to be so abrupt. Something had to be burning or war had just broken out.

'Did you do this?' Her mum held up shreds of paper. When she dropped them onto the end of the bed, Briony recognised photos. Family photos. They had been in shoeboxes under her mum's bed.

'Why would I do that?' Briony asked, pushing the laptop aside and shuffling closer. She picked up some fragments and let them flutter back down onto the bedspread. She could see parts of faces, floating arms and legs, flashes of different clothing, smiles and tops of heads.

Her mum cocked her head at her, as though she were seeing her in the street and didn't quite recognise her. 'Bri, there's only us two here... How could it be...?' Her mum paused, gripping the end of the bed with shaky hands, 'Anyone else?' she breathed out, remembering she didn't like confrontation.

'Maybe *you* did it?' Briony suggested.

Briony saw her mum's face redden slightly, an eruption threatening to spew out and burn them once and for all. Briony had been waiting so many years for it, almost prayed she'd finally let it out. Instead, her mum bowed her head and took a deep breath. 'Bri, these were pictures of all of us… Jason. How could you?'

Briony sprang towards her mum, making her jump back. Her mum slammed into the edge of the open door behind her and nearly crumpled. She massaged her back with a wince and attempted to stay upright.

'You blame me for everything, don't you?' Briony hissed.

There was a long moment of silence. Maybe her mum was finally going to say something truthful or maybe she was wondering if she was quicker. Her eyes kept darting towards the doorway behind like her eyes were arms of a clock constantly ticking, counting down… to what?

'I don't blame you, honey. I don't know where this venom comes from,' her mum said eventually, her mouth barely moving. It seemed that the less air she disturbed, the less angry it would make Briony.

Briony sighed. 'Venom,' she mumbled, shaking her head.

'What?' Her mum asked, almost sounding innocent.

'The venom has been in this family ever since that day. Maybe before that… Let's just stop trying to pretend that's not the case.' She sat back onto the bed and grabbed fragments of the photographs. She squashed them in her fists. They felt razor-sharp in places but didn't cut her. Even though the memories were like rusty old razors across her skin, the actual photographs were harmless.

'Shall I call SJ?' Her mum was staring at Briony's hands, her eyebrows getting closer and closer together.

'Why? What will *he* do?' Briony snapped.

'Um, I don't know. Talk to you?' Her mum's voice was high and desperate as if she had been screaming into a pillow for hours. Maybe that was how she dealt with things.

Briony laughed quietly, moving back on the bed until she was sitting against the headboard again. 'Why don't *you* try talking to *me* for once?'

Her mum hesitated, frozen for a moment except for her cheek doing a spasm like it always did when she got nervous, then she stepped nearer again. It took her mum about five minutes to approach the bed, move close enough to Briony and perch next to her. Her mum was right on the edge and Briony wondered how she had leg strength to hold herself up.

'You're right,' she coughed out. 'You *can* talk to me. You can tell me anything, I promise.' It always amazed Briony how deluded her mum was. She had been a virtual zombie for years after Jason died and even then, her efforts had seemed contrived. She merely had been playing the part of being 'Briony's mum'.

'Okay, *Mum*,' she spat. 'Let's talk – *where* were you?'

'Huh?' Her mum pretended not to know.

'When Jason died! Where were you when your two young children were in a lake, alone?' Briony gripped her wrist, pulling her closer. Her mum's eyes widened in panic, but she didn't fight.

'I told you, we were making lunch.'

Briony tightened her hold more. 'There was no food in the cottage. You had to send Dad out after we got back. He came back with those horrible sandwiches. I remember,' she informed her mum, watching the air seep out of her like she had a slow puncture.

'I'm sorry,' her mum sobbed. She wrenched her wrist away from Briony and covered her face. 'I'm so sorry. We were in the bedroom, Bri. We left the TV on. We thought it would all be okay...'

'You were... *having sex*? You were shagging in the bedroom when your son died?'

Briony didn't see it coming. The next thing Briony felt was her cheek stinging from a slap and her mum was examining hand as if it were covered in blood. Briony wanted to tell her mum she was small fry. Briony was the one who had hands covered in blood. It would always be there like the scars on Ed's face, and SJ's face, for that matter.

Briony massaged her cheek while tears began to well up. 'I needed you. I need you now,' Briony whispered. She suddenly felt cold and wrapped her arms around herself. She was seven again and world was the coldest thing she had ever felt.

Her mum was silent. She was cradling her hand like she was one who was injured. She did look pale. Briony wondered if she'd had her insulin. Her life was a balancing act these days; too much sugar, too little sugar, too much insulin, too little – it all affected her. It sometimes led to seizures. Briony had taken her to hospital a few times in recent years.

'I *did* cut up the photographs...' Briony admitted quietly. 'I can't stand the memories. *His* face. He follows me around this damn house like some demented shadow. The dreams, Mum.' She cut herself off and breathed in deeply. 'I don't have anyone left. Just you, and...' She watched her mum's face closely. 'You don't love me either, do you?'

Her mum's lip trembled and tears built quickly. She dipped her head for a moment but forced herself to raise it. 'You're my daughter, of course I love you.'

'Don't lie!' Briony demanded.

Her mum shook her head and pushed herself up, backing away. 'I think you need to leave. I think you need to find somewhere else... someone else...'

'There's no one else. Nowhere else,' Briony told her glumly. She had no friends, her home was gone, Ed didn't even want to see her again. She just had Ed's money, but was it enough to help her make a new life and find someone who actually cared about her?

'I didn't mean right this second but I... can't have you here anymore. I can't deal with,' her mum gestured to her, '*this* anymore.'

'*This?*' Briony stalked closer. 'You mean *me.*'

Her mum backed away until she was pressed up against the door. Briony wanted to laugh or cry; her own mum was afraid of her.

Jason appeared before Briony's eyes. With or without photos, his face was etched inside her mind. Little dimples. White blond hair. Perfect innocent smile.

'Jason was afraid,' Briony whispered and pulled her mum into her.

'Bri, what do you mean?' her mum choked out.

'In the water. Jason was afraid.'

The strange thing was her mum didn't look surprised. Her face settled into something like recognition or acceptance, as if Briony were an ever-developing photo that had finally settled into permanence.

'Briony, I can help you.'

'Help me with what? The only thing I wanted was for you to love me as much as you loved Jason.' She caressed the back of her mum's neck and pulled her in closer. Her mum was squirming but not properly struggling. 'But you can't.'

'Bri, I *do* love you,' she whispered urgently.

The lie made Briony inch her hand towards the front of her mum's neck. Not thinking. Just doing. 'You both loved him more. You *always* did… Can you tell me why? Before I… Before I do this.'

Briony pressed harder and harder. She pushed her mum against the wall. This was the most fight her mum had had in her since Jason died.

CHAPTER 29

SJ

I was quietly working on Marek Sitko's defence in my office when the landline buzzed, notifying me of an internal call. I picked up, already anticipating what it would be. Mari was earlier than I had predicted; it was only 4:30 pm. I thought she'd work later, even on a Friday.

'Sorry, Mr Robin, there's a woman here and she's demanding to see you. Should I–?'

There was a rustling sound and then Mari's voice came on, 'Let me in your bloody office, SJ. I'm sure you don't want everyone to hear all your business, do you?'

'Tell her to let you in.' I sighed.

A moment later, there was a furious knock at the door. I shouted, 'Come in!'

Mari burst into the room, clutching a phone in her hand. I didn't bother getting up, but I barely had time to think of doing it before she had stormed over to my side of the desk.

'What the hell is this, SJ?' she demanded, pointing at her phone where a message could be seen on the screen.

'Most people sit on the other side of the desk,' I observed as flatly as I could. She growled at me, still waiting for a response. 'You *can* read, can't you?'

Mari shook her head, open-mouthed. I noted then that her hair looked a bit wild as if she'd rushed here and the buttons of her jacket were in the wrong button holes. I tried to swallow the guilt rising up my throat. 'You're seriously doing this, after what a bastard you were eight months ago? I can't believe it.' Her sentence tailed off like she had just discovered I liked to drown puppies in my free time. She shook her head at the wall behind us. 'I deserve better than this,' she mumbled to herself.

'Yes, you do,' I said but my brain was screaming to take it back. My disloyalty to Aris and his comment just kept jumping out at me, although was it possible I was just afraid that I actually liked Mari? Aris might understand... *Or maybe not.*

'I know this isn't you, SJ... *I'm sorry but what happened was a mistake—*'

'Don't do that,' I interrupted, slamming my palm against the desk.

She jumped but continued, '*I hope we can still be friends but I'm not ready—*'

'Stop,' I commanded more firmly and jumped up to put my hand over her mouth. This didn't help matters. I was pressed against her with my hand over her lips, her hot breath against my palm and her gorgeous smell overpowering me. She smelt like oranges and coconut. I closed my eyes for a moment and shook myself out a little.

She wasn't smiling but her eyes were taking me in. I tried to keep my face composed but I was sure she could feel how much I wanted her. I carefully unpeeled myself from her body and stepped back, lowering my hand last.

'You're afraid, aren't you?' she challenged, pushing herself up and showing off her whole body to me.

'What am I afraid of exactly?' I asked quietly, leaning against the wall with my arms crossed. I was only wearing a shirt, but it still felt boiling in there. I wanted to open a window, but I was transfixed by her, wondering if she had the nerve to see this through. What would I do if she did? Or what would I do if she finally walked out, as she should've done already?

She edged closer, holding my gaze, and stopped just in front of me. Our toes were actually touching. She lifted her hand up and pressed her fingers against my stomach, right where the scar underneath was. Then I watched her raise it higher and press her whole palm against the scarred side of my face. 'That I'll see past these,' she murmured.

I let out a strangled laugh. I forced myself to look her in the eyes again. 'You think you're so clever.'

She let her hand wander down my neck, then slowly down my chest and under my untucked shirt. I hadn't been expecting her to storm in on me at work. I might've tried to make myself look more presentable, despite us having an inevitable bust up. 'Tell me I'm wrong then.' I shivered at her fingers scratching lightly at my skin.

'Mari...' I mumbled, pushing her away slightly. 'You really think you're the first woman to say something like that to me?' I shook my head and chuckled.

She didn't look taken aback as I expected. 'No, SJ, but I think I'm the first woman you might actually believe,' she told me in the sexiest voice I think I'd ever heard. It made me want to never wear clothes again.

Before I knew what, I was doing, I had pressed her lips against mine. One hand was in her hair and the other was lifting her onto my desk. Then it was all fumbling to release belts and buttons and knocking things on the floor. My hand still hurt but I ignored it. She tasted so sexy and her tongue was deep in my mouth, her nails digging into me with one hand and the other hand directing me into her like she couldn't wait.

We were interrupted by a knock at the door. We both nearly fell over, although I grabbed onto her and held her in place. 'For fuck's sake,' I hissed.

What the hell is going on today? And where has Alexis got to?

'Maybe if we just keep–' I was interrupted by another knock.

'SJ?' a voice called through the door.

'Briony?' I called back. *Seriously, who had let her in?* I growled and started trying to put my clothes back together. Mari did the same, turning red and trying not to meet my eyes. I picked up some of the things we'd knocked on the floor and turned back to her. She was trying to smooth out her hair. I approached her and ran my hands over her hair, pulling her closer and kissing her on the lips. 'This isn't over,' I promised.

Mari's face lifted as she glanced at the door.

'Could you... um, let her in?' I looked down pointedly at my crotch.

'You dirty bastard.'

'Your fault.'

Mari grinned as I sat myself behind the desk again. I wished we'd got to go through with it. Aris must be wrong about Mari. She hadn't seemed like someone who was faking it. She'd appeared just as into it as I had been. Maybe Aris was just being protective, or he'd misinterpreted how she felt about her ex. Either way, I didn't feel much like a 'parachute'.

'Briony,' Mari greeted as she opened the door. I noted the lack of warmth in Mari's tone.

Briony's eyes widened. She already looked like she'd been through the worst. Her eyes were red and puffy even from a distance, she was shaking gently, and her clothes were hanging off her. What was it with dishevelled and stressed women turning up at my door today? Surely, I couldn't be responsible for Briony as well...

'Sorry, I came to see...' Briony began and then spotted me behind the desk and added, 'SJ. There was no one at the front desk.'

Mari invited her in. I stayed in my seat, knowing I wasn't quite out of the woods yet. This had to be one of the pitfalls of being a man. I gave Briony a reassuring smile instead, trying not to let my irritation shine through. If it weren't for her, Mari and I would have been having sex right now.

'Is something wrong?'

Briony took a seat opposite, wringing her hands in front of her. She gave Mari a sideways look. I cleared my throat and turned my face to Mari. 'Would you mind leaving us alone, Mari? We can finish... *this*... off later?' I suggested with a raised eyebrow.

Mari nodded. 'No problem. See you later. And you too, Briony,' she called. She retrieved her jacket and phone from the desk and as she was leaving, she blew me a kiss behind Briony's back, but I couldn't react.

After Mari had closed the door, Briony looked around for a while, only settling on my face for a moment before continuing to scrutinise the room.

'Briony, are you here for a reason or just to take in the scenery?' I joked but acidly. This was far from what I'd rather be doing right now but she did appear distressed. 'Has something happened?' I leaned forward.

'DC Demetriou was following me last night,' she finally mumbled. I struggled to hear but when I did, I let out a sigh. 'Can I make a complaint or something...?'

'Okay, let's just talk about this first. Did you speak to him about it?' *What the fuck is Aris thinking?* 'I mean... Are you sure he was following you? Maybe he was just in the same place as you.'

'Are you defending him?'

I tried not to react but something in my face probably shifted a little. 'No, of course not. I just need you to be sure.'

'He told me to my face. He said he couldn't stop thinking about it and he wanted to know the truth. I told him, "Don't we all."' Her voice was monotone, as if someone had turned off every emotion. I shifted in my seat and thought about my next move for a few moments.

'Look, everyone's been pretty stressed out by all this. How about I just have a word with him? Would that make you feel better?'

Briony stared at me with dead eyes. Ever since Ed had attacked her, she'd seemed even more removed. *'Stressed out?'* she repeated, the words sharp on her tongue. Her eyes were bloodshot and when I examined her more, I realised she had some scratches on her arms. Where had they come from?

'Well, yeah,' I agreed, slowly.

'I haven't slept properly in weeks. Even when I do... the dreams, the crying out... My mum was in permanent denial, I still don't remember what happened with Ed, you think I'm nuts – all of you... So, *stressed out,* SJ?' Briony gripped the edge of the desk with both hands. 'I would say I have the lion's share of that here, wouldn't you?' Her mean jaw appeared to be daring me to contradict her.

'Okay.' I sat back in the chair. 'Like I said, the case is over but I'm sure Ma– Doctor Demetriou might be happy to continue some sessions with you. As for DC Demetriou, I'll speak to him and perhaps we can hold fire on the complaint for now. What do you think?'

Briony regarded me blankly for about ten seconds but then slowly nodded, dropping her eyes to the floor. 'Fine.' When she raised her head again, her eyes were wet.

'Briony, you need some sleep. Maybe you should get something to help you sleep.' I stood up. Her eyes darted to my fly and I realised it was undone. 'Shit.' I turned away to zip up and sheepishly spun back to her. 'Sorry.'

Briony was covering her eyes with her hand like I might still be flashing her my pants. 'Are you and Mari... together?' She asked hesitantly, peeking out at me.

I stepped back on myself briefly but quickly recovered. I picked my tie up from the desk and made a big show of looping it around my collar and tying it. Briony had finally removed her hand by the time I'd finished. 'No, Briony,' I told her firmly, walking around the desk to stand beside her. 'Yet even if we were, it wouldn't be your business, would it?'

Briony's expression hardened. She made no attempt to hide it. 'No...' she eventually agreed, 'I suppose it wouldn't.' Although, her edgy tone made it sound quite the opposite. She stood up too, casting one last dirty look at my fly to remind me of my humiliation, and backed away towards the door.

'Briony, if you need help, I'll try my best for you but...' I hesitated to say it aloud, but I swallowed and said it anyway, 'I have other work to do, okay? You'll have to start sorting this all out in your own head.' I held my hand out as though to shake her hand, but she was away, acting as though I'd jabbed her with a knife. She was being weird, even weirder than before.

'I'll be just fine,' she snapped.

'Whatever you say, Briony.' I nodded but inside felt far from convinced. I would speak to Aris and Mari about her, but it was true; now the case was over, I had no business with her. There was a question I couldn't keep inside though. 'Briony, they found some files on Ed's computer. Do you know anything about them?'

'Files?' she repeated, as though I'd said a dirty word.

'Yes…' I struggled to think of a way to explain it delicately. 'Porn. Choking porn.' I felt like an awkward teenage boy talking to his mum about it.

'Choking porn?' she echoed blankly.

'So, you and him… never…?'

'Choked each other during sex?' Most people would baulk or look embarrassed, but Briony appeared unfazed.

'Well, you don't have to tell me anything about your sex life. I was just–'

'*No*, SJ,' she nearly spat at me. 'Maybe that's what he was into. Perhaps that's why he grabbed my neck. Would explain a lot.' She stood up as though she was finished with me. 'You and that detective just won't stop asking questions, will you?' She turned her nose up.

'Okay, sorry. I just thought I'd ask… Look, why don't you call a friend, Briony? Get a drink, have a chat,' I suggested in a lighter tone. I guessed there was no point bringing up the fraud or the money transfers now. I was getting nowhere.

She puffed out air and repeated, '*Friend?*' She said it like it was an alien word to her. 'Bye, SJ,' she mumbled and left.

As soon as she was out the door, I rang Aris.

'Kiddo?'

'Jon, you okay?'

'You can't follow her for no reason,' I informed him as sternly as I could.

I heard him sigh. 'I *had* a reason.'

'A criminal reason,' I clarified.

'I know.' Another sigh. 'You still her lawyer then?'

'No, kiddo, I'm your friend.' *A friend who nearly shagged your sister, but nonetheless, your friend,* I added in my mind. 'Stop, okay?'

'Hmm.'

'*Stop,*' I repeated and put the phone down.

CHAPTER 30

BRIONY

She wasn't on bail anymore and Ed wasn't under police protection, so it didn't take much to sneak into his hospital room. She had found out where he was by waiting at the nurse's station until the nurse on reception had got distracted and Briony had been able to check the room records. Briony was surprised they hadn't moved Ed to another hospital, but she supposed they thought the case was done and dusted.

Once she knew he was in room five on Larch Ward, she made her way there with a bunch of flowers in hand. She wanted to look the part after all. There were no real checks on the way in, even though she had to be buzzed into the ward and someone was sitting at the desk when she went in. Briony simply said, 'Ed Porter, room five,' and they signalled the way.

When she reached the door to his room, she saw he was asleep. She tiptoed in and lay the flowers on the table at the end of the bed. Then, she settled in the chair next to the bed and waited for him to wake up. As she sat there, she thought about the first time she had met him. Briony had seen him around the apartment building and they had exchanged a few words. She had always thought he had the greatest hair, kind of like Lenny Kravitz's afro when it wasn't at its longest but with lighter brown running through it. He got the regal sounding name from his dad (Edward William Porter, which she had always mocked him for) and amazing hair from his mum's side. When he woke up in morning, he would always look completely wild. When he'd first stayed over, Briony had asked him if he had been fighting lions in his sleep and he'd laughed in that lazy way he did, like he was doing you a favour.

She reached over and touched his hand. It felt cold. She wanted to cover him with her body, but she was sure he wouldn't appreciate it. After all, the last time he'd seen her, he'd tried to throttle her.

Briony missed how he used to care about her. She had stopped pretending any other people could be there for her. As soon as they learnt about Jason, they could never shake that doubt, even if it was buried deep. It was a permanent hole in a bridge that Briony could never rebuild. She hadn't ever really revealed her true self to anyone properly. She was always worried they'd see right to the bottom of her and find the bottom of that lake.

Ed was the one. He was the person who'd got closer than anyone in only six months. Briony had told him about the nightmares, had introduced him to her mum, had shown him photos of Jason… Now, they were here. How could everything have gone downhill like this?

He stirred then. She tried not to jump towards the sound and gripped the edges of her seat. He took a few minutes to fully wake up, with her breathing only when necessary. Trying to stay invisible as long as possible. When he turned his head and his eyes took her in properly, he tried to shuffle away on the bed and clamber into a sitting position all at once.

'Wait.' Briony held her hands up.

'Get the fuck away from me,' he spat. He glanced down at himself, realising with his hospital gown and the drip how vulnerable he looked. She was sure he hated it. He'd even hidden from her when he'd hit one of his fingers with a hammer once, not wanting her to hear him whimper. She wondered then if she had shown him far more about herself than he'd ever shown her? Would he have opened up more if they'd continued going out?

'I just want to say sorry.' She lowered her hands.

'Fine, you said it. Now go,' Ed brushed her off.

His coldness cut through heart like a scalpel. She stood up. 'There's no need to be like that.'

'Like what?' His voice was high-pitched; afraid. *First, Mum and now Ed.*

'Mean,' she hissed.

He nodded slowly, eyes wide. They were bloodshot and watered down now. Normally, they were a deep brown, not dissimilar to Mari's eyes. Briony had always loved meeting them in the hallway and the lift before they had started going out. Now, she knew he'd never look at her with love in them again and she wanted to collapse to the floor.

'Okay, Briony,' he agreed, as if she were a landmine he was skirting around.

'Ed, do you hate me?' Briony asked, standing right beside his bed but not touching him like she longed to. He was watching her hands closely as though they might turn into venomous snakes that would sink their teeth into him.

'No, course not…' He was lying. When he told lies, he always looked down. 'Briony, what do you want? Want to threaten me some more?' She could see him eyeing up the alarm next to the bed, but she didn't think he could reach it quickly enough. He was breathing fast and she watched his chest rise and fall in fascination. She had nearly stopped his chest from moving. But here he was, so very alive.

'I never threatened you. I love you. I miss you.'

His mouth fell open slightly, but he clamped it back together. His face was still discoloured but he was looking better. However, there were stitches across his forehead, his nose and some over his head. They'd shaved off his beautiful afro to access the wounds. He looked like a patchwork doll.

'How many stitches have you had?' Briony tried to scan them.

Ed winced and kept his eyes on her as he answered, 'Thirty-seven... I think they said.'

She bowed her head. 'Ed, I never meant–'

'For this to happen?' he suggested darkly. He was sitting upright in bed now. She could see the muscles in his arms.

'Did I hurt you?'

Ed regarded her with a heavy frown. 'Are you saying you don't remember?'

'So, you *do* remember?' she clarified hollowly.

Ed was silent for a moment, then shook his head. 'Snatches, Briony. I'm not sure–'

'You looked down again. You're lying.' If he knew the truth, why wasn't he telling her?

He coughed and shuffled away from her slightly more. He kept sneaking glances at the door, hoping someone might save him. 'Briony, I don't want to talk about this. I just want you... to leave,' he said in a resigned tone.

'Ed, we loved each other.'

He took a deep breath, as if he was about to go underwater for a long time. 'Yeah, Briony, *loved*... but look at my face.' He pointed at it. 'Really, *look* at my face.'

She couldn't help but do as he said, taking in every fading bruise, the future scars, the haunted look in his eyes. 'I've seen it.'

He looked up as the door opened. A doctor stood there, assessing both their faces and taking a step backwards. Ed called out, 'Don't go, doctor. *Please.*' With the clear desperation in that one word, *'please'*, Briony's heart finally broke. Being alone with her was something he never wanted again. Their relationship was a sunken ruin at bottom of the lake she had been running from all her life.

'You did this,' Ed added quietly as she made to leave. He was gesturing to his face again.

'I did?' she choked out.

'You know you did too,' he added in a whisper. He looked to the doctor, who was pretending to examine a chart at the end of the bed but was clearly eavesdropping. 'Let's just move on... I won't tell them about you, and you don't tell them about me. We'll forget about the money – all of it.'

He was staring her down; one eye twitching. It sounded like a plea, not an ultimatum.

'I needed the money. I was going to pay it back... But now I've lost everything, and I need it to help me,' Briony revealed quietly.

He nodded slowly. 'I don't know why you took my money, Bri'. I would've given it to you if you'd asked me, you know. But I guess when you found out what I'd done...' He glanced at the doctor and said quietly, 'at work. You decided to take advantage. Maybe you thought I was going to break up with you?'

She didn't speak.

Ed continued, 'We could've worked through the problems – what you wanted to do,' he looked at the doctor again, 'in bed. We could've tried to fix the mistakes I'd made. But you just assumed things and took the money... And then, you did, what you did.'

It felt like a pile of rocks had landed on her, blocking out light. He'd said it all, out loud and it didn't make her mind any less cloudy. She had destroyed everything and everyone she'd ever loved. *And for what?*

'Ed...' she started but there was nothing left to say.

CHAPTER 31

SJ

When I arrived at Mari's I had a strange impression that I was being followed. I figured it was probably just after Briony's talk of Aris following her, which must've left me a little unsettled. I waited outside until someone pitied me with the pizza box I was holding and let me in, then I went up to Mari's door and hoped she would be home. I'd wanted to surprise her, so I hadn't called or texted her since earlier.

I knocked on her door and waited, a permanent smile on my face. When she opened the door, she grinned without restraint and pulled me inside.

'I was worried Briony had commandeered you for the night.' She couldn't reach me past the pizza box but even so, I wasn't sure how to greet her. Equally, she stood with her arms by her side, considering what the next move should be.

'The polite thing would be to invite me in properly,' I proposed.

She chuckled, a little nervously, and gestured for me to enter. 'Sorry, Tinkerbell, I wasn't sure of the etiquette when the last time I saw you, your trousers were down,' she sniped naughtily.

'Well, you weren't exactly Miss Prim and Proper either,' I noted with the same affection. I entered the kitchen and slid the pizza onto the worktop. Then I produced a bottle of prosecco from my jacket pocket. 'I took a punt. I hope you like chicken and peppers on your pizza.'

'I think I can live with it.' She smiled. 'Although did you really come here to eat pizza?' She ran her fingers over the box and even that seemed sensual.

'Well, partly...' I pretended to move to open the box. She pouted in response. 'What? Aren't you hungry?'

Mari started opening the bottle of prosecco instead. 'Can you grab some glasses?' she mumbled as though irritated. I managed to find them pretty quickly and pushed them across to her.

'Everything okay?'

'Yeah,' she assured me with the most non-casual shrug I'd ever seen. 'So, what did Briony want?' She handed me a glass.

'Oh, she's just stressed out about the case being over... strangely. I think she's expecting someone to jump out and handcuff her.' I clinked my glass with hers and said, 'Happy belated New Year's.'

She turned her nose up. 'Yeah, I think you were too busy sucking my face off to say that at the actual time.'

I smirked, reddening slightly. It wasn't because of her comment, it was because I remembered being pressed against the wall with her in a dirty alley, wishing I could take her home with me. Of course, I'd been far too drunk and worried Claire might waltz back in to actually do it. Then there was the Aris issue...

'So, what did you say to her?' Mari asked, bringing me back to the room. She had moved to stand beside me, both of us leaning against the worktop with a glass in hand.

'I tried to reassure her again and I suggested she could still see you.'

'Oh gee, thanks SJ. Palm her off to me!' Mari rolled her eyes.

'She trusts you,' I reminded her. 'Goodness knows why,' I added, nudging her in the side.

'Ha bloody ha. Do you think she felt better when she left?'

'I don't think so. I told her to meet a friend.'

'And how did she react to that?'

'Not well. She looked like she wanted to stab me with a pencil.'

'Standard response with the ladies for you then,' Mari suggested.

I put my glass down and grabbed her around the waist. 'Didn't see you complaining.' Our bodies were close again. She kept hold of her glass and took another sip. 'Look, I don't know what Briony wants from me now the case is over.'

'Maybe she wants you to write a diplomatic text message for her.' Mari smirked into her glass.

I tightened my grip around her. 'I said sorry.'

'Actually, you didn't.'

'Oh? Well, I *meant* to...' I scratched at my stubble and stepped away from her. I wandered around the kitchen, taking in the pictures and magnets on the fridge. There were magnets from Barcelona, Canberra, Paris, Berlin, Bangkok, Pretoria and Amsterdam. 'What's this?' I gestured.

'My capital cities' collection.' She looked down, blushing.

'You've been to all of these places. Even Canberra?'

'Yeah, even Canberra. I always pick up a magnet,' she explained, still quietly.

'Don't you get magnets from other places?' I hadn't seen fridge magnets like this on someone's fridge for a long time. Most people just took a selfie. I liked the way she had a physical collection.

'I keep those on the radiator in my room.' She finished her drink and turned to put the glass down, but I think she mainly wanted to hide her pink cheeks. When she spun back around, she crossed her arms in front of her.

'Can I see them sometime?' I dared.

She widened her eyes at me and glanced behind her, as though fearing I could see into her room already. A smile bubbled up on her lips though and she raised her head a few centimetres, pointing her chin in the air slightly. 'We'll see...'

'Mari, I wanted to apologise too – not for the stupid text message – for earlier.' I took out a candy cigarette and popped it between my lips as I joined her again beside the worktop, causing her to shake her head with a mixture of irritation and amusement. When she did, her silky hair rubbed against her shoulders briefly and I got a flash of her elegant neck, the neck I'd been kissing and nibbling at earlier. I closed my eyes momentarily and tried to shake the thought away.

'Another apology. This must be a first,' Mari noted. She was probably right too.

'You deserved better than that earlier – a quick shag on my desk in my office. I don't know what came over me... or us...' I fumbled, unbuttoning another button on my shirt. I'd already removed the tie. I wasn't sure if it was her flat or her that was making it so hot...

'Maybe I *wanted* a quick shag on your desk in your office.'

I stammered on words for a moment but eventually said, 'Well, that changes everything.' I paused and tagged on, 'I asked Aris if you were single.'

'You did?' Mari laughed. 'Brave.'

'For official purposes only, of course.'

'Undoubtedly.'

'He mentioned about your ex being at the wedding and he said something about me just being your parachute... Is he right?' I cowered at my own words, expecting a bottle to the head. Mari tutted and swivelled to face me. I turned my face towards her, wincing. 'You're going to chew me out, aren't you?'

She surprised me by planting a long kiss on my lips. 'You are an idiot. Of course Aris would say something like that. He'd fight his own shadow if he thought it was trying to see me naked. And my goodness, SJ, your self-esteem needs a deluxe treatment, doesn't it?' She pulled me closer and started unbuttoning the rest of my shirt buttons.

'I'm not that bad,' I claimed, unconvincingly.

'I've fancied you for ages, you know,' she informed me without a hint of embarrassment as she trailed her fingernail down my body from my neck to my hip.

'You have?' I coughed out. 'That's so weird... I've fancied you for ages too, but I thought, you were Aris's sister so...' I said, running my hand down her back, which curled under my touch. 'Just looking at you makes me want to rip your clothes off.'

'Is it the dress or me?' She smirked, unbuckling my belt.

'You. Definitely you. I would tear off a bin bag if you were wearing it.'

She moved back slightly and pretended to baulk. 'Oh my goodness, was that a compliment, SJ?'

I unzipped her dress slowly and she shrugged out of it. She was wearing matching purple underwear. She hadn't been wearing that earlier, so she must've been expecting me. 'Get ready for more of them,' I breathed and kissed her, both of us staggering to the nearest available surface, which happened to be the sofa. I concentrated on Mari and tried not to think about the sixty-seven ways that Aris might kill me for what I was doing.

CHAPTER 32

BRIONY

She had always been afraid of water, ever since that day. It wasn't that she feared she might drown; it was more that she thought the water hadn't forgotten. Every time she saw a body of water, it felt like it had its eyes on her. She had tried for years to flush the past out of her like a river joining the vast sea, trying to bury itself in volume. But trying to erase your past is like trying to lose a limb. Unless you actually cut something out, it will stay there forever.

Briony was standing in the park opposite Mari's block of flats. She had followed SJ there not that long ago. Of course, she couldn't see inside. She could only imagine what they were doing up there and none of it was particularly comforting. The two of them had been brought together by her and they were enjoying themselves, like the case had only been a minor preoccupation. As soon as they left their metaphorical offices, they forgot about her, Ed and the blood splattered walls of his bedroom.

She wrapped her arms around herself. Even though it was the end of August, it was spitting again. She was wearing an old jumper but nothing else. She hadn't expected to be out so long and was still wearing old clothes from her mum's house. She guessed they had every right to get on with their own lives but nonetheless, it grated. Whenever she saw the two of them individually or together in same room and they had that faraway look in their eyes, it reminded her of what she had lost.

She had only ever wanted someone to love her. *Really* love her. Was there something that stopped people from loving her? Even though she'd looked after her mum, since her dad passed away unexpectedly, it hadn't made her mum love her more.

Now Ed hated her. He just wanted her to keep his secret and he would keep hers. He wasn't even bothered about the money anymore. She pictured his patchwork face and wanted to cry but nothing came out. The only wetness on her face was light rain, but it was building above her eyes like a mini-dam holding off the world, although occasionally spilling over. She felt like *she* was a dam and had been for years – holding it all in because her mum and dad had wanted her to.

They didn't realise how much Jason still goaded her, always chasing her like a physical nursery rhyme rolling around in her head, a miniature shadow no matter what the weather was like. Sometimes he would say he could hold his breath for five minutes, but Briony knew it wasn't true. She had seen how long he could hold his breath for, and it was more like two minutes when the thrashing and the twitching had finally stopped.

She looked up at Mari's window again. The light was on, but Mari lived on third floor so Briony couldn't see any movement. She hadn't seen SJ leave though so he must still be in there. She wondered how long he would stay. She also wondered what Mari liked about him. Was it that she thought he was kind? Underneath it all, she wasn't sure he actually was. His words earlier had been bordering on cold.

'*I have other work to do, okay?*'

'*Why don't you call a friend, Briony? Get a drink, have a chat…*'

The only one who wasn't moving on was DC Demetriou, although she hadn't caught him following her again. Perhaps even *he* had better things to do. Maybe her whole problem in life was not letting things go.

Jason. It always came back to Jason. She sometimes wished she had been the one to drown in that lake and not him. She could be the one haunting someone instead and she wouldn't have to live with the suffocating memory. The way his eyes had begged her from below the water at first, then squeezed shut as though to pretend it wasn't happening, then nothingness.

Oh, little brother, who saw who she was and couldn't keep looking. No wonder everyone wanted her out of their lives but here she was, still clinging onto SJ and Mari because there really was no one else.

The rain got heavier, but she stayed still, trying to see through walls and shivering. If she curled up and died right here, would anyone even notice? Her next-of-kin list was basically non-existent now. She had ruined almost everyone she loved. She had ruined them because they couldn't love her back.

CHAPTER 33

MARI

'SJ, how can you defend someone you know is guilty?' Mari asked suddenly, as their bodies were still entwined on the sofa.

'That's quite the question… Is it multiple choice?' he played for time, stroking her thigh with more tenderness than she had imagined he might be capable of. He was surprising her in many ways. Once you got past the jokes and the scar, he could be serious, kind and affectionate.

'SJ… come on,' she urged him, grabbing his hand to stop him getting distracted.

'Okay, Miss Mari, I'll play.' He grinned. 'I think I convince myself that this is my job and because I want to do a good job, I have to provide my client with a good defence. And after all, everyone deserves to be represented in court. That's the law for you.'

'Hmm.' She was silent for a long moment, and then added, 'Even Hitler?'

He laughed heartily. 'Even bloody Hitler.'

She liked making him laugh. She stared up at the ceiling. 'I suppose you're just doing your job.'

'You know, not all of them *are* guilty or, at least, they don't tell me they did it.' He paused and added, 'You know, sometimes I think about giving it all up though.'

'So, what's stopping you?' Mari shuffled into his vision.

'I don't know… habit, determination, a sense of economy?' He suggested.

'Economy?'

'Well, I spent enough time and effort getting qualified. Seems a waste to piss it all down the drain, right? You wouldn't stop being a therapist, would you?'

'Who knows?' She fell silent for a moment. 'There are times when I find it all a bit fruitless, like I'm not sure if I'm helping them or not. Some of them come back and back and I'm not sure if it's just me not being able to help them, you know? Or is it that some people just need more help than others?'

Sometimes she thought about what job would she do instead of what she did. She didn't have many ideas. She'd considered working as a hospital doctor when she was younger but, in the end, it was the mind that had captured her attention. It felt good to help people, to see the relief in their face when they felt like they'd found someone to finally help them emotionally. She had had a big breakthrough with a long-term patient this week, which was hugely rewarding and didn't happen too often.

She wondered then if SJ was happy. Was he still feeling guilty about Aris? Was he thinking what they'd shared was more than a one-time thing? He had come over here and seemed happy when she'd told him she'd liked him for ages. Could they have really found something good amidst all the madness of Briony Campbell's life? Amongst all the drama of his life too?

'What did you want most for Christmas when you were a kid?' Mari turned so she was facing him. They held onto each other so neither of them would fall.

'Oh God, we have sex *one* time and then all the questions...' SJ mock-sighed.

'Don't be a prick.'

'Okay, okay. A beautiful woman.' He smirked.

She rolled her eyes. 'Okay, what about pets?'

'What about them?'

'Did you have any?' She persisted.

'An elephant.'

She tried to push herself up but SJ held her down, stifling a laugh. 'Oh, be serious for two minutes! Why do you try so hard to distance yourself from bloody everyone?' She tutted and pushed him in the arm hard.

He sighed and finally mumbled, 'Lego.'

'Huh?'

'I wanted Lego. Buckets of the stuff.' For once, there was no hint of a joke on his face.

'Oh...' She grinned victoriously. 'What did you build?'

'Castles and hideouts for the goodies and the baddies to have it out. Every Christmas or birthday for about seven years in a row, I got given so many packets of Lego that I had about six storage boxes under my bed. I would spend hours on Saturday morning constructing things. Once, my dad bought me a Houses of Parliament one too.'

'Wow, dedication. What were you: a goodie or a baddie?'

'No one imagines they're the baddie, do they?'

'I suppose not... What about now?' she questioned seriously.

'Well, I'm not a kid anymore.' He nuzzled into her neck.

'Are you a goodie though?' She pushed him back gently.

'You tell me.'

'I think the jury's still out...' She picked at his chest hair, making him wince.

'Thanks a lot, honey. And you?' He grabbed her fingers and transformed the gesture into holding her hand. Mari didn't complain.

'Am I a goodie or a baddie? Therapists can only be good, surely?'

'I meant the Christmas present... And as for you, I'm not sure you are so good actually.' He curled his arm around her and hugged her into him. When she'd imagined him being here a few times over the last eight months, she hadn't been able to imagine just how amazing it would feel when his body was next to hers.

'That's a different issue. And the answer is obviously a doctor's coat and a stethoscope.'

'Now, who's deflecting?' SJ whispered in her ear.

'I can tell jokes too. Okay, okay, one of those little kid's playhouses.' She relented and reluctantly pushed herself up to try and get off the sofa. She was starting to get hungry.

'Did you get it?' SJ asked, trying to pull her back down.

Mari chuckled and eventually scrambled away from him. She went over to the kitchen and turned the oven on. 'I was super cute, of course I got it,' she called back.

'Judging by how you look now, I'm not surprised.' SJ was easing himself up too and started pulling on clothes.

'Did I say you could get dressed?'

SJ stopped pulling on his trousers and looked up with a lazy grin on his face. 'Not finished with me yet?' he said half-joking and half-hopeful. 'I am kind of hungry though,' he added. He went back to his trousers and Mari put the pizza in the oven.

'SJ, why do you think Claire cheated?' Mari blurted out, instantly covering her mouth with her hand as though to stuff the words back in. 'I'm sorry… Aris mentioned it to me.'

SJ didn't even look up. He pulled on his shirt and started leisurely doing up the buttons like he hadn't heard her. He stood up, turning towards her, and she saw his jaw jut out briefly as if he was holding in an explosion. When he finally spoke, his tone was measured, 'I suppose everyone would blame her. Even I blamed her for a long time but…' He went over to stand by the window. 'I suppose I was cheating on her in a way… I was too fucking damaged to let her in.' He stared out the window for a long moment, before turning his face back to look at Mari. 'Not the best advert, huh?' His mouth was jagged, frozen between wanting to keep up the pretence and being in pain.

Mari maintained eye contact. 'Well, I won't kick you out of bed just yet. Probationary period.'

SJ nodded with a shy smile and turned back to the window. As Mari got out some plates and some coleslaw, SJ was silent. He seemed to be assessing himself in the reflection of the window. Did he feel haunted by his own reflection? Mari wished there was a way for him to forget the bloody scar forever. It was just a mark on his skin, it didn't define him. Was it what lay beneath that he couldn't let go of?

'That's a nice park over there,' SJ eventually said. He had his face pressed up to the glass as though contemplating jumping. Mari even made a step towards him, but he spun around abruptly and rushed over to his blazer.

'I need a cigarette.'

He was already halfway to the door when Mari shouted, 'SJ, it's raining and plus, it's a horrible habit. I can help you quit!'

He turned back. 'Tomorrow, honey. I'll be back in no time, I promise.'

Before Mari could tell him not to call her 'honey' (or some other pet name), he slammed the door. She rushed over to the window and watched. She expected him to hover near the door, but he barely checked the road before darting across it and disappearing into the park opposite. Where was he going and was he really coming back? Mari waited for a few minutes to see if he materialised again or if she could spot the light of a cigarette among the trees, but she saw nothing. She went over to the sofa that they had been lying on just minutes ago and wrapped a blanket around her shoulders, feeling suddenly cold.

CHAPTER 34

SJ

Briony's mum's house appeared empty from the outside. All of the curtains were drawn and there wasn't a sound coming from inside when I pressed my ear against the door. I rang the doorbell and waited three full minutes. I was standing near the front gate to see if any of the curtains twitched. Still, nothing moved. Although, suddenly, the door crept open and I saw Briony's haunting face peering out at me.

'You didn't go to your appointment with Mari. Are you okay?' I called as I stalked closer to the door. I hadn't seen her in about a week; although I still suspected that I had seen her across the road from Mari's the night I'd first stayed over. The last seven days had somehow passed in a blur of prison visits, a day in court for some in and out plea cases, only one night of Legal Aid and a lot of Mari. We'd holed up at my house and her flat, only venturing out to the cinema one night and a restaurant on Whetstone High Street another. It was suddenly Saturday, and I thought I'd pop by in the hope she'd be more likely to be home on a Saturday morning.

I tried to concentrate on Briony again, who had shrunk back into the darkness of the hallway and regarded me with distrust. I widened my smile to remind her I was on her side and remained on the front step. 'Can I come in?'

Her pale hand was gripping the door like a shield. She took a long glance over her shoulder and sighed. 'Okay, but it's a real mess in here so we'll have to be in the kitchen. And don't say a word, okay?' she hesitantly stepped back and allowed me to enter.

God, it really does stink in there. I wasn't even sure what the smell was… a mixture of rotting food and air freshener. Had she sprayed it while I'd waited for her to open the door? I wanted to tell her it smelt like something had died, but she'd said no comments, so I zipped my mouth shut.

'Don't go in there,' she snapped as I passed the living room door and nearly took my arm off as she wrenched it back.

'I wasn't going to…' I pulled my arm loose and held both my hands up to proclaim my innocence. 'I was just going towards the kitchen. Calm down,' I growled, losing my patience pretty quickly. There was no need for her to be that bloody rude.

In the kitchen, I surveyed the scene. She was right, it *was* a mess. The kitchen table was covered with duct tape, bin liners and various gardening implements. There were muddy footprints across the floor and I couldn't see the sink for the dishes that were piling out of it.

'What's going on in the garden?' I gestured as she turned the kettle on. Outside, there was a huge hole in the grass. I couldn't see the bottom, even when standing on tiptoes, so I figured it was reasonably deep.

She came over and stood beside me, a bit too close as her elbow brushed my arm. I shuffled away slightly, taking in the blank expression on her face. 'Building a pond.'

'Really? Interesting.' I didn't know what else to say.

'Not really,' she grumbled, moving away.

'Look, Briony, I need to talk to you about something…' I started but stopped as I turned around to look at her. She was beside the kettle but wasn't making tea. Instead, she looked like she was trying to burn a hole in me, specifically my chest area. 'Briony, I saw you. Last week,' I added.

She raised her gaze, a smile bubbling up on her lips like an extended yawn. 'Last week? You mean, at your office?' she clarified without an ounce of emotion. I could see how Aris felt suspicious of her. I couldn't deny I was starting to feel it too, and after last week… Perhaps I should've come round sooner but I hadn't wanted to come without an excuse, so her missing her appointment with Mari seemed a good chance to confront her finally.

'No, Briony, I mean later, at Mari's flat…' I explained, less forcefully than I meant to. There was still part of me that couldn't forget her dead brother and how she'd looked so vulnerable and small when I'd first met her in the interview room. Though first impressions weren't everything. I knew that more than most.

'I don't know what you're talking about. Coffee or tea?' she asked, turning back to the kettle again.

I walked over to her and grabbed her arm, pulling her towards me. 'I'm *not* an idiot, Briony. I saw you,' I informed her roughly.

She didn't say anything for a long moment, in fact, she was staring behind me like I wasn't even there. Even my grip on her arm didn't seem to be disturbing her thoughts. Then, instead of trying to escape as I expected, she stepped into me. She was so close, I could feel the rough material of the old jumper she was wearing, as well as the warmth of her body. I had guessed she might feel cold, but she was warm, just like anyone else.

'I'm sorry, I guess I just feel…' She put her hand on my chest, making me back away, but I only collided with the worktop behind me. 'Lonely,' she finally added, closing the space between us again. I didn't have time to escape before she tiptoed and kissed me on the lips. I didn't open my mouth, but I didn't push her off either. All I could think about was how this was the last thing I thought would happen today and how alone she seemed.

'Briony, please.' I finally eased her off me and stepped to the side, away from her.

She didn't look angry as I imagined she would. Instead, she licked her lips and settled against the worktop, wrapping her arms around herself. 'I didn't mean to make you feel uncomfortable,' she told me flatly.

'No, it's okay,' I said, but my voice came out low and shaky. 'I shouldn't have come by. It probably gave you… the wrong impression.'

'It was nice of you.' She smiled, almost normally, but it lasted for only about two seconds. She started pulling at a loose thread on her jumper and walked over to the garden door. She seemed to be considering the hole again.

'You're not going to do that yourself, are you?'

'It's keeping me busy.'

I turned to the sink and started rearranging all the dirty dishes. I'd taken the bandage off now but it was still a bit tender and unhealed. Though putting my hands in the dirty, soapy water was a great distraction. Briony came over and put her hand over mine. 'I can do that, honestly. And look, I'm sorry… about last week. I don't know what came over me.'

'It's good of you to apologise but please, don't let me see you doing that again. You need to sort things out in your head, Briony. When you do stuff like that…' I trailed off, swallowing hard.

'It makes people think I did it?' she suggested.

'Well, yeah,' I admitted.

'You still believe me, don't you?' she checked, eyeing me with something that looked like desperation crossed with intrigue.

'Of course, I do.' I had an urge to touch her arm reassuringly, but considering how she'd tried to kiss me, I kept my distance. However, I wasn't sure even I believed my own words anymore. 'You should keep speaking to Mari. It might help.'

'I will, thank you,' she said, but she was back to using her blank voice.

'Where's your mum?' I asked, belatedly. 'Is she doing okay?'

She regarded me with a vague smile and glanced at the garden again. 'She's out. Busy life, you know. You don't see her much around here.' I could have been being cynical, but her answer sounded scripted. I guessed it was probably something to do with Briony actually being disappointed that her mum wasn't giving her some extra time now, especially with everything that had happened. Did her mum somehow hold her responsible for her brother's death? How did a family move on from that? Mine never had, after all.

'Well, I have to go. I just wanted to—'

'Yeah, check on me, I know. I didn't mean to… freak you out.'

'It's fine, all fine.' Even the furniture knew I was lying. I was overcompensating big time. 'Anyway, I'll see you later, okay?' I was already half-way out the house. She didn't make a move to follow me, and I closed the door behind me. I didn't want to re-enter that cold house anytime soon if I could help it.

As I started up the car, I couldn't stop thinking about the hole in the back garden. I had wanted to go out there and see the bottom as though to reassure myself of something. If only I knew what.

CHAPTER 35

MARI

Mari was watching series two of *Race Across the World* for the second time and was messaging Selma, who hadn't seen it before, about the amazing places the couples were visiting. There was a woman who was pretty high-maintenance in one of the couples that Selma kept moaning about and Mari had to restrain herself from telling Selma that it was like the pot calling the kettle black.

Mari pressed pause when the doorbell rang. She found SJ at the door with a sour look on his face. He kissed Mari on the lips but pulled away quickly and went into the flat. She found him eating some grapes in the kitchen. He had made himself at home here over the last week, as she had at his. It seemed like he'd always been around. She kept finding his things everywhere – his clothes in the bedroom, a razor in the bathroom, his favourite pen beside the sofa.

'Everything okay?' she asked, touching his arm.

He turned to her as if he hadn't realised she was there. He forced a smile onto his lips and shoved a grape into his mouth to cover how insincere it was. 'Of course. Why wouldn't I be... okay?' He shrugged but his tight shoulders defied him.

'Bad day?'

He raised his eyebrows and made a 'huh' sound.

'Can I help?' She pulled him around to face her. He didn't fight her, but he wasn't exactly willing either.

'I went to see Briony, that's all,' he mumbled. 'I wanted to find out why she didn't turn up to your appointment. She seems... troubled.'

'You're not her father... or her friend even. Don't you think you're taking this Samaritan thing a bit too far?' She stroked his cheek with her thumb, trying to soften him, but his jaw remained tight.

'Do you switch off as soon as you leave your sessions?' he challenged her.

She rolled her eyes. 'Okay, but Briony... She unnerves me. I can't put my finger on exactly why.'

'So, it's just a gut feeling? Nothing more?'

'Don't you think it's slightly suspect that she's got absolutely no idea how her boyfriend came to be nearly bludgeoned to death, as well as the fact that she was there when her brother drowned? No witnesses both times and she's cried innocent.'

'So, you have a problem with her memory loss. Are all people who suffer from memory loss immediately guilty in your eyes?' His expression had a darkness to it, seemingly tilting his head away from her on purpose.

'Well, not immediately but you have to say, it's kind of convenient,' she suggested.

SJ finally met her eyes, but she almost wished he hadn't. His cool coloured eyes were devoid of emotional warmth. He suddenly pushed himself to his feet, but he wobbled slightly as though drunk or injured.

'Where are you going?'

'Do you even know what you just fucking said, huh?' he demanded roughly as he shoved his arm into his blazer. He left the jacket hanging like it was half a cape.

'What did I say? Why are you so intent on protecting Briony? Is something going on with her?'

SJ laughed but it sounded like there was sandpaper in his throat. 'Are you kidding me?' He shoved his other arm in. 'Can you think of anyone else in this room who has a memory lapse about an important event? *You?* No, wait, not you at all... *Me.*' He went towards the door, so she grabbed his sleeve to stop him. He allowed her to pull him back and gave her an expectant half-shrug, as if to say, *go on, explain this away.*

'I didn't mean *you,* SJ, I swear,' she blurted out.

'Yes, you did, whether you knew it or not,' he snapped and went towards the front door.

'SJ, come on, you're not like that at all. You didn't hurt your mum. This is totally different,' Mari insisted.

He stopped short a few feet from the door, not turning back and not leaving. His shoulders seemed to hunch over, and Mari only realised he was crying when the sob erupted out of him like a siren wailing, then immediately being shut off.

'What if it's *not* different?' She heard him ask, still with his back to her. He had lifted his head though and was looking at the ceiling as though asking God, not her.

'SJ, are you trying to tell me–?' Mari started but he cut her off.

'Answer the question!'

Mari shuffled closer. If she reached out with her fingers outstretched, she might be able to touch him. She'd feel his protruding shoulder blades, his strong and soft back that flexed under her hands, the back she'd grown to love pressing her body against in bed after only a week. She wanted to trace the leaves of his sunflower tattoo over his heart again. When she'd asked him about it, he'd just said, 'She would buy them on her good days.' She hadn't needed to ask who he'd been referring to; his glazed eyes had told her enough. Instead, she'd shown him the drunken tattoo of Pinocchio and 'Tell me no lies' she'd got when she was eighteen.

'I'm sure you didn't–'

'For fuck's sake, can't you understand English?' he snarled, finally spinning round. Mari didn't enjoy seeing his face as it was red with emotion and straining to hold his anguish in. His face looked stretched like he'd been shrunk, and nothing fitted properly anymore. 'What if *he* didn't do it? What if I, a nine-year-old boy, took a knife and stabbed her?' He stalked closer, grabbing her by the wrist and pulling her up against him. 'Ten times, Mari. *What then?*'

She twisted her arm out of his hold and massaged it with her hand, trying to ignore how being close to him had just taken a nasty and dark turn. 'I don't know what to say to make this better,' she confessed in a whisper.

He erupted in tears again, clawing at his eyes with his fingers but failing to erase them. 'It's because you don't know how to lie,' he finally sobbed out.

Tell me no lies. She hated to be told them and avoided telling them if possible. He knew her better than she liked to admit. 'SJ, please...' Mari started but choked on empty air.

'I'm sorry but I can't do this,' SJ announced, backing away from her.

'Don't you dare leave!' Mari stomped after him, grabbing him by the collar.

He eased her off him, shaking his head and still crying. 'You've discovered what it took Claire two years to figure out. I'm afraid of what's inside me more than I'm afraid of anything else in this world. And like you said, how can I ever really know if I can't remember?'

'You can trust yourself. *I* trust you,' she insisted.

SJ sighed, running his hand over his face, lingering longer on his scar without realising it. He trailed his fingers down it as though it were a secret code he had to decipher without being able to see it properly. She imagined how long he must have spent examining it, trying to remember exactly how it got on his face. She'd spoken to Aris about it recently. He hadn't wanted to tell her anything but eventually he'd relented and told her SJ's father had cut him. They'd found SJ with fractured ribs, a stab wound to the stomach, his face cut, a broken nose and numerous bruises and cuts. Those were the details her internet search had failed to tell her.

'If you really trusted me, Mari... If you really believed me, you wouldn't have said what you said about Briony.' He removed his hand from his face and touched the bottom of her hair instead. She recognised the gesture as a person trying to remember how you felt before saying goodbye.

'No, SJ,' she said, to stop him before he figured it out for himself.

'He told me I did it,' he whispered.

Mari took a step back before she could stop herself and tried to control her facial expression, yet she was sure he saw her eyes widen before she could stop them. 'What are you talking about? Who?'

SJ coughed gently, releasing the words from his throat. 'My dad.' How long had he been keeping all this inside?

Mari nodded slowly, squinting at him without being completely aware. There was too much raw emotion; it was like seeing rows upon rows of animal carcasses hanging in an abattoir. 'Why would he say that?' Mari heard her voice, but it sounded like someone else talking in a different room. Could

SJ really have killed his own mother? It didn't seem to match with the man she knew now.

'I don't know,' SJ croaked. 'Twenty-two years and… suddenly, he tells me that. Do you think he could be telling the truth?'

'That seems like a pretty horrible thing to lie about,' she admitted quietly.

He digested her words, his face turning from stricken to thoughtful. His eyebrows cascaded slowly together like a brown avalanche over his eyes. 'Yeah, horrible,' he agreed blankly. He looked down at his hands then. What did he see that she couldn't? What were those hands capable of? Had she let a murderer touch her all over her body?

'Ten times,' Mari repeated his earlier words, almost involuntarily. They had popped out of her mouth without her telling her brain to say them.

SJ jerked his head up, his lip trembling slightly but otherwise, he looked dried out. 'That's right,' he agreed again. He was looking at her in a way he never had, like she'd looked at the doctor who'd told her that there was nothing else she could do for her father.

'I'd better go. I'm sorry…' he mumbled.

He was out the door, leaving her stunned, as she went over his words in her mind: "Ten times, Mari. *What then?*"

CHAPTER 36

BRIONY

SJ opened his front door at 10 pm on Monday night, two days after he'd been to her mum's house. He tried not to baulk and checked behind her. What was he looking for? He plastered a smile on his face, and she took in his tired face and developing stubble.

'I'm sorry, my mum threw me out,' she told him with just the right amount of desperation. She stumbled into the door frame and gripped it tight.

He frowned and hesitated, hovering in the doorway like there was a force field stopping him from inviting her in. 'Don't you have a friend you can stay with?' he'd asked quietly, although appearing resigned.

'I don't have any real friends, SJ.' Briony swayed as she spoke.

'Are you... drunk?' He asked disbelievingly.

'Maybe a little,' she said slowly, pretending to think about it.

It didn't take long to get inside after that. She tried to walk into some things on the way in to emphasise she was drunk. He brought her a large glass of water and some ibuprofen.

Then he went to bed, after informing her he was a light sleeper. As she lay on the sofa, she thought about when she had last seen him. He'd allowed her to kiss him. Yes, *allowed* her to. There had been absolutely no reciprocation on his part, probably because of Mari. She didn't mind anyway; it'd been nice to step into Mari's shoes for a moment; to stand where she'd stood, to feel SJ's lips.

She threw the covers off and walked around. In the living room, she examined the photos on the wall. There were only three. The first was of a woman with dark brown hair and green eyes. She looked about thirty-something in the photograph. From the curve of her smile and the shape of her cheeks, she guessed the woman was SJ's mother. Briony wondered what her name was, where she was, and why there was no apparent photo of his father.

The second photo was of a couple. They didn't appear to have a family resemblance to SJ. The woman had bright red hair and the man had darker features, potentially Spanish or Italian. There was a dog by their feet, and they were standing in front of SJ's house. Could they be his relatives? Upon closer inspection, she also spotted SJ's current BMW in the driveway behind them.

The third picture was of a place. A cliff somewhere. It looked like Beachy Head. Briony had gone walking there once when she was a teenager, and she'd thought about all the people that believed it was best place to jump to their deaths. She would think it was a bit of a cliché to die that way. However, if you wanted to die, would you really care what people thought?

She had considered killing herself when she was younger. It had been the times when the doctors kept asking the same questions over and over, years after Jason had died. Briony thought it was more out of boredom than anything else. She didn't want to talk about it anymore, didn't want to hear him calling her in her sleep or think about his still face. Everyone was still obsessed with it though, even SJ and Mari.

The last appointment with Mari had been earlier that day. Mari hadn't spoken much. In fact, it had seemed like something was bothering *her*. She'd kept pressing her fingers against her lips absently and forgetting what they were talking about. Briony imagined she had something or *someone* on her mind. Was that 'someone' SJ? Briony didn't think there was much point in her talking to Mari anymore, but something kept drawing her back. She had those deep brown eyes that reminded Briony of Ed for one. There was something about her neck too, the way her hair hung down both sides of it like dark waterfalls framing it. And she didn't take any crap, not like some of the doctors she had seen in the past. The problem was, Briony couldn't really trust her, especially now she knew her brother was a police officer.

Ed had told Briony she knew what she'd done. *Remembered. Every. Blow.* Had she really tried to kill Ed, like she had told Mari that day? What was the lie? That she *wasn't* a murderer? How could she be one?

After all, SJ believed she was a good person. He'd seemed convinced of her innocence from the first day. He'd acted like there was a mystery to be solved, so she had given him one. She had played it all inside her mind like play she was rehearsing but it had come out like a final performance. How was she to know that Ed would wake up and go for her neck? That he would know she had stolen the money and want her to leave him alone so bad that he didn't even care anymore? Although, SJ still didn't know the truth, otherwise he wouldn't have let her in, would he? Even though she had looked drunk.

Ed hadn't wanted to do things her way. When he'd looked at her across worktop that day and said, 'Briony, I just love you. Is that a bad thing?' She had known he was going to say no to her request. He was overcompensating, trying to focus on how much he loved her and hoping she would forget. She had broached the subject a week after she'd told him she knew about the fraud. Briony had thought he would accept her flaws more when she knew his. Ed had only seen her a few times for brief periods until the Sunday night before the attack though. She'd guilt-tripped her way in and managed to stay the night on Sunday, but they hadn't properly touched. Going for a run had been his get-out clause.

'Is that a no?' Briony had asked him, pushing the bowl of fruit salad away.

Ed had spent long time talking, or more accurately rambling, after that. He'd talked about how good they were together, how he was willing to experiment but perhaps this was too far, how he hoped she could understand because he thought they had a good thing. They could get past it. But then she had thought about the stolen money. She'd only taken just a little at first, to help her get by for a bit longer. Then she had used his phone to transfer more, hoping to pay the rent she owed. Though he was an accountant, he didn't use fingerprint security. He used patterns and passcodes, which she had stored away in her mind just in case.

Briony had been planning all week to finally let him see her too – the real her. What she hid from everyone. She had seen his bad parts now after all. She had accepted them. Surely he could accept hers?

When they were in bedroom that Monday, she had done it. She had grabbed his neck tight and squeezed with all her might. He'd fought, scratching her hands, eyes bulging as he'd tried to push her off. Then he'd grabbed her neck too. She'd felt intense pleasure surging through her as he'd gripped more and more tightly. She'd been on the verge of coming when she'd accidentally released her grip. Ed had jumped at her, simultaneously gasping for breath and trying to escape.

Next, the ugly metal owl ornament was in her hand (that his mum had given him) and she had stared at it for a moment before bringing it down on his head. If he really couldn't accept her, if he really couldn't love her… *Well, it was definitely over.* He'd made a grunting sound and fallen sideways onto bed. She had struck again, causing blood to splatter up the wall. It had made a lopsided dotted pattern. She'd kept hitting him until his face and body were completely still. Blood was all over the sheets and the wall. She had looked down and saw that blood was also coating her hands and arms. She had carefully wiped the ornament down and left it beside him, like a mini-gravestone marking his death bed.

When she became aware of herself again, she realised she was standing beside SJ's bed. She must've walked upstairs without realising. SJ was facing the other way and she could hear his soft breathing. Was he really a light sleeper or had he just wanted to pretend he was so she wouldn't think of coming in? She nearly laughed into the darkness. Perhaps he should've locked the door.

It was then that she noticed the bundle on the empty pillow next to him. She picked it up and examined it in the light coming from the doorway. It was a woman's dress. She smelt it but it only smelt of perfume, oranges. She inspected the material more closely. It was red with random firework-like patterns all over it. It was a pretty dress. She thought about stealing it, but she didn't think it would fit and she also figured SJ might notice. The more she thought about it though, the more she realised she recognised it. She had seen Mari wearing it in one of their sessions. She remembered because she had thought it had lovely neckline. Mari had a long thin neck that she emphasised every time she was thinking. She often looked up at ceiling when she did.

'What are you doing?' SJ's voice came to her suddenly. She was holding the dress to her face, inhaling the sweet smell. She instantly lowered it and tossed it back onto the bed.

'Sorry, I was looking for a jumper. I'm cold.' She put her arms around herself for emphasis.

He sat up in bed and turned the lamp on. He glanced at Mari's dress and then looked into Briony's face again. 'Why were you touching M— *that dress?*' He'd nearly revealed his secret, but she supposed being woken up at two am by someone in your room might do that.

'I thought it was a jumper. Sorry.' Briony went towards the door.

'Briony,' SJ called out.

She stopped and turned back. He was clambering out of bed. He was wearing only pyjama bottoms and she couldn't help taking in the scar on his stomach and a tattoo of a sunflower on his chest. She wondered if he had any more scars or tattoos hidden away. He grabbed a jumper from the wardrobe and handed it over.

'Take this.' He kept his hand on it though so she couldn't move. He hesitated but finally added, 'I know I was your lawyer, but my private life is none of your business.'

Briony nodded earnestly and pulled the jumper along with her as she tried to leave. 'I'm sorry. I didn't mean to intrude. I was just cold.'

SJ nodded but he was squinting at her. 'Look, as the case is over... You may as well know; Mari and I were together.'

'*Were?*' Briony echoed.

SJ rubbed his hands over his arms, suddenly appearing cold too. 'Yes, *were.*'

'Then why do you have her dress in your bed?'

SJ's face fell and he stepped back into his room. 'I just thought I'd tell you… I don't know why,' he admitted, biting his lip. They were both quiet for a moment before he spoke again, 'Briony, did you know about the fraud?'

She tried to think of a quick answer but was too surprised. As she stayed silent, SJ was still staring at her, nodding gently. Now he knew everything – he knew about the porn Ed had on his computer too. She had found that early on in their relationship; she was good at finding hidden files on computers. Briony didn't really trust people so she always checked on them. It was a bad habit but when she had seen the files, her chest had flushed with excitement, she had felt completely drowned in it. She had thought maybe he could understand her like no one else and would want to explore it with her. Though it turned out he didn't. He only wanted to be a giver, not a receiver. *Typical man.*

It was kind of convenient now though. It made Ed look bad, not her. And the fraud. She had discovered it by accident – overhearing a phone call. When she had confronted Ed, he'd laughed at first but as they'd argued, the truth had come out.

A secret for a secret. There was no way he could ask for his money back now. It wasn't even his to begin with. He didn't ever want to see her again. He hated her now.

'Well, goodnight and I hope you sleep it off,' SJ interrupted, reminding her of another lie. He was back inside his room before she could say or do anything else. He closed the door carefully and a moment later, she heard the sound of something being shoved against it. He wanted to make sure she didn't come near him again. He'd made it physically and verbally clear he wasn't interested in her, not like that anyway.

After a safe amount of time, she continued searching around downstairs, wearing SJ's soft jumper. It smelt of washing powder. She remembered why she was there – DC

Demetriou. She had thought he'd have moved on, but she kept seeing him. In the supermarket, waiting for the bus, across the road from her mum's house. It was like he didn't care that she knew. She needed something to protect herself, something to keep him away. Then it had come to her – he and SJ were obviously friends. Maybe SJ was hiding something? Maybe she could divide them somehow.

A simple internet search had told her he got the scar from his dad. His dad had killed his mother when he was nine. Was it as straightforward as that? Even if she couldn't use it against him, she wanted to know more. Briony dug through some of the drawers in the living room until she found some letters. They were all addressed to Stanley Robin. On the back, the name *William Robin* was written, above a stamp saying *Pentonville Prison*.

She sat down in the kitchen and counted them. There were twenty-two letters. Only one of them was unsealed and it was from twenty-two years before. All of the others were sealed and looked untouched. There wasn't even a corner of them that had been picked at. SJ had never been tempted to read whatever was written in them but *she* was tempted. She promised herself to only read first one and then would take the rest with her. From where she had found them, she doubted SJ would even notice they were missing. At least not before it was too late.

CHAPTER 37

SJ

I found myself back at Barnet hospital on Friday evening after a long week of working at home, popping into the office only when necessary. Most of my time was spent trying to ignore how much I missed Mari, in between trying to dismiss thoughts of my dad waiting to die in his prison cell.

I was sitting beside Mary Walsh's bedside. She had been staring up at the ceiling for at least ten minutes, completely ignoring me. I had thrown my blazer over the end of her bed and was settled in a chair beside her. I didn't mind the silence; it was almost therapeutic. I focused in on her uneven breathing and tried to compare it to mine. Had my heart finally returned to normal after walking out of Mari's apartment and having Briony wake me in the darkness? I wasn't sure.

'Why are you here?' she whispered suddenly, turning her face to look at me. Her skin was deathly pale, and her lips were uncomfortably dry. It made me want to douse my lips in water. I stood up and lifted a glass of water to her lips. She took a small sip and shook her head weakly.

'I'm your solicitor, Mary. I'm concerned for your welfare.' I retook my seat.

She tried to laugh but the sound got lost in her oxygen-starved chest. It sounded like a wheeze more than anything else. 'I think that's the doctor's job, Mr Robin. Tell me the truth,' she insisted, staring me down.

I sat forward, pushing my shirt sleeves up. It was strangely hot in the hospital. I remembered them being cold. I remembered sitting there far too many times, with my dad's coat around my shoulders, wondering if my mum would survive each time.

'I wanted to talk to you, about the case. And it's SJ.' I did have other work to do, plenty in fact. Though when I'd heard the news about Mary, I'd turned the car around and driven straight here instead of onto my next client, who was in custody at Colindale. A few hours weren't going to kill anyone.

She blinked slowly, as if she could barely keep herself awake. 'He dropped the charges though. He says he can... forgive me,' she reminded me, her tone dipping as she spoke.

I fell silent for a moment. It had taken me a while to realise why this case had been bothering me so much. I had suddenly realised when I had been writing down some notes about charges being dropped. The words 'victim dropped charges without intimidation or influence,' had made me drop my pen. It made me focus in on the idea that intimidation and influence could come in many forms. I had pictured my dad, tired with the effort of trying to keep my mum from going over the edge. Who had been the real victim? Had she been at any fault too?

'You know... if you wanted to pursue anything, legally I mean, I could help you,' I offered, watching her eyes flit between me and the door. Was she expecting her husband? One of her children?

'We don't need help,' she insisted, but it felt like someone else's script she was reciting.

I nodded and tried to think of a different approach. 'Okay, Mary, all I'm saying is that if there was something you were unhappy about, that made you do what you did, we could try to find ways to make things better for you.'

She pressed her lips together and turned back to the ceiling. I was worried she would never speak again but her broken voice slid out a few moments later, 'You don't know what you're asking me.'

I stood up and leaned over the bed, making her look at me. 'You might think it's best to just go back, to let things happen like they were before, but you said some things... How he treated you badly, how he hurt you. That's right, isn't it?'

She sniffed loudly, perhaps holding back a wave of tears. 'He's my husband.'

I gripped the bed and told myself to breathe. I remembered the hospital beds in my childhood and how I'd wanted to smash the room up looking at the state my mum was in. I hadn't understood the anger then, but I understood now; it was because *she'd* failed us, but it had appeared to everyone else that *we'd* failed her.

'That's not the most important thing,' I said quietly. People always have options. Maybe Dad should have left my mum, taken me away from it. But he'd stayed and look how it turned out.

'I was taught divorce is a sin, Mr Robin, and I don't just intend to walk out on my family.'

I grabbed her arm without thinking. 'You wouldn't be walking out on them, you'd be saving yourself,' I urged but let go when she shrunk away from me in the bed.

'I'm sorry. I'm just worried for you. You took lots of pills, Mary,' I whispered, as if someone else might hear us.

She clenched her eyes shut. 'I didn't want to bother anyone anymore,' she confessed.

My brain was overloaded, and I sagged into the chair again.

Attempt one: slitting her wrists in the bath. I was seven.

Attempt two: stepping out in front of a car. It hadn't been going fast enough. I was eight.

Attempt three: pills in the bathroom. I'd found her vomiting on the floor. Eight again.

Attempt four. Attempt four. Attempt four. Was that technically a success? She hadn't survived that one. I closed my eyes and thought about her clothes sodden with black stains, blood as black as her diseased mind. Her mouth had hung open slightly, as though she was mid-frown or about to criticise something I'd done, but nothing had come out.

'Mr Robin?'

I shook myself out at Mary's voice and met her eyes again. 'Mary, I... What if it happens again? What if you try to defend yourself again and ended up in prison?'

The tears began to swell out of her eyes. She didn't even bother to wipe them away. 'I don't think that's how this will end, do you?' she finally asked.

I had to be professional; I'd already crossed some lines, but I couldn't stop thinking of this woman turning around and reacting after years of abuse. There was a long silence between us then as we both considered the probabilities. 'If you change your mind, you have my number,' I managed to say, despite the past thundering through my brain like a train without brakes.

She nodded gently, finally wiping a few tears away. 'He says it's because he loves me.' Her voice shook as if she wasn't even bothering to pretend to believe it.

I wanted to react but all I could see was my mum hovering over me. She was holding a knife. *This is because I love you, SJ.*

She was holding the knife in her left hand. Dad was right-handed…

I sprang up from the chair, making Mary jump. 'I'm sorry, I remembered I… have an appointment.' I hastily pulled on my coat and backed away towards the door. I felt like I was leaving someone in a car that was balancing on a cliff edge. But what if they moved closer to the edge instead of trying to escape? How could you save someone like that?

'Please look after yourself, Mary.'

I practically ran away from her bed and only stopped when I was outside the hospital. I immediately lit up a cigarette and tried to separate the truth from the fiction inside my mind.

I touched the scar on the right side of my face. Why didn't I remember? If my dad had done it, he would've had to hold the knife in his left hand. It would have been easier for my mum to have cut my face, natural even, being left-handed. What did that tell me about what had happened the day of her murder? Did it mean anything at all?

My only interruption was a text message from Mari, which read: *You taking me to this wedding or not?*

CHAPTER 38

BRIONY

It was ten days after she'd stayed at SJ's house. A Thursday. Briony was sitting across from a man who looked like a much older version of SJ. He even had the same shade of blue eyes. William Robin's mouth moved in ways much like SJ's, as well as sharing a similar build. It was slightly eerie. The major differences were that William looked incredibly pale and seemed to permanently slump his shoulders as if he wanted to be invisible. Though Briony supposed SJ often wanted to avoid attention too but his scar didn't permit that.

'So, you're SJ's fiancée?' he asked, scanning Briony's top half with his eyes, trying to spot traces of SJ on her. She nodded eagerly and put her hands on the table, hoping he wouldn't notice the scratch marks and the dirt under her nails. Briony had scrubbed them a million times but the mud seemed to have stained her like a non-removable tattoo.

'Did he tell you about me?' she asked quietly, knowing the answer. Briony had sent him a letter and had received a visiting order soon after. Maybe William had been curious. She'd hoped the letter would have that effect.

William bowed his head and glanced at the wall before turning back. 'He doesn't tell me much,' he croaked out.

'He's told me about you,' she offered.

He gave a strangled chuckle and nodded slowly with his whole body. 'I'll bet he did. Anything of interest?' His eyes darted to the prison guard behind them.

'He told me about what happened... with his mum,' she said quietly, glancing back at the guard as well. Briony wished they could be alone, but visits were done in the visiting hall with loads of other people. Aside from that, he was a category-B prisoner; not the worst but still a serious threat. He'd been convicted of murder after all, but he was too old and tired looking to pose much of a threat in her eyes.

She hadn't been surprised when she had read the letters, which had told her loads of information about SJ and his past. She already had the concrete facts she had found online; his dad had murdered his mum when was he was nine. SJ had been there but had no memory of the actual event. No wonder he was obsessed with mysteries. His life itself was one.

'He did?' William's voice was high; surprised.

'We've grown very close,' she clarified.

He chewed on his cheek and looked her over again, continually reassessing. Then he nodded again as a frown settled over his face. 'Have you been together long?'

'About a year,' she lied but her heart was pounding.

'A year, huh? Serious then?' He spoke out of the side of his mouth. Briony thought he was pained by the idea that she was closer to SJ than he was.

'I think so. Look, you probably want to know why I'm here...'

He tapped the table with his fingers as he continued to search her face. Perhaps he wanted to analyse her devotion for

SJ by her features. Briony thought about how much she had loved Ed and hoped it transmitted into sincerity.

'I kind of would,' he admitted, biting his flaky bottom lip. He looked like he hadn't had a drink in days. She knew it was actually because he was ill since the guard had told her.

'SJ let me read these.' Briony lifted the envelopes from her lap and laid them out on the table. His eyes widened at the sight of them. He reached across very slowly and brushed the edge of one of them.

'I can't believe that,' he whispered. 'They're very personal.' He sat back in his seat with a tight jaw. She saw one of SJ's looks again, disapproving of her when he thought she wouldn't notice, like at the hospital after Ed had attacked her. SJ had believed in her once, but now she wasn't sure he was on her side anymore. Most of all though, she wanted to know what the big mystery behind him was. What had happened the day of his mother's murder? Did he really not remember?

'Well, I'm telling you it's true. I came here of my own accord though...' she trailed off purposely. 'I want to know what I'm getting into with him, properly, before things get even more serious.'

'What did he think of my letters?' William asked, his eyes growing wet. Briony hadn't banked on him getting tearful, although the letters were full of over sentimentality and dramatic emotions.

'He says he can't forgive you, I'm sorry.' She clasped hands her together and gave him an apologetic smile. He didn't seem surprised. He just wiped at the corners of his eyes and cleared his throat.

'Then why are you here? To punish me more?' he demanded weakly. In the letters, William had mentioned how SJ visited him once a month. Twelve visits a year for how many years?

Since he was eighteen or younger? If SJ really couldn't forgive his dad, as the letters suggested, why did he bother doing it?

'I want to hear what happened, directly from you. Maybe I could talk to SJ for you?' As soon as she said it, he shot up in his chair. She could tell he hadn't been expecting her to suggest it and felt her insides squirm. He had no idea she was really only here for herself; to learn more about SJ, to hopefully give herself some leverage if Ed decided to talk. Somehow, Briony needed this to help her feel secure.

'You would do that?' He was sitting forward, almost on the edge of the chair.

'Of course I would. I just want to understand.' She reached across table and took his hand. It felt clammy and he was shaking; whether it was due to nerves or his illness, she didn't know. Briony glanced back at the guard, who was watching with interest. This was going to be difficult, though she had an inkling from the letters that all was not as it seemed. There were hints buried in there; mentions of *sacrifice* and that *he'd done what he had to for SJ*. If he was a murderer, why would he say he'd done it *for* SJ? It didn't make sense.

'Is he still angry with me?' William asked, then back-tracked, adding, 'I mean, about the last visit? I've never seen him so... livid. I mean, I know why...' He was rambling now, so she squeezed his hand to reassure him. She noticed he was now gripping tightly onto her. He probably hadn't had much physical contact for a long time, especially not from someone who didn't work for the prison.

'Yes, he was angry,' she agreed, hoping he would elaborate.

William sniffed, warning he might burst into tears at any moment. He leaned even closer. 'I wanted to protect him, I swear,' he whispered.

'I know that. He does too, deep down.'

'It's just it's been twenty-two years and we never really… I never really found out exactly what happened. Look, I'm dying, Briony. I want to make peace.'

She nodded. 'Of course you do, and SJ needs peace too. I see how he's struggling with all this.' Briony was ad-libbing but was hoping that William was so desperate to bare his soul that he'd eventually spit it out.

'It broke my heart. When I walked in that room,' he revealed, still quietly. She looked over at the guard, but she reasoned they probably couldn't hear from where they were. 'The blood, the holes… And my little boy,' he added, finally breaking into sobs.

Briony stroked his hand, waiting for him to pull himself together a little. He raised his head to look her in the face, his SJ-coloured eyes seemingly cutting her in half. She wanted to back out then. She wanted to kick back the chair and run from the room. Maybe she didn't want to know about SJ and his mother's death. Maybe SJ and everyone else weren't out to get her…

'Do you think he cares that I'm dying?' William croaked.

She swallowed hard. 'Of course, William. He definitely cares.'

CHAPTER 39

SJ

I'd been driving in the car with Mari next to me for fifteen minutes before she spoke. It was the Friday of the big wedding, one week after Mari's abrupt text, and we'd managed to patch things up enough to see each other again. This trip was probably a mistake though.

She looked amazing in the clothes she'd chosen for the wedding of course; wearing a fitted blue dress that showed off her curves and came off one shoulder. There was a slit that ran up the right side of it, all the way up to her upper thigh, giving me a view of her soft olive-skinned leg. It made me remember having that leg wrapped around me, and I had to keep thinking of her words when we'd last spoken to dampen my desire for her.

'You're a decent driver, despite your geriatric car,' she announced, smirking at the road ahead. She obviously wanted to get a rise out of me.

I snorted and stopped at a red light. 'This car is a classic and any damage was caused by third parties, I swear,' I managed to joke. I couldn't help giving her a sideways glance. I'd missed her – her profile even – demonstrating what a sad case I really

225

was. How could you miss looking at someone's profile? But I did. I remembered lying next to her in bed and turning my face to take her in. Her nose was curved at the end, much more delicate than mine. Her eyelashes were so long, you could see the tips of them even when her face was directed at the ceiling...

Shit, I've fallen for her, haven't I? The thought made me blush and I turned back to the road, realising the lights had already changed.

'You've gone all red. What were you thinking about?' Mari teased

'I was thinking about you naked,' I lied.

'And *that* made you blush?'

'I was thinking about that position, you know... When we were in the kitchen.'

She laughed. 'You *weren't* thinking about that.'

I went around a roundabout and took the third exit to Hertfordshire. It was all motorway for a while. Easy driving but potentially hard conversation to come. 'No, not right then... But I *have* thought about it over the last few weeks.'

'Good to know.' There was a notable silence as I moved between lanes and tried to get us there as fast as I could without killing us. 'Thank you... for not deserting me,' she said.

I cleared my throat awkwardly. 'I was surprised when you messaged me, but I try to keep my promises... if nothing else.' I could see her smile from the corner of my eye, but I tried to keep my face impassive. 'Anyway, how's work?'

'Oh, you know, a few clients making small steps. Though I have one guy who sits there and says nothing for a whole hour, which I wouldn't say is my favourite hour of the week.' She started fiddling with the radio but then turned on the CD player. Biffy Clyro started blaring out. She turned it down a little. 'I can't believe you still use actual CDs in here. Don't you ever want to upgrade?'

'I might one day. But I love this car. It reminds me where I came from.' I shrugged and started singing along, not caring what she thought of me. She surprised me by singing along as well.

'You like Biffy?' I exclaimed.

'Is the sky blue?' she called back, during an instrumental part. Damn, she was sexy, interesting *and* she liked good music. *Talk about making it hard for me to throw in the towel…*

'Have you seen Briony?' she asked when the song had ended.

I pretended to be focusing on changing lanes for a long moment, debating my answer. Mari had said she wanted the truth from me. I had to try to honour that even if I fudged it a little. 'I've seen her. She came by and… Well, her mum threw her out,' I mentioned.

Mari groaned. 'SJ, you didn't…'

'Didn't *what?*' I played innocent.

'You let her stay, didn't you?' Mari asked slowly. I couldn't tell if she was angry or not. She was staring at the road as though she couldn't stand to look at me, so I wasn't feeling too confident.

'I didn't know… what else to do,' I admitted quietly. 'She seemed drunk.'

'You could've told her it's not your job to rescue her?' Mari suggested between gritted teeth.

'I know, I know.' I paused, sighing. 'It won't be happening again though so…'

Mari detected the unsaid and put her hand on my arm. 'Did something happen?'

'What do you mean?' I forced out, moving my arm away. I turned the music up a few notches, but she immediately turned it down again. 'Hey, it's *my* car,' I protested.

'Don't avoid the question, SJ.' She sounded desperate now. I hated how it made me squirm in my seat.

'Look, she was on the sofa,' I emphasised because I didn't want any doubt. 'In the middle of the night, something woke me... She was in my room, standing right by the bed.' I winced, waiting for Mari to raise her voice.

Instead, her voice came out broken. 'What was she doing?' I realised then that I had been stupid to ever doubt that she cared for me.

'She was holding one of your dresses... that you'd left there. I don't know what she was doing with it really.'

'Do you think she has a thing for you?' Mari mumbled, fiddling with her handbag on her lap as if she wasn't interested in the answer but her bowed head told me differently.

'No, I don't think so... Even if she does, I'm not at all interested. You know that, don't you?' I brushed her elbow with my fingers without taking my eyes away from the road. I wanted to though.

'I guess so except–'

'Except *what?*' I snapped.

Mari repositioned herself in the old squeaky seat. 'I guess you've been quite defensive of her,' she offered quietly.

'Yes, because she was my client and because of the memory thing,' I emphasised, even though I'd wanted to avoid reminding her of my sobbing and our confrontation. I didn't tell her about the folder of porn on Ed's computer or the fraud. I wasn't sure why – maybe because it didn't feel like my information to give out.

She was silent for a moment. I was starting to wish I wasn't a man of my word. I could be at home today, sitting in peace, watching an old film. Strangely, I somehow knew I'd still rather be in this car having a difficult conversation like this than not see her again. The last few weeks had been a lot emptier than I'd wanted to acknowledge.

'About that...' she began cautiously, 'I wanted to say sorry.'

'Huh?' I blurted out.

'I'm a doctor but more than that, I'm your friend, and I should've been more sensitive than that. I spoke to Ollie about it – not specifically of course – but he made me realise I didn't deal with it very well.'

When I looked over, she had practically swallowed her bottom lip and was looking at me sideways. However, she averted her gaze as soon as I looked over. 'My *friend?*'

'Among other things...'

'Still?' I checked timidly.

'Yes, Tinkerbell, *still,*' she agreed in a bright tone.

'Even if–' I started but she cut me off.

'Even if *anything.* Obviously, it won't all be as easy as that, but I don't, in a million years, believe that you would hurt anyone intentionally. So, I'll believe in you *for* you.'

'Fuck,' I mumbled, trying to hold back the sudden tears that wanted to spill out. I focused on the lines in the road to distract me.

'What? Did I say something wrong?' Mari asked, leaning closer.

I managed to shake my head. 'No, you said something *right.*' I swallowed a few times in a row and swiped at my eyes.

'Do you need me to drive?' She laughed. There was only pure amusement and affection in that laugh. It almost made me want to cry more.

'There's no way you're driving this old girl.'

'Why do you love this car so much, Tink?' Mari dared to ask.

I took a deep breath. 'Oh boy,' I mumbled, wondering if she knew what a can of worms she was opening. I bet she thought she'd seen all I had to hide. 'It belonged to Debbie.'

'And Debbie was?'

'My family,' I answered curtly, no further explanation.

Mari made a strange noise with her throat. 'Don't tell me – she died?'

'Got it in one, although she died of natural causes. Well, as natural as cancer can be.' I shuffled around to find my candied cigarettes but couldn't get one out. Eventually Mari took them from my hand and got one out, slotting it between my lips, brushing them with her soft fingers. Then she got another out and put it between her own lips. It made me chuckle.

'You have a seriously bloody family history,' Mari informed me, moving the candy stick between her teeth loudly.

'You've only heard the half of it... Well, maybe the two-thirds of it.'

'Does this mean we're friends again?' she asked, biting down on the stick and crunching.

'Unbelievably, I guess so. Although you understand that I have some stuff to sort out...' I glanced at her, expecting her to be looking out the window but she was fixed on me with a small smile on her face. 'I really don't remember, Mari, but I'm ready to face it head on. I'm going to do some therapy. I *want* to know.'

'Okay.'

'If I do remember, it might be bad... You know that, don't you?' *Ten times, ten times, ten times.* It seemed to be floating past my eyes like an autocue. And my mum, holding a knife. In her left hand. The image kept returning to me since I'd left Mary

Walsh at the hospital, accepting her fate. Could my mind be making up the image, playing with me like my brain had for the last twenty-two years?

Mari sucked in her breath. 'One devastating revelation at a time, SJ.'

I nodded and made the turn off we needed. We weren't that far from the venue now; her family, her ex, my best friend, who would all see us there together.

'Can't you try to be a little more screwed up? It might make a guy feel better,' I suggested.

'Sorry, Tink.' She put her hand on my arm. 'By the way, you look fantastic in your suit.'

'Stop trying to sweet-talk me. I still have to go to *My Big Fat Greek Wedding* here.'

CHAPTER 40

MARI

She didn't know why she had thought it might be a good idea to invite SJ. By the end of the ceremony when they were taking some pictures outside the church, someone had asked him if he had had a face transplant, another person had asked him if he was in the mafia, and her aunt had not-so-subtly sent him off to do a job when there had been a group picture. Mari had watched him as everyone had smiled for the picture, his mouth downturned as he looked on from the cars, pretending to put the flowers in. The reception wasn't promising to be much better. The only upside was that her mother had looked over SJ when they'd arrived and said, 'You're Aris's friend, aren't you?', and not commented since. That amounted to approval in her mother's book.

As she caught up with him when they all went towards the cars to get to the reception, she brushed his hand, causing him to flash her a small smile. She wanted to take him away from all of her stupid family and their inane friends, most of whom didn't know her that well. Apart from that, she'd seen Justin staring at SJ with obvious contempt, which was odd because he was the one who had left her. Why did he care who she brought with her?

Finally arriving at the reception hall, where there was alcohol to numb the pain, Mari and SJ headed straight for the bar. She ordered two large red wines without asking. SJ leaned against the bar and surveyed the room. She wondered what he thought about her family; Uncle Theo was somehow already drunk, despite there being no alcohol at the church (though she suspected he had an individual flask hidden on his person) and had started asking everyone to act out scenes from *Romeo and Juliet* with him. Cousin Selma, who she actually liked, was being bossy and ordering literally anyone in eyesight around like she had become queen for the day, not a mere bride. Mari was, at least, pleased the family was so big she hadn't been given a big role in the wedding. While, Justin, the complete arsehole, had practically slammed the door of the reception hall in SJ's face.

'I'm not going to dump you,' SJ whispered in her ear.

She turned to him, chuckling quietly. 'That's a relief.'

'After what I told you the other week, I'm not sure there's much you could do to be dump-able really,' he joked, still checking she hadn't changed her mind about him. She elbowed him in the ribs softly to get him to move back. After all, Aris still didn't know about the two of them. Maybe a few drinks would help Mari break the news.

'So, I could sleep with everyone in the room, for example?'

'In *this* room?' SJ clarified with a naughty grin.

'You know what I meant.'

'I don't see the problem. Your uncle's Romeo impersonation is getting me kind of hot.' SJ gestured to the unfolding performance in the middle of the room. Her uncle was now forcing one of the bridesmaids to be Juliet, despite her not knowing any of the lines or being at all keen to participate.

'You're incorrigible… Oh God, he's going to climb on the table and then he'll probably fall off and we'll have to take him to the hospital,' Mari groaned, as her uncle did indeed try to scramble up the table. Fortunately, Aris intervened and steered her uncle towards the bar.

'Hey, you two, how about we all share a nice drink, huh?' Aris suggested, his eyes wide as he nodded to them both in desperation. 'A beer, Uncle?'

'Sure, sure,' he mumbled but he seemed distracted by the fact that the crowd had dispersed, and people were starting to find their seats. Aris hurriedly ordered a pint for them both and turned to SJ.

'You see how I've ended up buying again.' He had tamed his unruly hair today by using gel. It looked shiny and wet on top of his head, but he did actually look smart, even smarter than usual. His shirt had obviously been neatly pressed. Mari knew Aris regularly used his state-of-the-art iron, but he didn't like anyone else to know that, least of all SJ.

'I'll ignore the fact that it's a free bar... Anyway, I wasn't sure if I was your favourite person right now.'

'Why wouldn't you be?' Aris turned his nose up and glanced at Mari, as if he knew something was going on between them. Mari waved at a passing relative to hopefully distract him from her flushed face.

'Oh, Briony's case... I hope there's no hard feelings.' SJ held out his hand and Aris squeezed it readily.

'Seriously, has Mari got you only drinking wine now? I shouldn't have left you two alone for a minute,' Aris joked.

'I've always loved red wine, but I knew your immature palate would never appreciate it.'

'Oh f– Wait, where did Uncle Theo go? Oh crap, he's going for the microphone... Why is this *my* job?' Aris demanded, ditching his pint and running towards the stage.

Mari laughed at his departing back. Another face came out of the crowd then and Mari blinked a few times, almost hoping he might disappear. But no, here came Justin, with his angular features that permanently seemed to suggest he was looking down on people, and his mop of blond hair, that once she'd kind of loved but now looked slightly ridiculous.

'Mari,' he spat when he finally arrived in front of her. He didn't even glance at SJ, but SJ put his arm around her and made his presence hard to ignore. SJ wasn't taller than Justin, but he seemed to have a bulkier presence, maybe because Mari knew what a stupid coward Justin was. 'And this must be... outreach in the community? What are you, an ex-con or something?'

'Actually, quite the opposite. A lawyer.'

Justin ground his teeth in his mouth. 'So, you really started scraping the barrel after I dumped you, Mari. You could do better.'

Mari felt SJ straighten up, obviously trying not to punch Justin in the face. 'What, like you?' Mari challenged Justin. 'And where's your girlfriend anyway, the one you just *had* to cheat on me with?' She purposely looked behind him to check but she knew he had been at the ceremony alone.

Justin stepped back slightly, scowling. 'I thought it was better to come alone than bring some shoddy date.' He glanced at SJ pointedly.

'Seriously buddy, just leave it. I'm being polite right now but...' SJ let his sentence trail off purposefully but kept his arm around Mari's shoulders.

'Hey Justin, stop being an arse at my wedding!' Alex called, coming up behind Justin, and slapping him on the back. 'Oh hey, Mari. You look beautiful.' He turned to SJ. 'Nice to meet you, man.' SJ had to remove his hand from Mari's shoulders to shake Alex's hand.

'How do you know *he* didn't start it?' Justin snapped.

'Because I bloody know you. Now, go help sort out Panos, will you? He's as pissed as a newt and Selma's about to kick my arse if he starts singing "Livin' on a Prayer" before the speeches.' Alex was understandably beaming. Although Selma could be a tad demanding, he absolutely adored her. Mari couldn't have asked for a nicer guy to marry her cousin.

'It's been a beautiful day,' Mari said, despite hating the cliché.

'Thanks, cos'. You see that we're proper family now,' Alex joked.

'Are you being serious, Al? You're going to let this reprobate go out with Mari and say nothing about it?' Justin interjected, jabbing SJ in the chest.

'Oh my God.' SJ rolled his eyes.

'Watch your language,' Justin warned and before anyone could stop him, he delivered a punch to SJ's face, hitting him in the cheek. SJ stumbled back a step and took a moment to get his balance back. Mari tensed at the thought of his response but when he took his hand away from his cheek, he only smiled. If Mari had to classify the type of smile, it would be sinister, all teeth and insincerity.

'You absolute arsehole, Justin!' Mari pushed him hard.

SJ grabbed her hand and pulled her back gently. 'Alex, it's been a pleasure to meet you. Shame I can't say the same about the best man,' SJ forced out, before backing away and making his way to the exit.

'SJ, wait!' Mari called out.

He turned back and held his hand up. 'Just getting some air.' Then he shoved the door open and stalked out, not looking back. Mari turned back to Justin, but Alex was already grabbing him by the collar.

'How could you be such an arsehole today? It's not about you, for once, get it? You'd better apologise to him. Do you hear me?' Alex shook Justin like he was ten pounds lighter than him. Justin nodded tightly, pushing away from Alex but not aggressively.

Mari wanted to kick him. He had cheated on her, dumped her and then decided to punch her current boyfriend in the face. How was he not hiding under a table in shame?

'Don't talk to me, ever again. You've just shown me what a shallow arsehole you always were,' Mari informed him coldly. She sighed as she surveyed the room. 'And tell the rest of them to get a clue too. Just because someone has a scar on their face, it doesn't mean they did something bad to get it.'

'I'm so sorry.' Alex squeezed her arm.

'It's not you, Alex. You were actually nice to him.'

She glared at Justin then turned on her heel and ran off towards the exit.

CHAPTER 41

SJ

'Hi, Mr Robin? It's Yvonne, from the prison service. Can you talk?'

Oh fuck, what is it this time? 'Yeah, but not for long,' I lied, riffling through my pockets to find the emergency cigarette I'd hidden there.

'Look, your father has been in prison for twenty-two years and for all the time, he's only had one visitor,' the women explained.

'Are you telling me he had *another* visitor? That's not really my business, ma'am,' I interjected.

'But Mr Robin, the prison officer tells me your father was very upset. I thought I must inform you because you are,' she paused heavily, 'his son.'

'Be that as it may...' I trailed off but reconsidered. 'Wait, what did they look like?'

'She had light brown hair, quite long, blue eyes. Not very tall. Maybe thirty. You know her, Mr Robin?'

'Thank you for telling me.'

'The order says she was your fiancée. You have a fiancée, Mr Robin?'

'No, I definitely don't,' I mumbled, thinking of how close I'd been to proposing to Claire before she'd dumped me.

'I was correct to tell you, yes?' She sighed in relief.

'Yes, yes, you were… and thanks.'

It has to be her. Who else would it be? My father didn't have any relatives who matched that description. I could have asked for a name from the visitors' book, but the woman wouldn't have been able to tell me. Even prisoners had confidentiality and despite being a lawyer, I had no criminal reason to probe further.

What had she been doing there? I had begun to question both Briony's innocence and her motives. She'd known about the fraud too. It didn't exactly scream innocent until proven guilty. I shivered to myself and paced in front of a bench. I lit the cigarette and inhaled.

I liked to pretend Mum's scale of colours worked, but overall, most days started or ended as black anyway. If there happened to be spots of colour in between, the day was a success really. Maybe it was time I stopped trying to avoid my past, my predisposition to depression, and the fact that I didn't really want to be a lawyer anymore. I was going through the motions of doing my job, avoiding court as much as possible, trying to ignore the shame I felt when I realised a client was probably guilty of a serious crime.

I had somehow ended up defending the worst of the worst. Perhaps I was trying to save my father, by saving them? Though my tendency to protect my clients had gone too far this time. On Monday, I vowed to confront Briony.

'SJ, there you are.' Mari appeared out of nowhere and pulled me to a stop. She gave the cigarette in my hand a disgusted appraisal and met my gaze. 'Oh SJ, so much for your quitting,' she lamented seriously.

I stubbed out the cigarette, despite it being only two-thirds smoked. 'It's okay. I knew I'd need it today.'

'You mean, you knew they'd make you feel unwelcome.' She seemed disappointed in me, rather than them.

'I knew how they'd see my scar. It's like an unwanted third wheel,' I finally clarified. I looked past her to the reception hall. The doors were closed, and no one was loitering around outside. 'I don't want you to miss the party.'

'I'm so sorry about Justin.' Mari turned my face to get me to look at her. My eyes kept flickering as if I was staring into a bright light.

'Maybe he's still got a thing for you?'

'Are you okay?' Mari touched my cheek, where no doubt, a colourful bruise was forming. I pulled her hand away and sagged down onto the bench.

'Why did you bring me here?' I sighed.

She tentatively perched on the edge of the bench. 'Because I like you, SJ.'

'You can like me from further away. We could've met next week if you wanted to see me again. This is just such a highly stressed atmosphere. Emotions all over the place and your family think I'm some kind of day-release prisoner.'

I exhaled, trying not to lose it like I wanted to. Mari wasn't really the cause of any of my ills. Briony was. She must've snooped around my house. What had she found that had told her about my father?

'SJ, you're pulling a terrible face, like you're imagining someone torturing animals or something.' Mari touched my arm, jolting me back to the warm afternoon sun.

Mari shuffled closer and leaned her head on my shoulder. 'I brought you because I have strong feelings for you, SJ. I want to tell Aris about us now, so he knows how I feel.'

I dropped my hands from my face. 'Have you totally lost it?'

'What do you mean?'

'Aris will *not* take this well. Why would you want to say anything today of all days? Do you want to ruin your cousin's wedding?'

'You really are emotionally damaged, aren't you?' she retorted, biting her lip as soon as the words were out. She bowed her head. 'God, that was uncalled for.'

I stared out at the countryside, trying to decide if I should leave now.

'Briony kissed me.' I said, trying to end the conversation.

Mari jolted beside me, gripping my knee hard. 'What?'

I nodded as though to confirm it and turned to meet her gaze. Her brown eyes seemed to have darkened more than ever. I wondered if her eyes could burn Briony to ash with that look. 'I didn't reciprocate, of course. I just thought I should be honest with you.'

Mari clenched her fists, obviously trying not to explode. 'Don't you think you've let her get a bit too close?' she asked, surprising me.

'*Me* let *her* get too close? You think I've encouraged her?' I pulled a face like I'd just swallowed a cockroach.

'Not intentionally, but I don't suppose letting her stay helped.'

I sighed. 'I guess you're right. I just didn't know how to turn her away. She was in a state and she had no one...' I stared up at the sky. It was still bright and blue, not one cloud in sight. I wished I had been able to enjoy the day even more. I felt Mari take my hand and I didn't pull away.

'Obviously, she now thinks she has you.' Mari's voice was strangled.

I turned my head and saw she was staring up at the sky too, her forehead creasing up. I leaned over and kissed her cheek softly. 'She doesn't – *have* me.'

'I know,' she agreed quietly.

'Look, since you've stopped seeing her, I feel like you've been a little more disparaging of Briony. Why?'

Mari squeezed my hand and hesitated. I watched her swallow a few times, her long beautiful neck moving up and down a few times. 'SJ, I know it's unprofessional…'

'What ? Go on.'

'I just care about you. I can't just let her be near you and not warn you if I think she's going to do something dangerous.'

'And you really think she would?'

Mari sucked in air. 'I think so. What about you?'

My chest tightened. 'Maybe,' I squeezed out anyway. I kept picturing Briony in my bedroom, holding Mari's dress up against her face as though trying to inhale Mari's essence. Who the hell does that? No one with all their sanity, that's for sure. How had I just let that go so easily? I should've thrown her out right then.

'Wow, you must be worried. I really didn't think you'd say that.'

'Well, you know how to keep quiet, don't you?' I joked, pulling her closer. Kissing her again erased everything from our time apart. Even Briony was pushed to the back of my mind as I let Mari's tongue into my mouth.

'What the fuck?' a voice said. I didn't really need to look for the owner because I knew his voice so well. He was standing behind Mari, his hands loose by his sides and his mouth hanging open.

Mari tried to scramble to her feet, but I got there first, holding my hands up to him. 'Kiddo, I'm sorry. We didn't mean to tell you this way. I'm so sorry.'

'*We?*' Aris repeated darkly, like it was a terrible swear word. He ran his hand down his face as people did when they woke up from nightmares to check if they were actually awake. 'I came out here to find you, see if you were alright.' He frowned, more hurt than angry.

'My sister, man... What are you doing?' Aris continued, addressing only me. 'I thought you two were getting closer, but I didn't really think you'd do this.'

'I never intended for anything to happen. Things just... did.' I dropped Mari's hand and went towards Aris, but he stepped back.

'I stood up for you in there,' Aris protested, screwing up his face. 'And you were both laughing behind my back.'

'No way. You're my best friend, I would *never* laugh behind your back.'

'I told you not to go near my sister,' Aris grumbled.

'Hit me then. I deserve it.' I stepped towards him imploringly.

He chuckled sadly and shook his head. 'You have done some shitty things to me, but this really tops it.'

'I haven't done anything shitty. Look, kiddo, I'm serious about Mari. Really–'

'Save it, SJ. And do me a favour, leave us in peace here. I don't need your ugly mug ruining my day,' he added.

I tried not to let my face fall like it wanted to. Aris had never mentioned my scar before. I turned to Mari. 'I'm going. It was a mistake to come here.'

I walked down the long drive to the main entrance. I got my phone out and called a taxi.

When the taxi finally arrived, Mari appeared in the drive. She waved it down and jumped in the back with me.

I waited a few minutes to speak, 'I can't believe you walked out on the wedding reception.'

'It wasn't *my* wedding reception,' she reminded me. Then she reached over and grabbed my hand, and I didn't take it back for the whole journey.

CHAPTER 42

BRIONY

On Monday morning, she was loading up bags with possessions when there was loud banging on the front door. The landlord had told her she had to get her stuff out in next few days, or it'd be sold or thrown away. She grabbed a knife and approached. But she only saw a dishevelled looking SJ through the peephole and groaned.

'SJ, are you okay?' she asked through the door.

'Open the door, Briony,' he ordered. There wasn't an ounce of warmth in his tone.

'You sound angry,' Briony noted innocently.

'I *am* fucking angry. You know why.' He slammed his fist against the wood to reinforce his point. She jumped back slightly but straightened up again.

Remember: I am strong, he is weak.

She opened the door and gave him a smile. He scowled in return and pushed his way past, trying to ensure there was no way she could shut him out. He looked sweaty and flushed, and he stank of cigarettes and coffee. He wasn't wearing a blazer today, just a shirt that had the top two buttons undone and it was untucked.

'Explain yourself,' he demanded, then spotted the knife. A flash of fear crossed his face, but he quickly shook himself out and raised his hand. 'Give me the knife,' he said carefully. His hand was shaking though.

She laughed and pushed the handle of the blade into his open palm. 'I'm not going to stab you, SJ.' He raised an eyebrow like he didn't believe her and went inside.

He placed the knife in the sink, far enough away for her not to be able to grab it quickly and came to stand in the living room again. 'Moving out?' He nodded at the cardboard boxes and bin bags. The place was nearly bare.

'Yeah. Problems with the rent. Moving to... Mum's place.' She continued sorting things into boxes. She was currently loading up some old DVDs and books. Hidden underneath were weathered news reports about Jason's death she had found in a drawer at her mum's years ago.

Boy, 4, drowns at lake, sister survives.

Tragic death of young boy on family holiday.

'Your mum doesn't mind you moving back?' he asked, not able to stop himself.

'SJ, I'm sure you didn't come here to talk about my living arrangements.'

He glared and shook his head. 'No, I didn't.'

'So?' Briony didn't even look up from sorting.

'Will you pay some fucking attention?' he growled, making her raise her head. 'I know about the prison. Why would you go and see him?' He had his hands in his trouser pockets, perhaps to stop himself from trying to throttle her.

That would be kind of ironic...

'By *him* I guess you mean your father?'

She heard his teeth grinding in his mouth. 'You know who I mean,' he emphasised, unable to say it aloud apparently. He produced some cigarettes from his pocket and shakily shoved one in his mouth. He managed to light it after the second attempt and took a desperate drag.

'I was curious,' she explained, standing up. He appeared to take a definite step back, as if she had contorted into some horrific monster who was about to eat him whole. Maybe to him she *was* a monster now.

'Curious?' he repeated, the cigarette hanging out the side of his mouth. He didn't seem able to remove it, like a drug that was keeping him sane.

'I found your letters, well, *his* letters.' Briony watched his face shift from shocked to confused to angry in a matter of seconds. The cigarette dropped to floor, but he swiped it back up quickly and sucked on it again. He found an empty chair, pulled it out and took a seat.

'You'll have to explain to me what the hell is going on. You're not making any sense,' he paused, kneading his forehead for a moment. 'Are you saying you went through my things, my *most* personal things, when you were staying that night?' His big blue eyes looked so betrayed that she wished she could say it was all a misunderstanding, but she also knew she had to protect herself from all of them.

'I know you think I'm guilty, that I hurt Ed. I just wanted some leverage.'

He laughed, without a hint of humour. It was all bitterness and sharpness and disbelief. 'You really are a fucking piece of work. I've defended you.' He had made quick work of his cigarette. She only watched him as he stubbed it out on the tabletop, staring at her as he did.

'Because it's your job. You were starting to suspect me. I *know* you were.' Briony didn't react to his little act of rebellion. He just tore his eyes away and looked at the wall to the side of them instead. She remembered the same hopeless position of his father's shoulders and the way they both seemed to enjoy staring at walls. Did they believe the answers were hidden there?

'You had no right,' SJ said darkly, turning back. When he did, she saw his eyes were wet, despite his face being hard. Maybe he didn't know his eyes were betraying him as he attempted to lay down the law.

She flattened out her lips and kept her eyes on him until he finally looked down. 'DC Demetriou's been after me from the start. I know he's following me still… I'm sure he's been trying to turn you and I think it's finally worked.'

SJ lifted his head and blew out air in resignation. 'I just want you to stay away from the people I care about, including my dad.'

'You care about *him*? I thought he'd been convicted of your mother's murder, SJ?'

SJ sprang up, breathing heavily as though he wanted to lunge across the table. Instead, he shrunk back and closed his eyes. She watched him for a moment, taking in his lips moving and realised he was telling himself to 'breathe' over and over. When he eventually opened his eyes, he said, 'Do you think you need to remind me of that?' His voice was weak, as though he was speaking across a broken radio. When he stood there then, Briony imagined him as a nine-year-old boy; the one his father had told her about, the one she had read about in snatches on the internet.

'We all have things we'd rather forget,' she told him as she shuffled closer. She got close enough to place a hand on his neck. He glanced at her sideways but didn't try to shake her off. Briony wondered how Mari touched him then, how they fit together, whether they loved one another. But it was over now, wasn't it?

'Briony, I… want you to stay away from me. I think this has all got a bit unhealthy, don't you? I mean, coming to my home, trying to kiss me, now acting as my fiancée and going to see my father. What do you think you're doing?' SJ put his hand on her wrist and pulled her hand off his neck, pushing it back towards her, reasonably gently in the circumstances.

'You're just going to leave?' Briony called after him as he took a step away.

'Briony, what is it that you want from me?' He held out his hands, at a loss.

'I… don't know,' Briony admitted. A silence fell between them as SJ just stared at her, his mouth moving to speak but no words coming out. Finally, she spoke again instead, 'I don't have anyone… I thought you were there for me.'

SJ ran a hand over his face. 'Bloody hell – the reason you don't have anyone, Briony, is because you've hurt everyone!' he shouted abruptly.

'Hurt everyone?' she repeated blankly.

'What happened to Jason?' He forced out through flattened lips. His brain appeared to want to know but his body was trying to hold it in.

'Jason,' she said softly. 'He died.'

'Yes, but *how*, Briony?' SJ was more forceful this time.

'He drowned, you know–'

'Briony,' was all he said, raising both eyebrows.

She sagged back against the dining table and regarded him. This damaged man was really the only person she had right now? Her mum had made her feelings clear, DC Demetriou clearly wanted to throw her in prison, everything was over with Ed…

'Children can do terrible things, you know that,' Briony finally said.

'Are you saying–?'

'Not saying anything,' she interrupted him. 'Just that children *can* do bad things. You know about that, don't you, SJ?'

'I have no idea what you're getting at,' he said shakily.

'You did a bad thing, didn't you? He sacrificed everything for you and you didn't even read his letters.' She shook her head disapprovingly.

His eyes flashed with anger. 'You know nothing about what happened,' he spat.

She pushed herself up again, inflating her chest before him, keeping her chin high. He thought he was better than her, but he was no different. 'I read the letters and he told me, SJ. He told me he walked in and found you there, covered in blood.'

SJ stumbled backwards as though she'd hit him. He lifted his hand up and unconsciously touched his scarred face, staring behind her as if he was back in the room where his mum had died. '*No.* He was the one—'

She moved into his vision, breaking him from his trance. 'Sure about that, SJ?'

He dropped his head to the floor for a long moment. His body was visibly shaking. When he looked up again, his face appeared broken, as if all the seams were splitting apart. '*No,*' he whispered. 'No, I'm not.'

The truth seemed to suck the air out of the room. SJ backed up and leaned against the worktop behind him. He was breathing fast as if he'd been running for miles. He'd actually been running all his life, just like she had.

'It's okay, SJ. I understand you,' Briony said quietly.

He raised his head, his face coloured with distaste. Then he surprised her by laughing, but it sounded weak. He had his arms wrapped around himself as if holding his body together. 'That's what this is really about, isn't it? You think you've found someone who's just like you, but I could never be like you.' He paused. 'I don't know exactly what happened... but I know he loves me. No one loves you though, Briony. Even Ed has had enough of you. He saw who you really are, and he couldn't take it.'

'Yeah, maybe you're right, SJ.' She pretended it didn't hurt. 'But when everyone finds out what you did, are they going to keep loving you?'

He stared at her, his body swaying. He seemed like an object underwater, constantly in flux. He considered saying something else but in end, he walked to the door and left, without closing it. Briony watched after him, wishing he would come back. Then she thought of Mari and knew what she needed to do.

CHAPTER 43

MARI

Mari was walking back to the surgery after an hour-long break in a local café. Her weekend with SJ (once they'd got rid of her family of course) had been amazing. She felt as if they had really connected. He'd talked about going to therapy and sorting himself out. Somehow, she believed him.

She entered the surgery and popped into reception, asking them to give her ten minutes until her next patient. She went through to her office and took her jacket off. It was only a light one because for once, the warm weather wasn't disappointing; in fact, it was kind of an Indian summer, warm and bright. Mari still wasn't speaking to Aris. Or more accurately, he hadn't called yet and she hadn't bothered calling him.

She felt her phone buzz and took it out. There was a message from SJ, which read:

STAY AWAY FROM BRIONY. SPEAK SOON. X

Mari was about to text back when she realised there was someone in her office. It was Briony, who had managed to stay hidden until you took a few steps into the room.

'Um, Briony, I don't think we have an appointment, do we?' Mari asked, making a move towards the computer. SJ's text made her think she shouldn't be alone with Briony. What had made SJ so worried?

'Don't touch the computer,' Briony ordered.

Mari stopped and turned to her. *Damn, she knows about the internal messaging system...* Mari tried to look innocent. 'Sorry, I just presumed I must have forgotten.'

Briony shook her head, a sinister smile growing on her lips like bubbles slowly fizzing up at the top of a glass. 'I really enjoyed my sessions with you, Mari. I wanted to thank you.' Mari supposed it was meant to sound appreciative, but it sounded cold and menacing.

'Briony, there's absolutely no need,' Mari insisted. 'Look, why don't we talk later? I have patients waiting.'

'I know about you and SJ,' Briony announced suddenly. 'Are you in love with him?' Her tone sounded hushed, almost hurt. Although her face remained impassive.

'Briony – um, look, this really isn't any of your business.' Mari tried to edge towards the computer again but Briony mirrored her movements, not taking her eyes away from Mari's for a moment.

'Did you *ever* believe me?'

'About Ed? Of course.' She had genuinely wanted to help Briony, had treated her like her other patients, but there had been something about the whole thing that jarred her. Something she couldn't articulate.

'But you stopped believing? I thought you were on my side, once upon a time but when I think about it, I guess it was only SJ...' Briony trailed off. 'But now SJ's not so sure either I guess, with the way he left my flat earlier.'

Mari took a sharp intake of breath. 'He was with you earlier?' No matter how much she tried to keep her tone low, it seemed to jump out of her mouth like a mouse that had been stepped on.

'Yeah, he wanted to talk to me. I suppose he told you about our kiss.' She didn't even pretend to look sorry. Instead, she stepped closer, running her fingers over the things on Mari's desk – her stapler, her mouse, her pens. She did it in such a tender way, it made Mari stiffen up.

'He said *you* tried to kiss *him*,' Mari corrected.

Briony nodded slowly. 'I suppose that would be the best version of events.'

'Briony, it won't work,' Mari insisted, trying to sound bored instead of anxious. She wondered why the receptionists hadn't come in to see why she hadn't buzzed for a new appointment yet. She had said ten minutes. Hadn't it been ten minutes? And how had Briony managed to sneak in there anyway? It was probably because of the GP, Harry, who always left the back door propped open so he could smoke out there.

'*What* won't work?' Briony darkly teased.

'You won't make me jealous. I know you have something weird for SJ but he and I–'

'Are in love?' Briony mocked coldly, making Mari's arms erupt in goosebumps. She tried to respond but her mouth seemed to have forgotten how to form words. As Mari stayed frozen to the spot, Briony took the chance to come closer and grab her by the wrist. Her grip was like a vice. 'Is that what you think I came here to do, Mari?'

'Briony, please, there's no need to get angry with me. You need help. I've *already* tried to help you,' Mari tried to remind her, as calmly as she could. She didn't try to pull her arm away. She thought about her training; stay calm, speak in a measured tone, try to keep them calm, don't do anything rash. Briony might let go if Mari could just reason with her.

'You have a beautiful neck, Mari,' Briony suddenly said, reaching up with her free hand to touch Mari's neck lightly. She wished she hadn't chosen a V-neck this morning. They were standing hip to hip, Briony's right hand on Mari's left wrist and Briony twisting to touch Mari's neck with the fingers of her left hand. She moved them slowly from under Mari's chin all the way down to her collar bone, then swept back up and ran her fingers across her throat like the softest cut of a knife. 'I've always thought you were so beautiful, so well put together—'

'Briony, this isn't comfortable for me.' Briony's lips lifted as Mari's words vibrated against her skin.

'I killed Ed,' Briony revealed in a whisper. Her words tickled Mari's ear but slammed into her chest like a car at full speed. Mari gasped for breath, making Briony press her fingers against her throat. 'Stay calm, doctor. It's okay,' Briony pretended to reassure her, but Mari hardly heard. 'I waited until his mother left. He was asleep so I held a pillow over his face, held it down until he stopped thrashing. His hair had started to grow back. I always thought it was beautiful hair.'

Mari had dealt with some patients who had serious issues, but she had never dealt with a murderer before. Had Briony really killed Ed though? She could be making it up.

'Briony, maybe we should call someone. Your mum maybe? We could go somewhere else – to talk?'

Briony's fingers were still on Mari's throat, the pressure increasing slightly. 'I can't talk to her anymore. It's too late for all that.' Briony half-shrugged. She released Mari's wrist, but instead pushed her body up against Mari's like she wanted to hug her or trap her.

'Briony, please, I'm on your side,' Mari tried again.

Briony suddenly pushed Mari backwards, into the wall, making Mari smack her head. She was about to reach up and touch it but Briony shoved her head into the wall again, making Mari's head explode with pain. Her vision went fuzzy and she reached out hopelessly to find something to steady herself. It seemed like Briony deliberately stepped back because Mari only grasped at nothingness. She felt herself falling and her knees took the force of it.

'He's a murderer. You know that, don't you?'

Mari's ears were ringing but she still heard the words. Mari focused on trying to stand but she didn't have the strength. Before she could think about responding, she felt something strike her head and she fell sideways onto the floor. She rolled over onto her back and looked up at Briony, who was still standing, staring down at her. 'Did he tell you that?' Mari forced out, feeling like it was the most important thing to know right then.

'I knew from the moment I met him that he had a secret. It took me a little while to get to it but now I have. He and I are the same. I understand him better than you ever will, Mari.'

Was this what all this was about – some obsession with SJ? That they were kindred spirits or something? Mari snorted at the thought and only realised she'd done it out loud when she took in Briony's face, which was furrowed with confusion.

'What are you doing?' Mari asked, trying to push herself up. She managed to grab at Briony's top but Briony uncurled her hand gently, as though comforting her. Then she pushed her knee into Mari's chest to trap her on the floor and put her hands around her neck.

'I'm not pretending anymore,' Briony whispered. 'This is the real me.'

Mari tried to fight. She scratched Briony's hands and arms, but she couldn't get Briony to release her hold around her neck. She just kept squeezing until Mari felt like there was no air left inside her and things started fading.

All she could think about was SJ, the way he'd looked at her as they'd laid together in the hotel on Saturday morning. He'd asked her, 'Why are you here with me instead of with your family?' She'd kissed him in response. Now she realised she should have said it, she should have told him that she loved him. As ridiculous and fast as it was, she loved SJ Robin, despite not knowing what happened the day his mother died, despite not knowing if he'd held the knife in his hand or not.

Then there was black as Mari's senses lost orientation. She wasn't in the room anymore. She wasn't anywhere.

CHAPTER 44

SJ

I had driven around for the past three hours, wondering where I should go. I'd driven past Pentonville but hadn't stopped. I'd driven past the cemetery where my mum was buried but had missed the turn off. I had never fully understood it when clients had told me they felt numb about their crimes but suddenly it made sense. Everything I knew felt removed from me, even the old BMW I knew so well. It was as if I was a driver in a computer game, simulating driving instead of actually doing it.

When I finally parked the car and looked over at Briony's mum's house, I made the connection in my mind. I needed to check on the one thing that had nagged at me since I'd gone to visit Briony the other week. That hole that I couldn't see the bottom of out in the garden.

I went up to the front door and knocked. I waited a moment but when there was no response, I banged even harder on the door and the front windows. Still nothing. I checked out the side gate. I didn't hesitate before throwing myself against it a few times. It gave on the third attempt and I went sprawling through and into the alley beside the house.

When I got to the garden, I stopped. I saw the hole had been filled in and some plants planted. The job felt half-hearted and incomplete, though, like someone had got bored part of the way through. I approached the hole and got onto my knees beside it. I ran my fingers over the freshly disturbed soil and then plunged my hand in. Before I could stop myself, I was using my hands to fling the soil in all directions.

I jumped back when I finally saw the body. I took a few deep breaths but instantly regretted it because there was a putrid smell coming from the hole. I shuffled closer again and forced myself to dig a little more, higher up, where I eventually uncovered a face. I was confronted by the still and seemingly long-dead face of Briony's mum, Jessica. I sat there for a few minutes, staring at the face, expecting her to start moving again.

This must be a mistake…

Yet, it wasn't a mistake at all. She was real. I even prodded her skin to check she wasn't something I'd dreamed up.

'What are you doing here?' Briony was standing by the back of the house, craning to see how much I'd discovered. She appeared to be admonishing me, despite the fact that I'd just discovered a body in her back garden.

'I came to find your mum,' I explained, standing up. I tried to clean my hands on my trousers, but the mud didn't budge. I couldn't imagine how terrible I must look.

'Ah,' Briony said, as though I'd told her I'd found a dead bird, not a dead person. 'Are you afraid to die, SJ?' she asked, stepping closer. It almost sounded like she'd dug a hole for me and was about to put a bullet in my brain. I surveyed her for weapons but saw none. Though she had more scratches on her hands that seemed to disappear up her sleeves.

'You need help, Briony. We need to get you help,' I insisted, taking a step closer to her as well, mainly to prove

I wasn't afraid of her. Strangely, I didn't feel as afraid as I thought I might.

'None of this matters anymore, SJ. Can't you see? We're two sides of the same coin, we know each other's secrets.' She locked eyes with me determinedly.

How had I ever thought Briony was innocent? She was practically dead inside. I'd royally screwed up this time. I'd definitely been on the wrong side of justice before, but this was a new low.

'I'm not like you. I don't know exactly what happened, but I know I never would've hurt my… mum… without a reason.' Wherever the truth was deep inside of me, that was what my instinct told me. I hoped I was right.

Briony was giving me the warmest look I had ever seen on her face. I realised then what she had wanted all along, from the moment her seven-year-old self had decided to do a terrible thing: a friend. I remembered her offended look at my office when I'd suggested she call someone. She probably hadn't had many relationships with anyone and when she had, she'd probably reached an impasse soon enough. Except with Ed.

'Look, even if you have some weird obsession with me, it doesn't change the fact that you've hurt–'

I was cut short by her unimpressed laugh. '*You* think I'm crazy about *you?*'

'Well… you followed me, you were in my room, you tried to kiss me, so I thought…'

She crossed her arms and raised her eyebrows at me. 'I wasn't following you, SJ, I was following Mari… As for your room and trying to kiss you, it was kind of like role play. It felt kind of nice to see what it was like in Mari's shoes. People just like her, don't they? People think she's the kind of person you confide in. And she's so beautiful, isn't she, SJ?' Briony grinned inanely like a person deeply in love.

'What is wrong with you?' I blurted out.

Briony's face hardened. 'How many times did you stab her, SJ?'

'Shut up.' My muscles immediately tensed up. I tried to shake the sudden images that assaulted my brain. Blood. Mum. The knife. My hand.

'Did she die straight away?'

I had to focus on slowing my breathing down but thinking of Mum made my whole body go out of sync. *'Shut up,'* I growled again.

'Do you remember what you thought about as you stabbed her?'

'Shut your mouth!' I covered my face with my hands.

'SJ, did you get her blood all over your hands?'

'If you say one more—'

'What did he say to you, your father? When he saw the knife in your hand?'

She didn't even fight me when I grabbed hold of her and basically threw her to the ground. My muscles were telling me to tear her to pieces and a huge part of my brain wasn't going to argue. But I stopped. An image came to me. I saw his eyes as he'd stepped into the living room, how he'd scanned down my body, then to my lifeless mum on the floor. How I'd seen his heart split apart.

Briony took that moment to jump up and run towards the gate. I sprinted after her, not knowing what I'd do when I reached her. She was already in my car. I patted my pocket and cursed when I realised I didn't have the keys. She started the engine and I only managed to touch the boot of the car before Briony sped away. I fell to my knees and let out a howl.

I went back into the back garden without purpose, only to be faced again by the sight of that body peeping out from the dirt. Even though I kept telling myself I couldn't be a murderer, staring into Briony's mum's face was like looking at a scene from a film that I had been avoiding since I was nine years old.

What would a jury say about someone, who had spent his life living a lie, a man so dishonest that he had let his own father take the blame for his crime? Staring at the dead body in front of me, it felt like I should have known the truth long ago.

CHAPTER 45

MARI

She was bored of looking at the white walls of the private hospital room. It was three days since the attack by Briony and she was still feeling bruised and shaken. If the receptionist hadn't burst into the room and pulled Briony off her, she wouldn't have survived. She'd rolled on her side and taken one of the hardest breaths she'd ever taken in her life. It had felt like squeezing air through one of those tiny cocktail straws. Or how she imagined it anyway.

Aris wouldn't allow her to go back home yet. He was concerned about the psychological impact of the attack, and about her getting her strength up. Of course, his concern was mixed with guilt for not realising how dangerous Briony was. Though how could any of them have known?

She turned over in bed and tried not to look at her phone, but it was practically nudging her from the cabinet next to the bed. She snaked her hand across the sheets and grabbed for it. No messages. She'd heard from her family and friends of course but nothing from SJ. He'd tried to come and see her as soon as he'd found out from Aris what had happened, but she'd refused to let him in. She'd texted him with: *Give me a few days. I need to process all this. M x*

She dreamed about him whenever she managed to sleep. She also couldn't help imagining SJ lying beside her in the shaky hospital bed, wearing his understated smile that made her feel calmer. How he'd probably make some joke about her putting her neck on the line for her patients and then he'd kiss her so gently, she would wonder how he could make such a macabre joke.

She snatched sleep in between fending off Aris's concerns and trying to forget Briony's eyes as she'd tried to squeeze the air out of Mari. It still seemed surreal that someone had actually tried to kill her, let alone someone she knew.

'Sis, I got you a cordial,' Aris said from the doorway. He came around the bed and threw himself into the chair beside the window, placing himself right in her view.

'Did he call you?' Mari rasped.

'Um, no.' Aris shuffled in his chair. 'Look, weren't you the one that told him to stay away?' He paused, sucking in breath. 'I mean, as hard as this is for me to say, he cares about you and he's just doing what you asked him.'

'I didn't think he would disappear.' She held in the tears that she usually saved for when she was alone.

Aris sighed. 'I know… He left me a message though, saying there was something I needed to see at Briony's mum's house, and we found–'

'*What?*' she demanded.

'A body. Her mum. Buried in the garden,' Aris revealed, watching her carefully. 'And Ed's phone too. Buried.'

'Did she do it?' Every word crawled out of her throat like a meek fly trying to fight its way out of a web.

'We don't know, sis.' He stood up and put his hands on the side of her bed, as though asking for atonement. 'Look, there's a lot of evidence against her, wherever she is. You can break confidentiality now, Mari. You can tell me.' He tried to sound commanding, but his voice was high, pleading. Mari stared at her struggling brother, watching him pressing his tongue against that silver tooth of his over and over. She realised he was trying to keep himself together too; he wanted to keep her safe, he wanted to catch Briony, and he wanted to see his best friend again.

'Did she tell you anything important about Ed or her brother?'

'Only that she killed Ed.' Mari paused. 'I can't believe he's really dead.' Remembering how casually Briony had revealed the murder to her made her feel chilled, even now when she was covered with blankets. 'Nothing about Jason.'

'Okay.' He pushed away from the bed and went to stand beside the window. He pulled out his phone, checked it quickly, and shoved it back into his pocket.

'Did SJ talk to you about his memory loss?' Aris finally broke the silence.

Mari nearly got whiplash with how fast she turned her head to find Aris staring at her. His expression dropped slightly at her response, causing him to nod to himself. 'Did you believe him?'

'You're really asking me that?'

'I need you to tell me – what do you know?' he asked quietly. She saw his mind working, considering whether SJ had moved over from friend to criminal. The lines weren't grey for Aris, never had been.

'He said his dad told him he was the one who stabbed her. But he doesn't remember. He told me he was going to go to therapy.'

Aris snorted derisively then released her arm and sank back into the chair. 'SJ? Therapy?'

'He said he wanted to remember, Aris. He wanted to face it.'

'I don't buy it. This *can't* be right.' Aris shook his head. It was as if they were back in the room after their dad had passed away. He hadn't believed that either.

'What if he's not a killer, Aris?' She paused. 'What if he's your friend who was only nine when his mum tried to cut him open? What if he was a little boy who had already seen too much and fought back? What if he was so used to no one protecting him that he knew he had to stop her himself?'

'You mean it was probably self-defence?' Aris was going over things in his head, rerunning everything he knew about SJ, past and present.

Mari pictured SJ in his house. The photos on the wall. Only a photo of his mum, a woman called Debbie and her partner (who he'd never fully explained his connection with, just said she was 'family'), and Beachy Head. She'd asked him about the photo of the cliffs in particular, but he'd just mumbled something about it being a reminder. 'A reminder of what?' she'd asked. He'd taken a moment to answer, perhaps deliberating whether she deserved to know at all. He'd eventually said, 'To pull myself back.'

She'd wanted to ask him what from, but she knew now what he'd meant.

'You know I'm in love with him,' Mari said.

'I know, sis, I know. But–'

They were interrupted by a ringing. Aris pulled his phone out and frowned at the screen.

'Important?' Mari asked.

He looked between her and the phone. 'Uh, yeah, could be.' He pressed the answer button and put it to his ear. 'I'll be back,' he said before going towards the door. She strained to hear what he was saying but all she could decipher was, 'Okay, thanks. So, no news yet?'

Not SJ then. She grabbed her own phone and tried his number again. This time there was no ringing, no answerphone message. Instead, a cold voice announced: *Sorry. This number is no longer available.*

CHAPTER 46

BRIONY

Briony ordered her usual café con leche and churros in the lunchtime sun. Plaza de Tirso de Molina was bustling as usual. For once, she pulled off her hat and enjoyed the sunrays on her hair. Every time she caught a reflection of herself, she was still shocked by the blondeness of her hair, along with the lightened eyebrows and brown contacts. Would she ever be comfortable with herself?

It was November now, and she was wrapped up in a big coat, but the sun was out, which made a nice change from London. The waiter delivered her order and scurried away. It wasn't the usual waiter who liked to ask her about where she was from and whether she'd be staying a while. Everything she had told him had been a lie, of course, even her name: Carol.

'Briony,' a voice announced from the seat opposite. Somehow, they'd sat down without her noticing. Even before she fully turned towards him, she knew who it was.

'PC Demetriou,' Briony practically spat. There he was, with a smug smile on his face. His skin was more tanned looking than usual, and his eyes were adorned with sunglasses. He was even wearing a leather jacket. How could this be her captor?

'*Detective Constable*,' he emphasised and pulled his glasses off. He had huge bags under his eyes. 'Do you mind?' He gestured to the churros. She grudgingly shook her head, so he plucked one off the plate and took a big bite, crunching away at it and her nerves all at once.

Shit, six weeks of freedom and this is it.

'How did you find me?' she forced out, assessing the plaza with her eyes.

'How do you think?' He would've been teasing if he wasn't such a bastard.

'SJ,' Briony mumbled. 'Is he here?'

He shook his head. 'I got an email with lots of attachments out of the blue. SJ knows what you order every day, he knows where you're staying, he knows about the waiter, Jaime, who you chat to.'

'But how…?' she trailed off, feeling her stomach turning. *He's been watching me, that bastard.* She supposed he had only given her the same treatment she had given him. She was still astounded she had managed to miss SJ being so close. 'He's gone to a lot of effort then,' she finally added, resigned.

'Maybe he's mad about his car.' DC Demetriou shrugged. It was no time for jokes, though. Her freedom had evaporated right in front of her.

'I highly doubt he'd lose sleep over that old banger.' She took a long sip of coffee, feeling caffeine almost immediately surging through, or perhaps her body was already preparing for fight or flight.

'He's very sentimental.' DC Demetriou turned his face up to the sun briefly but didn't allow it to last because he clearly wanted to keep his eyes on her. He was almost bouncing in the chair at the thought of her in handcuffs. 'Mari's fine by the way,' he informed her, staring like he could slice her into pieces with his eyes.

'Oh good, not a murder charge then,' she retorted. She tried to sound blasé, but the news did result in a calmness settling over her chest. Part of her still thought of Mari fondly.

He clamped his teeth together and leaned back in the chair. 'You have other charges to answer to anyway. The evidence is so strong, not even the best lawyer on this earth could save you.' He moved his tight jaw into a smile and she almost heard the effort it took to manipulate his muscles.

'Not even SJ?'

He laughed dryly. 'Not a chance.' He paused. 'And SJ's not a lawyer anymore.'

'Huh.' She shrugged. What had made SJ quit? Maybe he couldn't live with guilt of knowing what he really was, pretending he wasn't just as much a criminal as his clients.

'So, you haven't seen him?' DC Demetriou asked, trying to sound casual but his voice went high, and he leaned in.

'I have nothing to say to him.' She paused. 'Where's DS Owusu?'

DC Demetriou grinned easily. 'She's around here. Didn't expect to bump into you like this to be honest.'

'You mean, you just stumbled across me?' She scowled disbelievingly.

He shrugged. 'Lucky I guess.'

'Though what's to stop me jabbing you with this knife and making a run for it?' she suggested, her fingers twitching beside a knife on table.

DC Demetriou eyed it up for moment but settled back on her face. He appeared completely unfazed. 'Aside from all the crimes you've committed, getting all the pen-pushers to green-light us coming over here was a nightmare so I'm not about to let you escape again.' He paused, sliding his hand towards the knife also. 'And you might want to watch out for the *policia* who just turned up. I gave them a call. They might just be looking for something to do.' He gave her a satisfied smile, not attempting to confiscate the knife.

Briony stared at him, unwilling to give in straight away, but slowly moved her head to scan the square. *Jesus, there's about seven of them...* They were huddled together in twos and threes around square.

'Are they really here for me?' She cocked her head at him.

DC Demetriou put his sunglasses back on and shrugged. 'Only one way you'll find out.' Then he got some handcuffs out of his pocket and threw them across. 'Put them on or we'll do it for you.'

So, this is it...

Whichever murder she was charged with, it barely mattered anymore. She raised her face to the sky and absorbed the sunshine for a minute. Then she plunged the knife into DC Demetriou's hand, shoved the table at him and started running. She could hear his screaming as she disappeared down the Metro steps. She scanned her transport card and ran down to the platform, shoving a hat on her head to hide her hair. She only had to wait about a minute for a train to pull in. She jumped on and leaned against the doors when they closed, seeing the *policia* running down the steps and onto the platform.

As the train moved, she finally caught her breath. She felt for the vials and the syringe in her pocket that she had carried with her every day since leaving England. It was finally time.

CHAPTER 47

S J

I followed Briony out of Atocha railway station and onto the busy main road. She started hurriedly walking towards El Retiro park. I quickened my pace to catch up with her and finally caught her arm near the big roundabout.

She started to pull away but froze when she saw my face. I'd been hiding from her for so long it felt kind of odd to meet her eyes properly. Her eyes immediately fell on my beard and she snorted in disgust, as though hiding my scar was a sin of some kind.

After finding my car abandoned near the coast and drafting in a private detective to help me, I'd found myself boarding a ferry to France. Then it'd been a long six weeks of tracking her and following her. Far too much driving later, suddenly, there we were, in the middle of one of the noisiest cities, finally face-to-face.

'Going somewhere?' I asked casually.

She shrugged off my hold but didn't move to run. Instead, she moved over to the low wall beside us and lowered herself down as though her body weight was ten times more than it was and perched there. She pulled her hat off and shoved it in her pocket. The walkway behind us led back to the station and there was a constant stream of people going by.

'You've been following me,' she noted quietly, less angry than I'd imagined she would be.

I nodded, not even pretending to look sorry. I sat down next to her but not too close, never really trusting what she might do. 'You have to face the music sometime, Briony. I'm going to do the same, when I get back,' I added pointedly.

She laughed but stopped as though it was taxing for her. She seemed to be drooping a little and breathing fast, despite us being seated.

'Are you okay?' I couldn't help asking and shuffled closer, as if we were two friends having a quiet chat in the winter sunshine. I caught the smell of her sweat and noticed her head was clammy, which was almost surprising. I had forgotten she might have feelings of fear like the rest of us.

'Like you care,' she muttered, blinking hard. 'Get on with your lecture on redemption, SJ. Not all of us have all the time in the world.'

I examined her face and saw that she wasn't as carefree as she was making out. Her eyes were bloodshot as if she had barely slept and her hands were shaking. When she saw me looking, she shoved her hands in her pockets.

'I'm sure you don't care much for my redemption, Briony. Or anyone else's for that matter. Definitely not your own…'

She gave me a twisted smile that looked sad more than anything else. 'I care about things. I did care about things anyway. I also care whether you've stopped lying to yourself, SJ?'

'I'm going to own up to it. I know what I did now. I have to clear my father's name before he…' I sucked in the dirty air. It still felt strange to say it aloud, that I even had something to confess at all. 'I just had some unfinished business to attend to.'

'What are you talking about? You're going to tell everyone you're a murderer?' She raised her eyebrows at me disbelievingly. Then she put her hands on her knees and leaned forward as though she might be sick. She took a few deep breaths and looked back at me.

I shrugged as if it wasn't important, but it felt nice because my shoulders felt lighter than they ever had. 'If that's the way you want to put it, sure.'

Her mouth dropped open slightly. She was about to say something, but a loud group of tourists walked past and she lowered her head to her chest.

'It would be better if you handed yourself in too,' I suggested.

She zoned back in on me, giving me a dark look. 'I think it's too late for that, SJ.'

'I heard about Ed,' I told her, watching her face.

She did a good job at keeping it flat; one of her key skills it seemed. 'I don't know what you mean.' Her voice faltered though. Her vulnerability was in there.

'Briony, they found his phone in your garden. And anyway, who else would kill Ed? Come on.'

She stared me down and didn't respond. After a moment of silence, she said, 'What was your plan; to follow me everywhere until I handed myself in?'

'Whatever it takes. And I do have a phone, I could call you in, Briony.' I paused. 'Well, a *second* time.'

She narrowed her eyes at me. 'But how did you know I'd get on the train, SJ?' she half-whined like a child throwing an exhausted tantrum. 'I just wanted… to be alone,' she added in a hushed voice.

'You chose that table every morning. Took me a while to figure out why. It was the shortest distance to the Metro steps, right?' I asked.

She snorted in response.

'And you kept your travel pass in your coat pocket. Easy access. In case you ever had to make a run for it. Easy to follow you from there.'

'Wow, you could be a detective.' She oozed with sarcasm, but she appeared woozy as if she'd drunk too much. 'You make me sick, SJ. You're not some goody two shoes. Your whole life is a lie.'

I reached out and touched her arm briefly, trying to remind her that she wasn't some cold, untouchable statue. She had nerve endings and blood inside her. She felt things.

'No lying anymore, Briony.' I paused and squeezed her arm. 'You don't look too good,' I commented, suddenly concerned that she was ill.

She edged away from me, brushing my touch off her. 'I tried so hard to make them love me, but they couldn't. What does a person do when no one can love them, SJ?' She appealed, wobbling as if the earth was moving below us.

I gave her a flat smile, thinking of Mari. Could she have loved me, despite the truth?

'You should keep trying, you never know,' I told her honestly. I didn't feel particularly angry with her anymore, I just felt sad for Briony and the people she'd hurt.

She pushed herself up but fell back onto the wall almost immediately. 'I think I'm too tired,' she confessed, which was hard to hear over the roar of the cars speeding by. She was swaying even more, and I reached out to steady her. She didn't seem to register my touch.

'I'm sorry,' I told her genuinely.

'And *I'm* sorry,' she mumbled, suddenly collapsing to the ground, taking me with her. We both fell to the pavement.

'What–?' I started to ask and pulled at her arm, but her eyes had rolled back and her body was jerking. She was having some kind of seizure.

As I tried to get her into the recovery position, I tried to figure out what had happened. I patted Briony's pockets down and found two empty vials of insulin with her mum's name printed on them.

A police officer appeared and pushed me out of the way. He started checking Briony.

'I think she took these.' I shoved the vials in his direction.

'*Insulina?*' he asked, meeting my eyes with a frown.

'I think she took too much,' I tried to explain, gesturing with my hands.

'*Compras zumo,*' he shouted to his partner, who was beside Briony's head, trying to check her pulse. I vaguely remembered '*zumo*' being juice.

'Stay!' the police officer snapped at me as I went to get up.

I nodded and placed myself on the wall I'd been sitting on only moments before with Briony. It hit me then that she'd planned it. She must've injected herself after she'd escaped from Aris, not wanting to take any chances. When she'd been talking to me, she'd known she was going to have a seizure, that she might die.

Looking down at her, it felt like there was no coming back from this. I had to admit she'd outsmarted me again. Always a step ahead, always another surprise. And somehow, she had known – seen me as I was, known what I had done.

The police officer was trying to keep her comfortable, while his partner had gone to call an ambulance. As I sat there contemplating the death of the person who'd hurt so many people, I thought about Mari. I shouldn't have left her, not without explaining, even if she had told me to stay away.

I took my replacement phone out of my pocket and dialled her number from memory. The ringing felt like years at a time. The longer it rang, the more the time stretched out like something I couldn't imagine ever filling up.

Finally, she answered. 'Hello?'

CHAPTER 48

SJ

It wasn't my usual visiting day. When I arrived at the visitors' reception, Cam looked up from his battered copy of a Stephen King thriller, with an instant smile. 'Hey, son, what brings you here without an appointment?' He placed his book face down on the counter and took in my appearance. 'And looking more casual than normal,' he noted.

I was wearing jeans and a long-sleeved turtleneck top. I had a hoodie in the car for later, when I knew I'd want to be comfortable. No lawyer clothes anymore. I'd quit my job seven weeks ago and got away with barely any notice period except for wrapping up a few caseloads over the internet. I think my boss, Rebecca, was hoping I'd change my mind. I wasn't bothered about leaving most of the cases, but the case of Mary Walsh remained in my mind. If she didn't ask for help though, there was nothing I could do.

'I'm sorry I didn't ring ahead. This was a last-minute decision. *Had* to be a last-minute decision. Could you help me out?' I appealed to him. It was a risk – you were meant to make an appointment or be sent a visiting order by the inmate. I was hopeful though that our history gave me some leverage on this occasion. 'And ideally, I'd like to chat in a legal visits' room if you can swing it?'

Cam pretended to think about it for a full five seconds before coming out from behind the desk and physically opening the gate for me, though he didn't have to. He could have buzzed me in automatically. I walked through the scanner and went through the motions of being searched, which was as familiar to me as brushing my teeth.

'You missed your monthly appointment,' he noted, as he handed me back my possessions.

It felt odd that someone was keeping tabs on me. It had been a while since anyone cared enough to do it. 'There was something I had to sort out.' I tried not to recall Briony's still body on the pavement in Madrid, but I did remember how everything had continued around her regardless. I had pictured it a lot over the last week. She hadn't regained consciousness.

'You in trouble, son?' Cam asked, putting a hand on my shoulder.

I wanted to laugh or cry at his simple gesture of kindness. 'Not really. Just time I got all this sorted out.'

'I've been told to report if William gets any visitors,' Cam said quietly, confirming my suspicions. He was examining my face carefully and saw my jaw twitch.

'I see.' I pushed a package into his hands.

'What's this?' he asked, transferring it like a magician into the booth without making it obvious. He wasn't meant to take gifts from anyone.

'Thought you might need some more reading material, but you'll have to pretend it's something official.'

He put his hand on my shoulder again and squeezed. It felt like goodbye. It made me woozy at the thought of it. These simple 'hellos' with the same prison officer for years outside my dad's prison have clearly been significant. The way he always smiled when he saw me, ignoring the constant reminder of my past on my face. I wasn't sure he'd ever stared at me.

'I think I might've misplaced that number. For a while anyway.'

'Thank you, Cam.'

'I'll call ahead for you, son. Wait here and we'll get someone to escort you in. But I think I'll have a little tea break before I get to that number someone left.'

'Police officer?' I checked.

'You know which one.'

Aris had been looking for me? Why? It was probably just for evidence reasons – wanting to find out how I'd known about Briony's mum. Maybe he had CCTV from Madrid and he wanted to arrest me. I wasn't sure I cared about any of it anymore.

What I mostly thought about was that one word: 'Hello?'

Mari had sounded tired, sad. In just one word, everything about her rushed at me and left me breathless in the frantic city, watching Briony's life slip away in front of me, but I hadn't heard anything else. I had tried to speak but nothing had come out. I'd dropped the call and scolded myself for being such a coward. Most of all though, I'd felt adrenaline rushing through my every nerve and muscle and tendon. It was as though I'd been struck by lightning.

Before I'd cut off my phone, she'd left a few messages. I hadn't been able to listen to her messages. The last text she'd sent had read: *I miss you.*

'Tom will be here in five minutes to take you in,' Cam informed me, having made the call.

A few minutes later, a younger prison officer brought me into the waiting area like a new inmate waiting to enter custody.

I wondered what they'd think if they stripped off my clothes and saw the broken body I was inhabiting. I wondered if the crime that I'd been hiding for so long would be clear for them to see, like a lighthouse projecting the truth and blinding them.

The bars were starting to tighten around my chest when they finally called out my name and a bored-looking officer opened yet another gate for me. How many doorways would I have to walk through to feel reinvented, to enter a room without my past following behind?

As I walked towards the legal visits' room, I concentrated on my feet. All the times before this, they'd been innocent feet. Now, they felt like concrete dragging against the dirty prison floors. How would I be able to continue walking like a free man out of there when I was the one who deserved to be locked away like he had been for twenty-two years?

In the room, he was waiting for me. There was no-one else with us for the first time in twenty-two years. When he stood up to greet me with his ever-expectant face, I rushed towards him and threw myself at him. He squeezed me into him and whispered 'Stanley' over and over, stroking my back like he had when I'd woken up from nightmares as a child.

I eventually pushed back but held onto him, my eyes puffy from the tears I'd finally let out in front of him. 'I'm sorry.'

'I love you more than anything, more than myself,' he croaked out. His eyes were wet with tears too, but he somehow looked happy. Suddenly, I saw him in the past, the last times he'd really been my dad: when he'd let me lie on his shoulder on the sofa, standing across my mum's hospital bed with his shoulders slumped, throwing me a ball in the garden, laughing at me sneaking out of bed to watch a detective film late at night. How had I forgotten how much he had loved us? How had I let him take the blame? I thought I'd come to see him all these years to find the truth about that day but maybe unconsciously, somewhere in the very depths of myself, I'd always known I was the guilty one.

'I was afraid. I thought she might...' I trailed off, unable to finish under his desperate gaze.

He shook his head and reached up to touch my face. 'I should've taken you away from her before it got that bad. I tried to get her help, I swear, but I failed. I was wrong to leave you with her...' His voice broke.

'I don't know how I can live with this,' I mumbled, staring at the wall behind him. The walls had been watching us all this time and it felt like they were laughing at me now, literally quivering at how stupid I'd been.

He contorted into my vision, grabbing my face with both hands. 'Stanley, if you don't, all this,' he gestured to the barren room we were in, 'what was the goddamn point?'

I laughed like a sneeze, which quickly turned into sobbing. I wasn't sure how long he hugged me for but no one came in and interrupted us. There was nothing else to say when we parted, except, 'I love you, Dad.'

'Oh Stanley, I love you too, son.' He held onto my hand, but I forced myself to pull away.

'I'm going to tell them the truth, Dad. They'll find what they need, and I think you'll be out of here soon,' I revealed, watching his face transform through about a million emotions all at once.

'You're going to tell them? *Why?*' He lowered himself back into his chair like a child waiting to be told what to do.

'You don't deserve to be in here, Dad.' I hoped my dad would be walking out of here in the next few weeks or months.

'But I confessed,' he reminded me vacantly.

I sat down again and reached out for his hands. He readily gave them over and I squeezed hard, causing him to grin. For the first time in twenty-two years, I saw myself reflected in him and I felt proud. He had sacrificed his own life to protect me. He'd taken the metaphorical knife out of my hand and taken it into his own.

'I love you for what you did but it's time I owned up to it. All of it,' I paused, considering how his hands looked so different – wrinkled and worn. 'I'm sorry, so sorry, that you've been in here for so long and I couldn't see… myself.'

He lifted one hand up and touched my face, the side that was scarred, and I tried not to flinch. 'You were afraid, Stanley. But you were, and always will be, my beautiful son.'

I chuckled sadly and pulled my face away from him. 'Now, don't tell lies.'

He frowned and sat back in his chair, examining me. 'Don't tell me what to think of you,' he mumbled. After a moment's pause, he added quietly, 'Stanley, if I get out of here, can we go look at the sea? I can't remember quite how it looks. I have pictures but they seem so flat, so still, you know?'

'It's *when*, Dad, not *if*. And yes, we can. I can do that for you.'

'Okay. But don't be long about it.' He raised his greying eyebrows at me knowingly.

CHAPTER 49

SJ

I arrived at Holborn police station with no files, no briefcase, wearing my casual jeans and a hoodie. I had been in there a few times before but not so often that many people would recognise me. The man on the front desk showed no inkling of recognition as he asked me what I wanted.

I had rehearsed this moment about one thousand times in the last few days. I'd even stood in front of the mirror practising, but now the moment was here, I stumbled on words and felt my cheeks growing hot.

'I need to report a crime, please,' I finally forced out. I took a deep breath. 'I need to report a murder.'

The man wrote a few words on the pad and looked back at my face, raising his eyebrows expectantly. 'Do you know anything else about this crime?' he asked, carefully.

'I want to confess to murdering someone twenty-two years ago,' I said, as firmly as I could, but held onto the counter in front of me to steady myself.

'Okay, can you give me your name, sir?' The man watched me carefully as if he might need to react to a sudden attack.

'Stanley Jon Robin.'

'Okay, Mr Robin, follow me.' He opened the door beside the front desk and led me through to an interview room. He gestured to the chair and I sat down, waiting patiently for the moment I'd been delaying for twenty-two years.

It was about ten minutes later when the door opened, and a woman stepped in. She was wearing smart trousers and a black shirt with rolled up sleeves. She looked too busy to be dealing with a twenty-two-year-old crime. I looked down at my own scruffy attire and shrugged. It felt weird to be wearing jeans in a police station.

'Hi. I'm Detective Sergeant Gregory. Mr Robin, is it?' She held out a hand and allowed me to shake it, as if she could tell everything about me by my handshake.

A man entered behind her, leaning over to shake my hand briefly.

'Detective Constable Nayar,' he introduced himself as he sat opposite.

'Do you mind if I record our chat?' DS Gregory asked from the corner.

'I know the drill. Feel free to do what you need. I'm a defence solicitor. I usually defend murder charges. I work out of Colindale a lot, so I came here because I don't know many people here,' I explained.

Her face changed slightly. It wasn't that she softened, more that she relaxed when she knew she probably wouldn't have to deal with my anxiety too. I knew the steps and I'd come here willingly. Perhaps she could get back to her caseload sooner than she'd thought.

When the video was set up, she sat down.

'Mr Robin, because of what you've said, I'm going to caution you now.'

'Okay.'

DS Gregory reeled off the caution, 'You do not have to say anything. But it may harm your defence if you do not mention when questioned something which you later rely on in court. Anything you do say may be given in evidence. Any questions?'

I shook my head.

'So, tell us, Mr Robin, about this crime.' Direct, to the point.

I started speaking, describing the incident I'd been running from all my life. The incident that my mind had blocked out, with my dad's enabling, to allow me to have my freedom. I needed to confess and get him out.

'The day my mum was murdered, we had breakfast in bed. It was the 23rd of July 1998 in my family home in Barnet. The address is 29 Barclay Road. She got angry with me because I burned the toast. She always got angry about stuff; was always calling me names and sometimes she would hit me. Not often and I think I always made excuses for it, but she was a mess. She was always taking pills, or *not* taking pills, or drinking, or trying to hurt herself. She started saying everything had turned dark. That she had to get the darkness out of us before it was too late. She went searching for her pills. She said they were white – they could stop the darkness from getting us if we swallowed them.'

'What happened next?' DC Nayar said, as I halted abruptly.

'I tried to message my dad on a secret mobile he'd given me. I told him to come home, but she saw me and accused me of lying to her. She hit me across the face. Then she dragged me downstairs to the kitchen and she…' I rubbed my hand over my mouth and my trimmed beard and pictured the old kitchen. I hadn't thought about it in so long. I remembered the awful yellow-brown tiles behind the oven that we'd never bothered to replace. I remembered the large sliding glass doors that led out to the garden.

'She grabbed a knife. She said I was hiding behind my skin. That she had to save me from the darkness and let the light in.' I pressed against my scar as I recalled the burning sensation of the blade down my face, the stinging as the air hit it. 'She cut me,' I breathed, swallowing hard.

'Where did she cut you?'

I wanted to give the detective a dirty look, but of course, she had to ask. Nothing was obvious in police interviews, even my scarred face. Everything had to be transparent and recorded. 'My face. She got me on the floor, and she cut me. I tried to push her off me, and I did for a moment, but she grabbed me and pushed the knife into me.'

'Where did she stab you?'

I pressed into my abdomen, exactly where the scar was underneath. 'Here.'

'Can you tell us what happened next?'

I nodded but the words wouldn't come at first. Instead, a few tears rolled down my cheeks and landed on the glossy table in front of me. I wiped them away from the surface as though it would remove them from my face. I sat back in the chair and prepared myself.

'I managed to grab the knife from her. And it went... into her.'

DC Nayar sat forward. 'Can you be more specific for us, Mr Robin? Can you tell us exactly how you stabbed her?'

'Yes, okay,' I agreed, swiping at the tears but feeling my body shake at the effort of keeping them in. 'I stabbed her in the leg. The left leg.'

'What happened then?' DS Gregory asked.

I pictured her falling towards me, how heavy she was in my arms. 'I tried to catch her, but we fell to the floor. I thought she was trying to hug me, but she pressed her fingers into my wound and...' I covered my eyes for a moment, trying not to look at the memory but there was no escaping it. 'I stabbed her again,' I sobbed out. 'I stabbed her in the chest. The left side. She stopped moving, but I was afraid. I pushed her off, and I stabbed her again and again.'

'Do you know how many times you stabbed her, Mr Robin?'

I uncovered my eyes and stared into DC Nayar's eyes, wondering what he thought of the child killer in front of him. 'Ten times. I wasn't counting but people told me later. How many times *he* had stabbed her,' I finished. I wiped my eyes on my sleeve.

'What happened to your mum after that?' DS Gregory asked.

I turned to look at her. She had the type of face that didn't give much away. 'She was dead,' I whispered.

'And what did you do after that?' DC Nayar inquired, more gently.

'My dad came home. I was on the floor, crying. He came in and he just stared at me, at her. Then he pulled me up and made me scrub my arms and hands. I kept telling him I was sorry.'

DS Gregory frowned. 'Did your father call anyone?'

I shook my head, feeling like my nine-year-old self again. 'He cleaned me up and he said to me, 'You tell them I did it, Stanley.''

'I'm sorry, I don't understand,' DC Nayar said, furrowing his brow.

I took a deep breath and tried to swallow the years of guilt, but it didn't work. I wasn't sure it ever would. 'He took the blame. For me,' I paused, pressing against the scar again. 'I said no at first but then he started to hit me. He'd never hit me before, but he kept doing it. We were both crying, and he just kept hitting me.'

'What happened then, Mr Robin?'

I sagged in the chair, mimicking the fight flowing out of me as it had then. 'I told him, "You did it. You killed her." And he stopped and nodded. He wiped his tears away and went over to her and pressed her against him so hard, like he was trying to squeeze blood out of her. He put some of her blood on his face. Finally, he called the police.'

'What did he say to the police?' DS Gregory asked.

'He told them *he* did it. They arrested him when they got there. He's still in prison.'

DS Gregory glanced over at the recorder as if to check it was still running. 'How old were you when this happened, Mr Robin?'

'I was nine.'

DC Nayar looked over at DS Gregory and sighed quietly. 'You're aware that the age of criminal responsibility is ten in England?'

I clamped my lips together and nodded. I was a murderer, but the law wouldn't even let me take the blame. 'Look, I know how it works. I know you need something that only I would know, to prove it was me, right?'

Her mouth twisted slightly, not wanting to admit I was right. 'Where did you stab her and in what order?' DS Gregory asked.

I sat forward with my hands clasped together on the table, trying to stop myself from falling to pieces in front of them. 'Ask him where he stabbed her first. I remember stabbing her in the leg because I thought that might stop her trying to chase me, to hurt me... Ask him where the second wound was.

Which side of the chest? He wouldn't know I bet. And the forensics can back it up.'

'Anything else?' DS Gregory persisted.

'Okay, the knife then,' I said quietly.

'Excuse me?' DC Nayar leaned in.

'The knife they found. It wasn't the knife I used. He grabbed it later and put blood on it because he couldn't find the knife I used. It was a similar size. He kept asking me where it was, but I wouldn't say.' I paused, composing myself. 'I hid it. Behind the boiler. There was this space that was really hidden. I hid things there when she tried to hurt herself and he wasn't home. I'd show him later and he'd lock them away somewhere.'

'You hid the knife behind the boiler?' DS Gregory repeated. She exchanged a surprised look with Nayar.

'Yes. It might still be there,' I agreed.

'Mr Robin, thank you.' DS Gregory stood up. 'I'm going to place you under arrest while we investigate further.'

I nodded, feeling my body slump with release. 'I understand.'

'I am arresting you on suspicion of murder. You do not have to say anything, but it may harm your defence if you do not mention when questioned something you later rely on in court. Anything you do say may be given in evidence.'

CHAPTER 50

SJ

The beachfront guest house that I'd found us looked out to the sea. I had promised Dad to take him somewhere warmer once we were no longer on bail and able to travel, but, for now, Whitstable in Kent would have to do. I wasn't sure how much time we had left together, and I intended to make the best of it. I had no job, so I had time to spare apart from one new 'project' – Mary Walsh had finally asked me to help her to leave her husband.

The sun was beginning to set on the water as I sat in one of the comfortable chairs on the front terrace of the guest house, wrapped up in a winter coat. Sometimes when the icy wind blew, I wondered why I had been stupid enough to think early December was really the time to make good on my promise to my dad. Though, when I'd got the call to say he was coming out, I'd gone online immediately and booked us into the place without a second thought.

Dad was having an afternoon rest in his room before we went out for dinner. He wanted to try some fancy seafood restaurant nearby. Apparently, prison food was not particularly gourmet. He'd spent hours fawning over the crisp white sheets and the soft mattress in his room when we'd arrived. He'd nearly passed out at the free tea and coffee. Every small yelp of excitement from him stabbed my heart a little. I'd taken all these years away from him. How could I ever atone for that?

Suddenly, we were both 'free' men, acquittal pending, but still weighed down by the past that would never leave us. I should have known the truth about Mum's death, but my mind had buried it so deep, like that knife had been buried in the depths of my childhood home. Although the boiler had been replaced in our old house, no one had even noticed the bloodied knife that was hiding at the back of that cupboard until the police had found it.

'Hello,' a voice said, which sounded remarkably like Mari's. It had gone through my mind a thousand times since that moment in Madrid, so I didn't look up. Even when a shadow fell over me, it took me a few seconds to register and lift my head.

My mouth fell open. Part of me was screaming to get up and run but the bigger part of me, somewhere behind my rib cage mostly, demanded that I stay still and let Mari's familiar face wash over me. Her dark chocolate eyes regarded me seriously, her big soft lips looked as kissable as ever, her long neck stretched up from the ridiculously huge purple winter coat she was wearing. How can someone look hot in a winter coat? God, I knew what people meant when they said it hurt to look at someone. My chest shrunk rapidly, and my mouth seemed to have forgotten how to work.

'The traditional greeting is "hi",' she eventually said. I wanted to kiss her neck, every bit of her skin, actually. I closed my eyes and savoured the sound of her voice, her voice saying more than the 'hello' I'd been holding onto.

'Hi,' I breathed out like a prayer, opening my eyes. Miraculously, Mari was still there.

'Is this seat taken?' She gestured to the seat next to me.

I shook my head, daring myself to keep looking at her. She sat down and suddenly seemed smaller, as if she had pulled into herself in the process of sitting down. My eyes strayed to her forehead where there was a mark. *No, a scar.* Slightly raised and pink. Had Briony given her that?

'I thought about coming to see you so many times.'

She cocked her head at me. 'Did you now?' She didn't sound convinced.

I clasped my hands together to stop them from shaking or reaching out and gave her a strained smile. 'You asked me to give you time, after what had happened.'

Mari lowered her head for a moment and took a deep breath. She took another one, perhaps remembering what had happened. 'I was messed up.' She raised her head again, frowning and holding in tears. 'I thought I should take time to process it but I... I missed you so much.' She smothered her tears with her hand.

I couldn't help but grab her and pull her into the chair I was on. We hugged briefly but I pushed back before I could relish the feeling of her close to me.

'I'm sorry for not calling you.'

'You did call me though, didn't you? You just didn't say anything.' She raised her eyebrows at me.

I cleared my throat uncomfortably. 'I wanted to speak. I just didn't know what to say.'

'Come on, SJ. You know the basics of conversation.'

'I know,' I admitted quietly, looking down at my hands.

She reached over and took one of them. 'She tried to kill me, SJ. And all I could think about was how I should've told you that I loved you. Can you believe that?'

'That you – *what?*' My mouth gaped.

She swallowed her bottom lip for a moment, perhaps losing her nerve. 'You know what you *should* apologise for – leaving me in the hands of my over-protective brother. How could you?'

She had changed the subject, thank goodness. *Why is she talking about love?* Maybe the months of silence had somehow transformed her apparent caring for me into some misguided sense of love. I met her eyes, and they were softer. I'd missed the softness of her eyes when she was amused. I'd missed the hardness of them when I pissed her off too. Basically, I'd missed her.

'How did you find me?'

'I asked around if anyone had seen a man buying copious amounts of red wine.'

'Ha, ha. It was my scar, right?' I frowned with a sigh.

'Actually, I used this.' She held up a photo on her phone that she'd taken the day of the wedding when we'd been in bed back at the hotel. I really hoped she hadn't been showing that around – I was shirtless and had been lying next to her in bed at the time. 'And shut up about that bloody scar.' She rolled her eyes dramatically.

'It's not easy to forget.'

'I do it all the time. You should try it,' she suggested as if it was no big deal, like I'd got it in some stupid accident and not in the process of fighting off my mum. 'And as for finding you, you do realise you and your dad are both on bail, right?'

I snapped my head up. 'You know, about my dad?'

'Aris found out when he was looking for you. He told me everything as soon as he was allowed.' She grinned, forgetting any anger for a moment. 'I'm so happy he's out, SJ.'

'But you understand what that means?'

She still had my hand and she squeezed it hard. 'I *understand* what that means, and we can work on it.' She pointedly met my gaze and held it. It wasn't like when I'd first told her about my dad's accusation, before I'd realised the truth, and she hadn't been able to look at me properly. She had had two months to process it.

'Why would Aris want to find me? For the case?' I asked, pulling my hand away. Trying to separate myself from her, even though I was beginning to think I never could.

'No, Tink, because you're his best friend.' She tutted.

'But he knows what I did, right?' I breathed out. I scanned the area belatedly but no one else was in earshot.

Mari leaned against the arm of the chair behind her. 'SJ, just answer me one question. And look at me when I'm talking to you about this,' she ordered. I forced myself to look at her. 'When it happened, when you were nine, did you think about doing it before you did it? Did you plan to do that to your mum?' She was trying to keep her face still, but she couldn't stop her forehead from creasing unconsciously.

I thought about that day. Strangely, I could now hear every word, feel the searing pain down my face, even feel the carpet burning my skin as we'd fought on the living room floor. Thinking about how to stop her.

'It was a reflex, I thought she was going to kill me,' I forced out, clawing at my face as the tears erupted out of me.

'SJ, it was a horrible thing, and you can't take it back, but I know you're a good person inside. Where it counts. And Aris knows that too.'

A good person. She thinks I'm a good person?

She pressed herself against me and absorbed my pounding heart, my shaking body.

'Jon,' I breathed out.

'I'm sorry?'

'You can call me Jon,' I said into her hair, inhaling her familiar smell. Coconut.

'That's nice, but what about Stan?' She lifted her head up, moving her lips dangerously close to mine. I couldn't help eyeing up her wet lips.

'You want to call me Stan?'

'Or Stanley?' She fluttered her eyelashes at me jokingly.

I wanted to laugh, despite the tears still on my face. 'Okay, Stan it is.' I finally leaned down and pressed my lips against hers. It felt like my lips suddenly knew what to do with themselves again. I pushed away a fraction. 'Are you saying you can really live with all this?'

'I've had the hardest time living without you the past few months Stan, so yes, I think I can live with you.' She held me close.

'I feel like I should tell you that,' I took a breath, 'I love you too, Mari.'

'Talk about making a woman wait!'

'Okay, how about you marry me, Mari?' I raised an eyebrow.

She blew out air, clearly not taking me seriously. 'No way am I subjecting us to a big fat Greek wedding. Uncle Theo is itching to act out *Twelfth Night.*'

I rested my head on her forehead. 'I wasn't joking.'

'One step at a time, Tink. I was just hoping you'd buy me dinner or something.'

'Did I ever tell you who Debbie was?'

She shook her head.

'She was my adoptive mum.'

'I had no idea,' Mari mumbled.

'I don't make a habit of sharing that information. Look, what I'm saying is, you know all of my deepest darkest secrets now and these last few months have been terrible without you. So, will you bloody well marry me?'

'Okay, Mr Robin.' Mari grinned.

'Really?'

'I said yes, didn't I?' Mari rolled her eyes.

'I suppose you'll have to meet my dad too.'

'Is he here now?'

I nodded and she looked taken aback.

'Well, I did actually buy you a Whitstable fridge magnet, so we'll have to go back to the room.'

Her face lit up. 'I would say that's a cheap way to get me into bed but, frankly, I don't care.'

I stood up and pulled her up after me. 'By the way, I quit smoking.'

She laughed. 'Great but where will I get my candy cigarettes now?'

I pulled a packet out of my pocket and grinned. 'How do you think I gave up?'

Acknowledgements:

Thanks to: Spread the Word and Book Outure editor, Therese Keating, for the feedback which helped me to hugely develop the novel. My dedicated and generous beta readers – Leia Butler, Louise Mather, Teo Eve, Rachel Dennis, Mari Maxwell, Cara V. Bland, Iqbal Hussain and Evia Kyriacou. Especially Trini Decombe, for always giving honest feedback. And to Trini's friend – Ewa Przytula for confirming a plot point.

Sam, Joe, Pip and Martin for helping me refine my blurb. Dónal and Margarita Fogarty for the help in researching some of the technical aspects. Rebecca Varrall for letting me quiz her about her training as a therapist and being an awesome friend. Paul Dudley for helping me choose a car for SJ and Marcin Bober for checking out some of the law aspects. Astra Papachristodoulou for helping me rename Aris. Dr Louise Tondeur for reviewing my contract.

The PWA course on Custody and Interviewing, run by Graham Bartlett, who had endless patience for answering all of my questions. He was also hugely supportive throughout the whole process! Also the Facebook groups – Writers' Detective Q&A and Trauma Fiction, whose members answered loads of my questions.

Martin for his thoughts on a very rough draft and for always saying nice things about my writing. My mum - for telling everyone she knows I've written a book. And to the rest of my family, who keep buying things I write, even though they probably have a small forest by now.

Greenie and Diane, who would have been one of the first in line to grab a copy. Pip and Martin once again, for believing in me at every turn. My friends who always champion me. Special mentions to KTK, Ayana, Izzy, Anna, and Alison.

My partner and best friend, Joe – for keeping me going when I wanted to quit, being proud of me, and listening to me ramble on about ridiculous plot points and issues that he had no idea about. As well as for helping me write, even if it meant losing out on time together. He has always valued what my writing means to me.

The Virginia Prize for Fiction is named in honour of the literary icon Virginia Woolf who lived near to the publisher's offices in Richmond-upon-Thames from 1914-1924. Her first novel *The Voyage Out* was published in 1915 and she and husband Leonard set up the Hogarth Press from their house in Paradise Road in Richmond, publishing authors such as T.S. Eliot, E.M. Forster and Katherine Mansfield.

Established in 2009, the biennial competition is open to women of any nationality from any country, aged 18 and over.

The competition accepts completed, unpublished novels for adults or YA readers, of at least 45,000 words in length. You can find out more about the competition at:

www.aurorametro.com/virginia-prize-for-fiction/

Aurora Metro initiated a campaign to commemorate Virginia Woolf with a full-sized statue of the author in Richmond in 2017. Read more about it at:

www.aurorametro.org/virginia-woolf-statue

Twitter @aurorametro
Facebook.com/AuroraMetroBooks

Why not read other Virginia Prize winners?

Pomegranate Sky by Louise Soraya Black
9781906582104 £8.99

Kipling and Trix by Mary Hamer
9781906582340 £9.99

The Leipzig Affair by Fiona Rintoul
9781906582975 £8.99

The Dragonfly by Kate Dunn
9781911501039 £9.99

The Walls Came Down by Eva Dodd
9781911501152 £9.99

Shambala Junction by Dipika Mukherjee
9781910798393 £9.99

To find out about other titles from
Aurora Metro Books
please visit
www.aurorametro.com